More acclaim for *The Tomcat's Wife and Other Stories*:

"Deep, complicated, American stories....Everything from symbol to diction works to effect. Ms. Bly knows that a story is about its network of personal secrets and about the tug that every word, every detail, exerts to make the web tremble....Every story in the collection, each for its own sake, is recommended."
—Louis B. Jones, *New York Times*

"Like Garrison Keillor, Carol Bly can 'speak Minnesotan' with the best of them. Bly's small towns have more in common with Sinclair Lewis' bleak Main Street than Keillor's lovable Lake Wobegon, though...like all good writers, Carol Bly maps her own imaginative territory. We're emphatically not in Lake Wobegon or on Main Street: Bly's is a clear-eyed vision of small-town life...the 'local color' is painted on a canvas as big and as broad as the human soul....Bly is both a teacher and an artist."
—Diana Postlethwaite, *Minneapolis Star Tribune*

"[Carol Bly] brings rural Minnesota to life...[in these] stories that couldn't be written by anyone else...each of these stories deserves a long review of its own....Bly makes these landscapes live in astonishing ways. Twin themes of suffering and rescue float through these tales....I think that's regional literature talking, a rural Midwestern-Northern voice. And thank God for it."
—Carolyn See, *Los Angeles Times*

"Ms. Bly reveals simple truths in appealing packages."
—*Dallas Morning News*

THE TOMCAT'S WIFE

And Other Stories

Carol Bly

HarperPerennial

A Division of HarperCollins*Publishers*

"My Lord Bag of Rice" first appeared in *The Laurel Review* in 1989.
"The Ex–Class Agent" first appeared in *Triquarterly* in 1985.
"After the Baptism" first appeared in *Western Humanities Review* in 1988.
"A Committee of the Whole" first appeared in *Triquarterly* in 1988.
"The Tender Organizations" was first published as "All the Tender Organizations" by the Minnesota Center for Book Arts, 1989.

A hardcover edition of this book was published in 1991 by HarperCollins Publishers.

HarperCollins books may be purchased for educational, business, or sales promotional use. For information, please call or write: Special Markets Department, HarperCollins Publishers, Inc., 10 East 53rd Street, New York, NY 10022. Telephone: (212) 207-7528; Fax: (212) 207-7222.

First HarperPerennial edition published 1992.

Designed by Alma Orenstein

The Library of Congress has catalogued the hardcover edition as follows:
Bly, Carol.
   The tomcat's wife / Carol Bly.—1st ed.
     p. cm.
   ISBN 0-06-016504-9
   1. Minnesota—Fiction. I. Title.
PS3552.L89T6   1991
813'.54—dc20   90-55564

ISBN 0-06-092264-8 (pbk.)

92 93 94 95 96 NK/HC 10 9 8 7 6 5 4 3 2 1

FOR
Donald Hall

Contents

THE
TOMCAT'S
WIFE

The Tomcat's Wife

THE GALLS had not been in Clayton two weeks before my husband, Furman Hastad, got a crush on Tom Gall. The first I suspected it was when Mrs. Beske, a woman in our church, told me while our Circle was putting together the spread for the Dollum funeral. We were making up the usual funeral spread—ground-up roast pork, ground-up roast beef, two onions chopped, three boiled egg yolks ground up, and Miracle Whip. Mrs. Beske said she was trying to get a deal on some chick starter and oyster shells at the elevator. I believed that much straight off.

She told me my husband, Furman, was hunched over his desk on the telephone the whole time, so she had to talk to one of the girls there instead. The girl said there was one price for small lots of starter and she couldn't give discount. Mrs. Beske asked if Furman was ever going to get off the phone. She had to shout to get herself heard over the sudden noise of the blowers when one of the men opened the office door and brought in a sewn bag from the machine. The girl shouted back that Furman was pretty much on the phone recently. Then the door shut, which made the office suddenly quiet. The man balancing the feed on his shoulder, the office girl, and Mrs. Beske all heard Furman say, "I guess this has to be goodbye for now, Tom."

I did not pay attention to it, because in our town Mrs. Beske wasn't much. When she wasn't trying to clip Furman at the elevator and all the businesspeople on Main Street, she was complaining that the interim pastor was perverted or crazy or senile. Everyone knows you don't criticize an interim pastor. She always angled to cause trouble, and her one kid, LeRoy, was as ugly-minded as she was.

In the next week, Furman started having long telephone conversations with Tom Gall from our house. Tom had been hired as Clayton's first school psychologist. He invited Furman to go with him when he drove down to Grand Rapids or over to Bemidji or even all the way to Duluth for psychological conferences. Until Tom Gall came to town, Furman was an ordinary, nice man, a good father to our Freddie and Faye. After the Galls came, Furman asked me to be especially nice to Mercein. I agreed it would be hard to be new in town. Furman said, "It isn't just that: it's that Tom has told me that Mercein has many serious problems, things that blocked her from being happy like a normal woman." Then I knew there was some kind of new situation here: Furman and I used to talk about a lot of different things, but they weren't about someone being blocked from being happy. We talked about the kids' artwork at school and the Clayton football team and ordinary incidents at the elevator and work around the farmstead. Furman part-time farmed our eighty, as well as working at the elevator.

By the middle of October, Furman joined the Jaycees, which he had never been interested in before. I was glad, because I thought he could have more ambition than he had. Then I found out he joined the Jaycees because Tom Gall was offering a Business Psychology course to them on alternate Monday noons and nights. Furman also asked me to arrange going to the PTA and

Artmobile and other doings at the same time Mercein and Tom
Gall would be there.

We were shaking hands after church with the interim pastor,
and Furman told him he had always wanted to sing in the choir
but he guessed he was too shy to ask. The interim pastor told
the choir director to get Furman in there.

Next Sunday, there was Furman in a navy-blue robe beside
Tom Gall, with the tenors. Tom Gall could read parts, so Furman said he kind of got the note from Tom and then bellowed
it out because they needed more sound from the tenors and
Furman's voice was all right. When you have lived with an
ordinary man for fifteen years and know him, it is a peculiar
feeling to see him decked out in those navy-blue robes up there.
And instead of coming right back to the farm on Wednesday
nights after practice, Furman went for coffee with Tom.

Mercein had a five-sevenths appointment to teach art at the
Elementary and help Grayzie, the Artmobile director, with the
exhibits. She had time on her hands. She and Tom hadn't any
children, the way Furman and I and all our other friends had.
None of us people in Clayton, even the ones right in town and
definitely those of us living in the country, really ever hung
around with the high-school teachers. Since Furman asked me
to hang around with Mercein because it would mean so much
to Tom, I got to know her all right but also I got to know
Grayzie, a twenty-seven-year-old art teacher, who was famous
for being someone the kids really liked. He was gay, but he
never made passes at anyone in our town or in any of the six
other towns where he took the Artmobile, so we all trusted him.
He was a slow-moving bear of a man. He and Mercein could
do British accents together, not just ending every sentence with
"old son" and "old chap," which even our Freddie could do,
but real-sounding ones. Grayzie was kind, too. He told me not
to worry about Furman and Tom. Furman wasn't going to be
homosexual, he said. Tom wasn't homosexual. Grayzie said
Furman had longed for a mentor and now he had one. Give it

a year and it's gone, he told me, patting my shoulder with his big, soft hand.

Day after day in October and early November that year, Mercein drove fast into our farmyard around two o'clock, promising to get me back to the farm before the school bus dropped off Freddie and Faye. Then we drove fast into town, the half-mile of township road, the three miles of Minnesota 73. She parallel-parked the Chevette very snappily alongside the football field. There were other cars parked along there, too. I never paid them any attention until Mercein told me they were doing the same thing we were doing.

Mercein was opening her box of charcoals and settling her sketchpad against the steering wheel.

"Now, that much I know isn't true!" I said with a laugh, but it was a nervous laugh, because even though I was one hundred percent sure those other women in those cars weren't making charcoal sketches, I always turned out to be wrong when I disagreed with Mercein about anything. Worse than wrong: I always turned out to have said something that had been acceptable before Furman and I met Mercein and Tom but now was either false or shabby-sounding. Mercein was the first human being I had met who didn't lie about anything.

"I know those guys are not sketching," I said.

"Neither are we," Mercein said, throwing her head back. She had long black hair, with some silver very noticeable in it. Her facial skin was unusually white, and there were dark circles under her eyes. Her face was finely made. She had shadows under her cheekbones the way comic-strip women characters have—the ones who smoke cigarettes in long holders and lead astray men like Steve Canyon or Rex Morgan. That was another thing: she smoked hundreds of cigarettes every day.

Mercein was drawing the football team members' legs.

"You are too sketching," I said.

"No," Mercein said in her languid way. "No—no. I am doing the same thing you are doing. I am looking at the butts of the boys when they bend over for the huddle. Yup," she said leisurely. "Looking at how those silvery pants made of that snaky stuff draws tight against their incredible butts. However, nothing in life lasts forever. Soon they straighten up and go running off to their line. Then I sketch for a while."

She checked the rearview mirror and all around the car. Then she loosened the fifth of Vat 69 wedged between the hand brake and the passenger seat. She offered me a swig in her mannerly way. I always took a small sip. In 1975 it was not yet O.K. to turn down an alcoholic beverage, even if you were getting to think the person offering it was on the way to alcoholism. While the whiskey I had taken made me shudder a little, I daydreamed that I was an intense person like Mercein. I dreamed I had not married Furman because he was uncomplicated and I thought I could trust him.

A few snowflakes swung down. They were scant, but it was the first snow of the year and I had the whiskey inside me, so I felt something. I felt special. Mercein had told me just the week before *never* to talk about anything or anybody being "special," but the fact is that snow looked that way to me. The boys struck each other in the scrimmage: we heard the creak and thunk of their pads across the cold field.

Mercein said, "Yup, that's right, fellows, go to it, all you junior Einsteins. Men have been doing that since the Lascaux caves," she remarked. "One! Two! Hike! Everyone hit everyone else as hard as you can."

I was just about to say, "I guess you don't think too much of football, then," but I could tell it wouldn't have the right tone. In my few weeks' friendship with Mercein I had learned from her, and from Furman indirectly after he got it from Tom: if you haven't got any particular opinion or feeling about something, don't say anything. Don't say, "That's the way it goes, I guess" or "If there's one thing that doesn't change, it's human nature." Whenever I said things like that to Mercein she said, "Christ, Cheryl" or "Jesus, Cheryl." That was another thing.

Literally no one else in Clayton, no other women I knew of, said "Christ" or "Jesus" to each other about anything. I don't expect anyone else said anything that brought it on.

Mercein lighted a cigarette. "Here's something f.y.i.," she said. "See how the boys' socks fall down when they bend over like that? See that? What happens is, the pants tighten up behind their knees, and the lower leg, the calf part, bulges, so their socks fall down. O.K. Notice how their socks lie around their ankles in those messy, chaotic rings?"

I have to say one thing: if I had to be thrown together with Mercein so much of the time, at least it never got boring.

"Folds," she said slowly, drawing quickly with her charcoal. "Folds and shadow in them. No matter whether you're working in charcoal or crayons or oil or anything. Whenever cloth folds it makes shadow. After you draw in the shadow, you take and wipe a thin rim clear around the outer edge of each fold, so it shows how it picks up light because it is uppermost and outside."

She did it awfully well. Her drawing looked exactly like those boys' socks and legs.

She glanced at me and smiled. "Yes," she said, as if agreeing with whatever was in my face. "A good drawing is a wonderful thing, let's face it."

She added, "So if someone comes up to the car and knocks on the window and says, 'What are you two nice ladies doing sitting out here staring at those young fellows' behinds, anyway?' I would instantly show them this drawing."

I said, "You really *are* an artist, though. Everyone in town knows that already. Grayzie says without you the Artmobile would go total zip. And even my little Faye loves the drawing lessons with you."

Mercein rolled her eyes. "But that is not why I am studying those boys."

"Why are you, then?" I said. "You mean you don't really study those boys the way an artist studies things?"

"Jesus, Cheryl," she said. "Next you'll be telling me a doctor doesn't see a woman patient as a woman."

I thought of all the prenatal examinations in the state of Minnesota alone, including the sixteen of them I had had for Freddie and Faye. Then I thought of all the Pap smears in the world, not just those in the past but those in the future. I was thirty-four then, so if I had one every two years and lived to be seventy-eight or eighty, that would be twenty more Pap smears still coming up just for me alone, and people live longer these days, so I might get to be ninety-five, even.

"Jesus, Cheryl," Mercein said, tossing back some more whiskey. "Next you'll be telling me a psychotherapist doesn't see his women patients as women."

I told her, "You're the one who's lived in the Twin Cities and Grand Rapids and everywhere and knows all this stuff. How would I know any psychotherapists?" Back then we didn't even have a mental health center anywhere near Clayton.

"Well," she said slowly. "You know Tom. Of course, he isn't a real therapist yet, but he has sat in on a lot of workshops and he looks forward to taking on some clients. He's going to talk to the Lutheran Social Service guy about sitting in on some of their sessions here too."

Then the coaches blew their whistles. The tinny windblown sound of it came across the fields to us. We watched the boys, hulking under their pads, drift away in bunches, like dark clouds.

"Mind you," Mercein said, in the foreign accent she sometimes got when she had drunk a lot already that day, "to watch those boys, now . . . it makes your heart stop, actually."

"Why?" I asked. "I like watching them O.K."

Mercein matter-of-factly wedged the bottle back into its place and started the car. "Yup," she said. "I like watching them, too. They look wonderful. And fortunately from here we can't hear anything they are saying. But if we were closer we would hear all their stupid remarks and their stupid jokes, and it would remind us that they will grow up to be really pointless. They look good—right now—from here. In three or four years they will mostly be idiots. Makes your heart stop to think of it."

Then she said, "Cheryl, how about just driving around another five minutes?"

We went through this every time. "Take me home, please, Mercein. You can come in, though, when we get there. The kids're always glad to see you. You can talk to me while I start supper."

She laughed. "Jesus, Cheryl. Next you'll be telling me that mothers are thrilled to get home in the late afternoons so they can start supper for the kids and show an interest in their schoolwork and sit around the kitchen table and praise their art projects!"

I felt ashamed, because I was feeling just the way she supposed I was feeling. As she drove down 73 I made a mental picture of me already home, cutting up green pepper and onions, melting butter, and then frying all that a little. Then adding chopped raw potatoes and the better part of a can of Carnation milk, then coarse pepper, and then putting it in the oven for about a half hour. I could not decide one way or the other about browning hamburger to go in. I half wanted to, but sometimes it is nice to have a dish that has not got any browned meat in it. Also, since Furman had been talking to Tom Gall so much, he had this new idea that he would go vegetarian.

Mercein took her eyes off the road to glance at me. "I see you *are* looking forward to seeing your kids." She gave me one of her deep-voiced laughs. I looked into my lap.

Back then, people always smiled when they had their pictures taken. Ordinary people had the idea you looked prettier when you smiled. We would all put on a full, open-mouthed laugh for our pictures.

"You don't like my laugh," she said, looking at the road, making the turn onto the township road. "Never mind. Tom says that people in pain always have ugly laughs. Also, the rich have ugly laughs. That's why they always pose for pictures very sober."

With a person like Mercein, there weren't a lot of places where I could jump into the conversation with confidence. She knew more. She analyzed things. I never analyzed anything before the Galls came to town. People were what they were. They knew what they knew. Whenever there was a chance for me to tell her anything I really was sure of, I would try. Now I said, "People always smile when they pose for pictures."

"Not the rich," Mercein informed me. "They—the women—know it is shallow to spend your whole life improving your tennis backhand or your parallel turn, so they put on sad looks in photos so you will be struck with how classical and womanly they are. If they are all that sad and classical and womanly, they should slit their wrists," Mercein said with one of her laughs.

Mercein was remarkable-looking when she wasn't jeering at herself or laughing. That word, "remarkable," got going around the Jaycees when the Galls came to town and Tom Gall started the course in Business Psych. When Furman took to Tom that much, he started using his language, which is how I got used to it. Tom had told Furman that Grayzie was remarkable. He said Mrs. Beske was remarkable. I didn't see the sense in either of those remarks. Mrs. Beske was extra poor and extra stingy. She slept with not one but both of the drivers who carried the bus service up from Minneapolis to Clayton. The buses stopped overnight in Clayton, because we were so near the Canadian border. Next morning, the drivers drove the morning service back down to the Twin Cities. When they changed drivers on that route, everyone in our church said, "Good. Mrs. Beske can keep her pillowcases cleaner now." Then she started sleeping with the substitute driver. All that was interesting and got talked over at Circle meetings, but I couldn't see it was remarkable. I didn't think Grayzie was remarkable, either. He was unique, being the only gay whom no one even thought of running out of town, but basically he was overweight for a person in his twenties, and lazy. A lot of his Artmobile exhibits, including I am sorry to say the recent one called "Ancient China and Her Arts," were really boring, even for us people who didn't exactly expect Mona Lisa to step off the bus at our Jack Rabbit station.

Furman started saying that things and people were remarkable. When he watched football with Freddie, our thirteen-year-old, he would say, "Here, hand her over here a second, Freddie," and Freddie would hand over our Mother Cat, who was allowed in the house on Sundays and at special times. Furman told the cat, "You are a remarkable animal. Also very pregnant." I felt two things at one time: I was happy I had a husband who enjoyed his family life and was a sweet-tempered father. I also felt doom, because all that September and October and part of November he said words and whole sentences he got straight from Tom Gall.

When we got home Mercein followed me right into our house. She did what lonely people do: they learn quickly the customs of your home and then they pour into any space you don't physically lock them out of. Mercein thoughtfully brushed the new light snow off her shoes and then sat in a kitchen chair and leaned both elbows on the table. She was nice about not smoking. I started to cut up vegetables.

"Do you have time to talk now?" she said from behind me.

The school bus was due in four minutes.

"Oh, well," she said. She started going on about how well Faye drew in class. I didn't listen much because the chopped pepper smelled strangely fresh; although the snow was settling down to serious fall outside, this quavery smell of pepper coming up to me from the knife was like a pang of summer. Someone in my Circle at church once said she was cutting an orange in August and the smell brought her a pang of Christmas, like pine smell. I am not saying that the kind of feeling is deep or remarkable or anything like what Mercein was talking about from behind me, but it gave me a feeling, so I stopped listening to

Mercein and thought about the pepper smell. Anyway, I wasn't used to listening to anyone hours on end the way Mercein seemed to want me to. Grayzie said, "Oh, one more motor-mouth won't break the town wide open."

Now she said more loudly, "I wanted to tell you something Tom said last night, but I suppose Freddie and Faye will be home in a second, won't they?"

"They get a kick out of it when you're here when they get home," I said. I quit cutting peppers and went to onions. "Especially Faye when you look at her pictures and help her."

"I can tell Freddie would rather get home and find just you here," she said.

"You know kids," I said from my repertoire of things to say when nothing you say is going to do it. Every day when Freddie got home he followed me around, whatever I was doing. He had not gotten his height yet. He was a fine-made boy, with huge hands hung at the delicate wrists like upside-down parachutes. Every day he was hassled by a bully on the bus, Mrs. Beske's rotten kid, LeRoy. LeRoy teased him on the way in to school, and then on the way home. Freddie was nervous about it all the time.

"Freddie is always real tired when he gets home," I said.

"Tired, shit," Mercein said. "Jesus, Cheryl, can't you see that when people act tired what they are is distressed?"

"Well," I said, not trying to be pleasant since I didn't cotton to being told I didn't understand my own children. "There's such a thing as making a—"

She interrupted me with her ugly laugh. "No! No! Cheryl! Don't *do* it!" she shouted. "Don't tell me not to make a mountain out of a molehill! Aaagh!"

Right away I felt hot.

Mercein said in a quieter voice, "All the molehills are mountains, Cheryl. I got news for you."

That was another of Tom Gall's phrases: "I got news for you." Furman said it all the time.

Mercein said, "Christ, Cheryl, next time you'll be telling
me that if a person just looks on the bright side . . . Shit, I
don't even want to finish the rest of the sentence."

Then the children came swooping in. Mercein greeted them
and did not sound especially drunk. She and Faye leaned over
one of the construction-paper drawings Faye laid on the table.
Freddie came over to me and jammed himself between me and
the trash can beside the stove. "You can stir," I told him. "The
Mother Cat keeps trying to get in," I told him. "I think she's
having those kittens pretty soon now. She scratched at the
kitchen storm door all morning."

Freddie said, "Yeah, Mom, she did? She did? Mom, what
do you think? You know what happened last time! You remember, all right! All those little kitties except the one?"

Around our county, the tomcats never stayed on the farms.
As soon as a male kitten grew up, it wandered off and joined a
pack of wild tomcats that roved around from farm to farm,
living wild. The females stayed if you let them, and became
what we called good farm cats—that is, they kept the outbuild-
ings free of mice. What they didn't care to eat they killed, anyway, and brought up to the kitchen door to show you. Our
Mother Cat left all her kills on the iron-grate boot mat. Whenever our Mother Cat had new kittens, she had all she could do,
night after night, to fight off the roving tomcats. The toms
systematically went around from farm to farm, biting new kittens in the neck. I had handled the situation in two ways. The
first time the toms killed a litter, the children wanted a funeral.
They dug a mass grave south of the machinery building. They
found a Bidding Prayer in the front of the old red hymnal. Faye
said the prayer, and Freddie pushed the shoveled dirt down onto
the crowded little shoulders and heads. The next time we lost
a whole litter to the toms, I didn't tell the children at all. I said,
"Something must have happened to the kittens, I guess." Anyway, the church stopped using that hymnal with those ancient
prayers in it.

"So, Mom? So, Mom?" Freddie said.

"You fix her up some place either in the cellar or in your closet, but she doesn't get the run of the house. She can be in the living room during television, but someone has to be watching her. I don't want the house smelling of cat's business."

He was gone fast as light.

Mercein wanted to know if I could walk her out to her car. On the way out we passed Freddie coming in, with his arms full of the Mother Cat. His face was all grins, hers very cool. I said to Mercein, "I am always surprised how cats keep their cool. A human being can be all the way excited about something, but a cat just keeps its cool." Before Tom and Mercein got to be such good friends of Furman and me, I didn't say those observations if I had them. *If* I had them. I could hardly remember if I thought about things before Tom and Mercein came to town.

"Cool! Christ, Cheryl," Mercein said. "Cats aren't *cool:* they're inimical!"

I got sick of asking Mercein what different words meant that she used, so I decided I'd wait and look it up later. Inimical. What I mean to say is, it was something new in our lives to have such interesting people around. Ask Furman, who was always trying to get to any meeting he thought Tom would be at. And offering to drive Tom to the out-of-town psychology things he went to, in case Mercein needed their car or anything. The interim pastor said Tom Gall was stimulating. What I mean, though, is I didn't want to be stimulated all the time. I wasn't used to it. Sometimes I just wanted to live the way I lived before, doing the things adults do when they are married and raising kids on an eighty near an O.K. little town and their husband runs the eighty and also the elevator.

We stood outside in the falling snow a moment. Furman had put in one of those yard lights that knows to go on as soon as it gets dark. Now it cracked on with its blue-green glow. Mercein leaned against their dirty Chevette and took out a cigarette.

What went through my mind is: Now she will have to send that raincoat to the cleaners.

"Wait a minute," she said. She bent into the car and came back out with the Vat 69.

"You?"

"I got the kids home and all," I said.

Mercein said, "Last night here is what Tom said. It was just last night, and he said this. Now, what he said was . . . Let me see now. Let's see," Mercein said. "I need to get this right. What he said . . . Well, what he said was, the reason that we didn't . . . Christ, Cheryl, this is going to be worse than I thought."

She took a huge drink, which I thought she didn't need.

"What he said was, the reason that I didn't have kids is that my vagina is frightened and so it has turned to steel and iron and it is locked out of fear."

She drank again and then smiled. "Yup! That's it!" she said. "That's it! Other people's vaginas are made of blood and skin, and mine is made of metal, and it's locked. Locked out of fear of womanhood. Yes—that was the last part: locked out of fear of womanhood. I nearly forgot that part."

We both looked out to the edge of the driveway, to where the yard light didn't reach. It just barely picked out the tassels of the headland corn, which Furman always picked last. My problem was whether to act surprised that Tom said that. I had heard that he knew all about locked wombs and vaginas before, because he had told Furman, and Furman had explained it all to me. Once I remember we were lying in bed, and I said, "That's hard to believe," and Furman said, "Well, the remarkable fact is that the truth is always hard to believe. The real, inner truths are, but once you learn to believe them," he added, "Tom says life is never the same again because you are alive in ways you never were before." It sounded like something to think about, all right, but it had to wait, because we were both tired, and I know I fell asleep then.

I didn't know what to say to Mercein. Who wants to be told, "Oh, I didn't know you had a iron womb!" Finally I decided to say something not completely loyal to Furman. "I don't guess I believe that, Mercein," I said. "I guess if it was me and I wanted children, I'd go get tested or whatever they do."

After another minute or so she climbed into the car. We arranged that both couples would meet at the Artmobile at seven o'clock the next night. Grayzie and Mercein had finally closed down the exhibit on Ancient China and Her Arts and were starting "Artists Look at Our Life: Our Kids' Art." It was expected to be a success. No one had gone to the China exhibit except the people who support all community efforts at anything. "Artists Look at Our Life" was present times at least, and even if kids can't paint well, they're just kids, so you can allow, especially when it's your own kids.

On the way back into the house I figured out the rest of the hot dish and decided to brown some hamburger and dump it in, after all. Tom and Mercein had argued Furman into being a vegetarian, but it didn't completely take. Furman explained to me about three thousand times that if you eat lightly—vegetables, not hamburger—you will have remarkable insights flying in and out of your head, but I noticed that when we had hamburger, Furman put his elbows and forearms on the table and he ate as much as Faye and Freddie. As long as I didn't use the actual words "Do you want seconds of meat, Furman?" he would help himself to more. One insight I had before the Galls ever got to town was that if you don't use actual words about what they're planning to do, people will do pretty much whatever they've always done.

When the hot dish was in the oven, I went upstairs. Freddie lay on his bed with the Mother Cat. She was absentmindedly clawing up tufts out of the chenille bedspread.

"Do you think she will have kittens tonight, Mom?"

I said, "You'd think all the years we've had that cat around,

I'd know. But I can't tell." I sat down and we both petted the cat a while. I lifted the claw that was tearing up the chenille; old Mother Cat instantly drew her claws in. I pressed the pads, though, and sharp tips of claws stuck out again.

Freddie and I talked about where cats get their purr.

After a few minutes, Freddie said, "That sucker told me that if he felt like it he would push me all the way out of the bus some day."

"The Beske kid," I said.

Freddie told me three or four cruel things LeRoy Beske had said, right in front of all those girls who rode that bus and the little kids up front.

Finally I said, "Here is this mean kid giving you a bad time, while his mother is always hanging around the elevator trying to skin Dad in some deal. She always wants money off everything, even though she's the tiniest customer he's got. Her with her half a pound of chick starter and then could she have some oyster shells thrown in. Anyway, she is losing her farm, it turns out. My Circle's serving that auction on Saturday."

"Mom, you won't say anything to anyone about LeRoy pushing me around?"

"No."

Freddie said, "Maybe you could poison the barbecue at the auction, and he would die a very painful death. They would think it was suicide."

"Yeah, that's right, Freddie," I said. "They *would* go around saying it was suicide, but you and I would know it was murder but we would never let on." I gave the Mother Cat a last scratch under her ears. "I would have to spend the whole day at the auction trying to keep other people from eating the poisoned batch of barbecue mix."

Freddie said, laughing, "They'd say, 'Mrs. Hastad, how come you don't let us have any of that wonderful-smelling batch over there in the crock pot? How come, Mrs. Hastad?' "

I left Freddie talking aloud to himself: "So then you'd say, you'd say, let's see, you'd say . . ."

The best way to get through a kids' exhibit at Grayzie's Artmobile was to do it on a double date. Furman and I met Tom and Mercein, who were standing around smoking in the lighted area beside the trailer. The Artmobile trailer was a project of Minnesota Citizens for the Arts and a whole lot of other organizations, mostly located in the Twin Cities. When Grayzie had it in our town it would be parked on the far edge of the football practice field, and everyone who had anything going for them in community leadership made sure they were seen checking out every new exhibit. There were men standing around breathing smoke, with their blousy Hollofil jackets open, delaying going in. Their wives would be inside the Artmobile, pretending to be as interested in other women's kids' artwork as they were in their own. We all stood around, stalling before going up the little staircase to the Artmobile show.

Mercein said that the Artmobile would be the perfect place to hide spent plutonium rods. I had to ask her what spent plutonium rods were, since I could see Furman didn't know, either, but would feel foolish to have to ask. "They could paint two or three thousand trailer rigs like this," Mercein explained, with one of her laughs, "white, with 'Art' or 'Culture' written in Bold Caslon on the sides big as life, and then pick up the rods in Charleston harbor and drive them wherever they like in the countryside and just park them in some schoolyards. No one ever goes into any culture site unless they have to because the town is behind it. All that radiation could just sort itself out slowly over those schoolyards for the next fifty thousand half-lives."

Tom turned to Furman and said that when women got into what sounded like animals but was something he called animus, they got sharp opinions on every subject that came up. The way you could tell, he went on, that they were in their animus was that their opinions were always unpleasant and were designed to make people listening feel just slightly more miserable than they may otherwise have been feeling.

Furman said, "Yeah, Tom. . . . I think I get the sort of thing you mean."

I did not marry Furman Hastad for his brains, and he never said he was Einstein, so I told myself there was no reason to feel hot when he pretended to understand things he probably didn't.

Now Grayzie shouted to the fifteen or sixteen of us standing around in the half-dark, "Welcome, everybody! Welcome, folks! Come on up now! Welcome the true art done in your community! Hi, everybody! Come on, Tom and Furman, lead the way! Hi, Mercein—come on, Cheryl—all right, everybody! This is something special!" We all went in.

People in Clayton envied Mercein and me because our husbands went into church affairs and art affairs without being herded. The other men in town would drive their wives there, all right, but then they would hang around outside in their thick jackets, making jokes. "Yeah, you got a deer license, Orrin? You need a deer license like you need a hole in your head," and then someone else says, "What *you* going to do with a deer license, Merv? Use it to prove you're old enough to quit drinking, or what?" (Haw, haw, haw.) I never could figure out the humor in men's jokes. Furman told me that October that Tom had explained it to him: The jokes did not have to be especially funny; the point was to keep up a jeering level to prevent self-pity.

Mercein said, "That is why the boys are so cute in football practice. They haven't got the joking perfect yet. But every locker-room shower session takes them closer and closer. Makes your heart stop to think of it."

Finally a whole group of us were slowly going around the U-shaped aisle of the Artmobile. Clayton Elementary School kids' drawings were matted and hung on the walls, and flat projects of various kinds covered the long, narrow center table. Grayzie had followed us in, and now he stood on a housewives' stepladder at the rear. "Your attention for one second, folks!" he called to us. "Welcome to Art of the Present! Now, we had art from the far past, and starting this coming Monday we will be having a very special look at things *future*—but for the weekend, here it is: the present, and best of all, your own children's interpretation of it. As you walk around, of course you want to find your own kids' work first and admire it! After all— it's the best of the bunch!" This got a laugh. "But then I suggest you go around and say, 'Well—here is how kids see the world around them. Here's something they're trying to say.' Now—have fun, everybody!" And Grayzie let his large body down, his hands outward, delicately balancing as he came off the step.

Freddie's "America at Night" project lay on the center table. It was a wide, shallow box, whose lid was a dark-blue painting of a United States map, with tiny flashlight bulbs at each of the capitals. On one edge there were forty-eight halves of tongue depressors on springs. Each had a state name rub-off-lettered onto it. Wiring ran from the depressors under the map to all the capital cities' locations. Since Freddie had used paper clips for part of the electric wiring, you had to be careful when you touched the project.

Furman hung over the map a second. I could see he was pleased with it, but Furman never shows much. He was about to continue on around the trailer, when Tom Gall gave a shout. He gathered us all around the map. "This is one hell of a wonderful project!" he shouted. He pressed the Minnesota lever, and not just Saint Paul lit up: Grand Rapids and Clayton and Saint Cloud and Duluth lighted up too. "Look how bright the cities are at night," Tom said, smiling down at the map. "Then look at all the countryside asleep in all that navy-blue darkness!"

Freddie's project looked better now that Tom explained it

that way. I imagined all the unlighted millions of farmsteads like ours.

Tom turned to Furman and me. "You can be proud of Freddie," he said. "They always assume a boy gets his abilities from his father, but some of it *definitely* comes from the mother—don't let them tell you different."

Then I felt sorry I didn't believe some of the things Furman told me Tom had said.

Mercein had walked over to one of the walls. She said, "Look. Here is someone in pain." She said it quietly so no one but us four would hear.

The drawing showed two semis that had just struck each other on the Interstate. Every detail of the trucks' brake lines and spare-wheel carriers showed. The Interstate sign was drawn exactly. Some black crayon lines radiated from the trucks' smashed engines; the words "Pow!" and "Smash!" appeared in clouds at the outer ends of those lines.

Tom jerked one shoulder and said lightly, "That's not pain. That's just TV imprinting. Imprinting on a kid's mind is all. Who did that?" He bent his tall body so he could make out the signature. "Oh, yes! That kid! No," he said, "that's just your regular old U.S.A. violent-culture imprinting."

Furman said, "Cheryl and I have cut down on the amount of TV Freddie and Faye get to watch."

"That's very good, Furmy," Tom said. "Very good! A strong stand like that, especially from the man, makes a difference."

By then our group had made its way all around the trailer. Grayzie asked us to go down the front little staircase so the next group could come in the back. Mrs. Beske came running up. She looked rapidly over Furman and Tom and Mercein, as if to see if she dared interrupt. "Do you have a minute?" she said to me.

She took me by the elbow over to the parked cars, out of the streetlighting.

She said, "I wanted to tell you I heard about how your Church Circle didn't want to serve lunch at my auction."

"We *are* serving your auction," I said. "My Circle is the one that's doing it, Mrs. Beske."

"I heard that," she said. "I heard you were the one made them do it, too." She went on in her slaty voice: "I heard people talked. . . ."

She heard right. Every month, the Stewardship Committee and the Circles met in the Fellowship Hall. I happened to be chairperson in 1975, so I was at the meeting. They planned all the weddings and they planned a schedule for the funerals, so when anyone died, each Circle knew if it was their turn to serve the funeral. Then they planned the lighter-weight stuff, like serving barbecues at farm auctions. We never even baked for those: we bought the doughnuts at the two bakeries, the Catholic one and the Lutheran one, so there wouldn't be feelings. We used the same barbecue recipe that had been thumbtacked inside the custodian's closet for as long as I had worked in that church at all, which would have been when I was in Luther League. It was a pretty good recipe; kind of a big sugar hit, but it tasted good at a freezing-cold auction.

At the end-of-August meeting, someone said that as a Christian Circle chairperson she didn't feel she could ask her Circle members to serve at a whore's auction, and she was very sorry but you had to draw the line somewhere.

When I rejoined Furman and Tom and Mercein, Tom was explaining to the other three that Grayzie was most likely unconscious of his own sexuality. Tom said, "In an unconscious little town like this, it is perfectly possible for a homosexual to be absolutely unconscious that he *is* a homosexual. Very likely the case with Grayzie."

Furman agreed, doing the nodding-several-times thing he had picked up from Tom.

Furman knew perfectly well that Grayzie was openly careful to have his social life in some other place. Two years earlier, some people had gotten juiced at the VFW and they beat up someone they said was homosexual. At an Artmobile meeting the following week, Grayzie had said cheerfully, "Probably get me next time!" and we all assured him that he was perfectly safe and very well respected. We told him that because he was originally from Grand Rapids or the Twin Cities, he didn't understand how the very small towns work: nine tenths of the time men said they were going to straighten out some gay at the edge of town, they never got around to it. Furman knew that Grayzie was not unconscious of being gay, so I felt cross that he went along with Tom's remark.

On the way home I said, "How come you went along with Tom about Grayzie when you know better?"

Furman kept his eyes on the road. "I don't know," he said finally.

The next morning was very cold. Two distant relatives of Mrs. Beske's set up a cylinder-shaped gas blower-heater for us in the tools building of Mrs. Beske's farmyard. Mercein and another lady and I tied our price list to the stringer behind us. We plugged the crock pot of barbecue mix and the two coffeepots into the drop cords and then spread our tables with white roller paper. We had twelve muffin tins for the nickels, dimes, and quarters. We kept the dollars and fives sticking out from under a breadboard, the way children keep their Monopoly money during a game. The blower roared and sent old hay wisps flying, but the feeling came back into our feet as we stood waiting for trade. Mrs. Beske herself came in and of course asked for a freebie. Since we were ready a quarter hour before anything really started, we took turns going out and walking around the flatbeds full of junk for auction, keeping our arms crossed over our chests, the wind lifting our aprons. Returning to duty, we discussed how none of the pillows or sheets would go, not even the old ones from the 1950s, when people embroidered them for wedding presents. We figured that about one hundred times that day people would say you never knew who slept on *these* and how many at a time. I saw Mrs. Beske's son, LeRoy, go by, dragging a rolled-up carpet. I took his measure and realized he would be a handful for Freddie, all right. He looked at least five foot ten.

Grayzie wandered in and ate a barbecue. "I love auctions," he said, keeping us company for a few minutes. "I always pick up old satin and velvet dresses. Oh, don't look so shocked, Cheryl. It's not for drag; it's for costumes for the kids' art projects and all."

Then, just when the crowd started coming and we had our hands full, Mercein said to me, "I have to go home, Cheryl."

"Oh, no!" I said.

"Don't discount what I say," she snapped. "I said I have to go home. That means I have to go home. I think I'm coming down with something."

That afternoon Furman was going along with Tom to a Psychological Outreach to Rural Communities session in Saint Cloud, so I didn't see Mercein again until Sunday in church.

She looked even paler than usual in the navy-blue choir robe. When they all stood for the anthem, Mercein in the second row with the other altos, Tom and Furman in the tenors' row just behind her, I could see she wasn't paying attention to the director. I still didn't worry about her, because everyone is absentminded some of the time, my guess being those deeper-thinking types are like that even more than us others. I don't know that; it's just a guess. Still.

I didn't pay much attention to the sermon because we still had just the interim pastor. We didn't know him very well. He didn't know us. You can't get terribly interested in people who obviously aren't going to stay in town. As we shook hands in the doorway, I told him thank you for the interesting sermon.

The first part of that afternoon was happy. Furman and Faye and Freddie all sat on the living room floor. They were going

to watch the Vikings play the Steelers and told me to watch if
I wanted to see something good. Freddie explained that I
couldn't go out in the kitchen and expect to be called when there
was a Bradshaw-Swann pass, because a pass situation comes up
so fast it'd be over by the time I got back to the living room to
see. I had things I wanted to do in the kitchen, but I remembered
how Mercein was always telling me, Put people before things,
Cheryl. People before things. I told the family I'd watch the
first quarter, then.

The game had just started when the telephone rang. It was
Grayzie. He was at the hospital, because Mercein Gall had tried
to commit suicide an hour before, and did I know where Tom
was? I explained he was back in Saint Cloud, at the wrap-up of
yesterday's conference.

"Furman!" I called into the living room. "We need to reach
Tom. Where is that conference at? Mercein's bad."

Furman called back, "I wouldn't bother Tom at that meeting."

Finally Furman got the idea I wasn't going to shout what
was wrong over the children's heads. He came and stood near
me at the telephone. He took the receiver then and told Grayzie
he should call the Sunshine Motel in Saint Cloud and ask for
the school psychologists' conference.

Furman followed me to the far end of the kitchen. "That
was really a hostile thing for Mercein to do," he said. "What a
terrific guilt trip to lay on Tom! To do a thing like that when
Tom's away. Boy, that's hostile."

"Hostile" was a word like "remarkable": I wasn't just sure
about it, so I didn't say anything.

Freddie gave a whoop, so we both went and stood in the
kitchen doorway. On the television behind him I saw a player
rise up way above the others like an acrobat: his ams clenched
around the football up there, and then he fell down amidst a
crowd of players on both sides.

"That's your Lynn Swann!" Furman said. "That's him!"

Furman decided to wait at home with the kids. He thought Tom might telephone and he could stand by him—go with him to the hospital if he wanted.

I certainly was not much at prophesying. As I drove from my healthy and happy farmhouse to town and the hospital, I thought sure I would get depressed when I got into room 101, which was where they put all the emergencies. I imagined Mercein lying there with her wrists all bandaged up, looking pale the way she always did anyhow, and me trying to say something appropriate and her scarcely answering, and Grayzie stalking around the waiting room feeling miserable and helpless.

It was not like that at all. For one thing, the moment I got outside 101 I remembered how back when Faye was born someone in 101 had moaned and cried aloud, rhythmically, nearly all the night. The maternity wing was just east of the nurses' station; 101 and 102 were just west of it, so we could hear across. When they brought me my fresh-juice ration at around two in the morning, I asked about who was crying and groaning. That was a stroke victim, the nurse explained. They do that, she said, in a reassuring voice. Then she added, This one needs to die. Don't think about him, she said. Drink your juice. I'll bring you your little girl in a sec.

All the rest of that night I had off and on thought about having a baby and then perhaps forty or fifty years later coming back to the same hospital and trying to die.

Now the memory returned. I pushed open the door of 101. Mercein was sitting on a wooden chair near the window; Grayzie was standing. They were laughing. Only one of Mercein's wrists was bandaged.

Mercein was telling Grayzie that she was the only person she knew who had tried to commit suicide who wanted to have the theme from "Masterpiece Theatre" at her funeral. "I know you don't get to choose the music for your funeral if you have done a suicide attempt," she said. She and Grayzie both laughed.

"You can have any music you want," he told her. "You just

can't have it *now*. You have to live awhile. I wouldn't mind
having the 'Masterpiece Theatre' theme at my funeral, now you
mention it."

They were very high without drinking anything. I partly
felt left out. I had prepared to say something like "I am so sorry,
Mercein," but then I got into the room and there was all that
hilarity. Finally I sat on the edge of the bed and smiled, because
that's what both of them were doing.

They talked about "Upstairs, Downstairs" for a while. I
couldn't join that, either, because no one in my family liked it.
It just seemed like a soap with the wrong accents, we thought.

"I live in some other world for about two hours after each
episode," Mercein said.

"I have a fake British accent for two hours each time," Grayzie remarked. He gave Mercein a friendly smile. "I say," he
said. "Mind *you*, that fellow looks a proper sod if ever I saw
one."

A nurse came in and sang, "Time for temperature," as if
Mercein were there with a head cold.

The interim pastor stuck his head in, looking shy. "You can
come in," Grayzie said respectfully. "She has a thermometer in
her mouth."

"Well, I just wanted to give you God's blessing," the pastor
said.

We all lingered around a while, but there didn't seem to be
anything to do or say. The hospital was keeping Mercein for
the night.

"I suppose Tom is on his way?" she said to me when I picked
up my jacket to go.

"He should be here soon," I said.

When I left through the waiting room, Tom came through
the revolving door, his cheeks brilliant and red from the cold
or from hurry.

"Don't leave," he said to me. "I want to talk to you."

"Mercein's been expecting you," I told him.

"Just a second," he said. "You see, Mercein has a lot to bear. She has a lot of real sadness to face. Frustration and anger. I knew that, but I didn't know she was this depressed."

We sat down on the plaid-covered chairs. Tom leaned toward me. "You see, Cheryl," he said, "she isn't in touch with what a woman is, the way you are. She has to face the fact she hasn't had any children. She definitely must be feeling that she has failed in some deep, horribly sad way. She's got to be feeling that. How else could she feel?"

I felt off-center, somehow—from so many surprises in the last hour. An hour earlier, I was trying to understand how a ballet dancer could turn into a wide receiver. Then I was trying to understand how two good friends could be laughing and making gags in a hospital room right after one of them had made a suicide attempt. Now I was trying to understand whatever this point was Tom was making. I spoke up sharply, to my own surprise.

"I don't know how much Mercein feels about having children," I said.

Tom gave me a soft look. "Ah, Cheryl," he said. "You are a good loyal friend to her. But you mustn't get into denial about it, you know. She and I have openly talked about her feelings of failure, dozens of times."

That dumb waiting room with its dumb plaid-covered chairs and the beat-up magazines showing macho men dressed in sports clothes was not a kind of place to have a big personal-discovery experience, but that is what I did. I suddenly hated Tom. I stood up.

"She's been waiting in there for you, Tom," I said. "You're this big psychologist. Why don't you go in and talk to your wife once?"

When I got home, Freddie had the large cardboard box he had fitted up for the Mother Cat on the living room floor. The Mother Cat kept lying down in it, then standing up, arching her back, turning around, and sitting down again. Then she would lie down for a moment or two and stand up again. On the flannel-covered bottom of the box were her new kittens. They needed another week to get cute-looking, but they already had the wonderful quality of kittens: you can't keep your eyes off them.

Furman wanted to know how Tom was bearing up. Then Faye came out of the kitchen and started drawing kittens, so Furman and I were distracted and couldn't talk.

All night I felt changed. It was certainly a new experience for me. In recent years there had been some prayer groups in our church, since prayer groups spread all across the United States in the late sixties and early seventies, so I had heard people in town going around saying they were changed, and they could tell you the exact moment they got changed. I didn't pay much attention, because most of those people who did all that religious changing were the lightweights around town anyhow, and besides, I had Freddie and later got pregnant with Faye. Just recently Mercein had told me there is a moment, now and then, when your life comes to a dead stop.

Next morning, the snow still covered the ground. After Furman and the children had left for work and school, I went around turning off all the lights they had left on: the yellow of the electric lighting gave way to the blue and gloomy snowlight from outside. The house was shadowy. I sat down at the kitchen table without even looking at the dishes. I suddenly decided a lot of things *fast*. I decided I was a happy woman and I would live my life to the end, although I was in the middle of a somewhat boring marriage. I decided that although my marriage was a little boring I would stay in it. I decided I was a little bored with Mercein, too, no matter how insightful she was about everything. I decided I admired her honesty a lot but not completely and I was going to go back to saying things people around Clayton always say, since it didn't do any harm. I decided Tom was a mean man. I decided Grayzie was a human being to be taken seriously.

Grayzie! It brought me to the fact that in an hour or so he would be working on his new exhibit in the Artmobile. I decided I would drive into town and look at it.

He opened the trailer door with one of his fake-gallant bows. I peered into the darkness. "Come in, my dear, come in," Grayzie cried in one of the various accents he could do. This one was what he called his Basic Fulbright foreign accent, a kind of Transylvanian-blood-drinker-plus-Parisian-lady-killer accent. Grayzie was wearing a French Foreign Legion–style hat, with the visor in front and the neck flap in back, the whole thing made out of what I recognized as a blouse of Mrs. Beske's. I'd know that pink-and-light-green rayon plaid anywhere. He looked wild, but inside the shadowy Artmobile he had done something that knocked me out.

He had plastered the entire inside ceiling and walls of the trailer with brown and gray dirt—or plaster made to look like brown and gray dirt. Uneven strata of metamorphic rock stuck out here and there. Some roots and twigs hung from the ceiling. In one rounded, dark corner, two bright eyes looked out from an absolutely black hole. It was hard to see, since I had come in from the snowlit football field: in here everything was dark. Grayzie had laid old straw and some gravel on the floor. On the center table stood three lighted globes of the earth.

"Grayzie, how did you do it? Who helped you?" I put a finger on one cave wall: the substance of it was still wet.

"It took me all last night," he said. "Isn't it wonderful? I have been dreaming of it for ages. I know we all long to go back to the cave times. I know it! I know it! So I have been dreaming it up, in bits and pieces, for years. Then I had this meeting set with Mercein for yesterday afternoon to do the center-table stuff," and he pointed at the lighted globes.

"We were going to plan the earth in the past, the earth in the present, and the earth in the future." He went on, "I got to her house at two-thirty. She had just done it," he said in a low voice. "She had just done it, Cheryl. Not five minutes before."

He brightened. "Well, so all last night I couldn't sleep! I thought I might as well work, so I came over and decided to get the whole thing done myself. It's a kind of present to her and to myself, too."

I went down the aisle to see the globes. Each one was lighted at its center, then painted with stained-glass paint. In the first globe you could see the fiery gases of zillions of years B.C., already some molten and premetal, the crust still showing cracks full of fire; the seas were beginning, but they were seas the way Freddie and Faye free-drew the world when they tried to show Furman and me how much they knew in geography. The second globe was our world now, in its mantle of blue and white cloud, the way the world looks behind TV weather anchors. Tom Gall told Furman and Furman told me that some famous psychoanalyst had nearly died once, and when balanced between life and death he dreamed he was flying away from the globe and that it looked heartbreakingly beautiful in its blue and white winding cloth of cloud.

From the rear Grayzie called, "There's going to be sound effects, too. Here it is. French horn. Elgar. What do you think?"

Under the final globe, a plaque read: OUR EARTH, A.D. 65,000,000 YEARS. California was half gone. The Aleutians were too prominent. The East Coast was under water. Other things were wrong. The Midwest, my country, didn't show, because Grayzie had positioned blue-and-white cloud above it, but I knew it would be changed, too.

Grayzie now came over and stood next to me. We listened to what he called Elgar. I would have called it "Pomp and Circumstance," and I thought it was beautiful. I kept staring at the lighted earth.

"We'll all be dead by then," I said, not even caring if that was a dumb remark, because I was still in my strange new mood.

"That's my idea," Grayzie said. "The very thing I thought to myself."

I looked at him to smile. I saw now he was wearing a dickey

of white cotton with handmade embroidered flowers on it. I knew instantly that he had bought a pillowcase of Mrs. Beske's at the auction and then sewn it so the embroidered part would show under his open shirt at the neck. He gave the plaid visor a soldierlike yank down. "Right!" he said snappily in the working-class one of his British accents. "All the shit that is going round now will be ended by then."

When I got outside I drove up to the hospital, but the nurses told me Mercein was sleeping and they didn't want her disturbed. They were going to keep her at least another night for observation. They added, "She's pretty anemic, you know."

I went home to wait for the children. I decided to make them a treat so I would get to feeling less strange.

"Cocoa!" they shouted, pleased.

"Yeah, but listen," I said. We all sat at the table. "I have been thinking about that little drip LeRoy Beske."

"*Big* drip LeRoy, you mean," Freddie said, but he looked respectful and interested.

"I've been thinking about him," I repeated. "It's going to take the two of you, I figure. So here's the idea. Tomorrow morning, Freddie, you go to school but don't take your bookbag. Take your books loose. You get into the bus, as usual. You sit halfway back, as usual. And Faye, you sit where you always sit.

"Now, as soon as the bus gets to the school grounds, let the little kids off first, the way you always do. Then, Faye, you hurry those sixth-grade girls. Tell them anything. But once they get off, don't let them start for the school building. Keep them around there."

"This is weird, Mom," Faye said. "What do I tell them?"

"Just lie," I said. "Now, Freddie, you will have to hustle so you are down on the ground fast. Take each of your books and hand one to each girl and look her right in the face and say, 'Hold this for me, will you?' They'll take the book because people don't think fast. Believe me, kids, take it from your mom:

people do not think fast. Then, Freddie, you'll see that the girls will stand around in a half-circle. They may say a lot of negative stuff, but don't pay any attention."

"Will they *ever* say a lot of stuff," Faye said richly. "Words you hear only on school buses, Mom. They'll think it's really weird."

"But they'll stay around to see what's going on," I told her. I turned back to Freddie. "Freddie, now you turn around to face the bus doorway. When LeRoy Beske comes out and has one foot in the air but not on the ground and the other foot still bearing his weight on the lowest step, then you say very loudly, 'I forgot to tell you I don't like your tone of voice,' and you slug him as hard as you can just where the nose meets the forehead. If you get a second chance, hit him on just one eye. You need to get blood fast. Don't count on the second chance, Freddie. I looked over that kid at the Beske farm auction. So as soon as you've hit him, once or twice, don't get smart and decide to stay for more. Turn around and walk up to each of those girls and thank each one for holding your book for you. Take the books and go up the sidewalk to the doors. Don't turn around, whatever you do."

"Mom, that is a very dumb idea," Faye said. "LeRoy will go right after Freddie and hit him from behind."

"If I get *that* far," Freddie said. "I'm thinking about it, though, Mom. Things sure can't go on the way they are."

"They won't," I said. "Nothing's going on the way it was."

The three of us went over the plan again. Freddie modified it some. Faye decided to call up each girl that evening, not tell her what was going to happen but tell her that *something* was going to happen, so they would be geared up. Then she started drawing fists. She rested her own left fist on the kitchen table and then drew it, freehand, without looking at her drawing, the way Mercein had taught her. She put shadow between the knuckles.

In the next weeks our lives changed. Mercein had always

told me, "Never, ever say, 'You just never know how things will turn out,' because it is such a boring thing to say." I felt like saying it a thousand times during that next week, however.

The local hospital staff didn't get in touch with the Mental Health Center psychiatrists, but they did arrange some chemical-dependency counseling for Mercein. They were going to arrange for Mercein to see a social worker from Grand Rapids, but Tom reminded them that after all he was a trained psychologist: Why drive down to Grand Rapids on all this new snow and get killed on the road? The hospital staff said Mercein should get psychiatric care. All right, Tom told them, he was all for it, but not this very minute. All right, they told him back, but they wanted to do a complete physical for both of them, because she seemed upset about not being able to have a child.

The test indicated that Mercein could bear children perfectly well. Tom's sperm count was five percent of normal.

The following Sunday afternoon, Tom and Furman went off to a retreat for school psychologists and intake officers in Saint Cloud. Grayzie had the Artmobile on the road that weekend, so after the police found Mercein and took her to the hospital, they called me. She had slit both wrists this time. She succeeded in dying.

After that, attendance at Tom Gall's Business Psych class dwindled. Even Furman missed some times, and right after Christmas he said he guessed he had had enough of singing with the choir. In April the school did not renew Tom's contract, and he moved out of town in June.

I never forgot all the interesting conversations I had had with Mercein. In the years following 1975, Grayzie and I often reminded each other what a wonderful exhibit he had made in the Artmobile, with those three globes lighted at their centers—especially the last one, showing the earth sixty-five million years from now.

I also remember the details of Freddie's fight with LeRoy Beske outside the school bus.

He and Faye did everything by their plan. When LeRoy came off the lowest bus step, Freddie slugged him one. Freddie decided fast not to try for a second hit. He turned around and started thanking each girl for holding his book. Then, he told us, a semitrailer hit him in the small of his back. He felt himself caving. As he went down, another semitrailer hit him in the back of his neck.

Next he lay on the concrete sidewalk, face up. Snow was falling. The remarkable thing about it was that all of the snowflakes were angled straight at him. Some came from straight above, but also some came at him at a slant from left and right, and some from above his wet eyebrows and from below his chin. Then he noticed that in a ring all around that gigantic gray sky were the faces of little girls. They were all looking down at him. He saw the baby fat under their chins. The girls were cheeping and crying his name. Freddie could see they looked very respectful. As I listened to him, I thought: Maybe they'll grow up to be dull or dispirited like the football players, but for now, as Mercein would have said, they were enough to make your heart stop.

My Lord
Bag of Rice

WHEN VIRGIL had been healthy and mean, Eleanor had loved him; now that he was dying, his pain grinding his shoulders and hips into the bed, she sometimes found herself daydreaming: If Virgil died this week instead of next, I could start everything that much sooner. "Do you feel guilty?" B.J. at the Women's Support Group said. "You have a right to your own life." It sounded 1980s O.K. to have a right to your own life; it did not sound so good to say: If Virgil Grummel would only die this week instead of next, or tonight instead of tomorrow night, I could inherit the farm and the engine-repair service all the sooner. I could sell it all and take the $180,000 cash that their neighbor Almendus Leitz said it was probably worth. She would start a boardinghouse in Saint Paul and never, never again hear cruel language around her. *Never,* she thought, patting Virgil's ankle skin.

It was three in the morning, the hour when she usually visited Virgil at Masonic Hospital, because then the drugs didn't cover the pain. She also drove over from Saint Paul during the day.

35

Sometimes, like tonight, when she walked right into the hot, wide doorway of the hospital, no one sat guard at Reception. The flowers leaned on their stems in the shadowy glass cooler. The crossword puzzle kits waited motionless in the gift case. Someone could perfectly well walk in and hurt people, and steal things, and trot back out into the August night. Eleanor always walked past the dark counters to the elevator and came up to Three.

Despite his morphine, Virgil once again was awake and in pain. He wanted to talk about the good old days. His agonized, liquid eyes watched her as she cut in half each sock of a new woolen pair. Then she slipped the toe half over his icy feet. Whole socks didn't work because of the Styrofoam packed around Virgil's insteps to prevent bedsores.

In his wispy, pain-throttled voice, he said, "Do you remember how we went to Monte to get you your stone?" Dawson was their town, but Montevideo was the town that counted, the place for buying major things like wall-to-wall carpeting and diamond rings. Eleanor smiled down at Virgil's face in the shadowy hospital room, but she was thinking how he had never called the ring an engagement ring; he called it a "stone," just as meals were "chow" and making love was "taking your medicine." One day their older neighbor lady had come to the house, Mrs. Almendus Leitz, and told Eleanor how Almendus was always telling her to "just roll over and take your medicine." Mrs. Leitz was sick of it. She and Eleanor stood on the stoop, both of them with their work-strong arms folded, looking out over Virgil's steaming acreage of corn and beans. It crossed Eleanor's mind at the time that the whole breathless prairie was full of farm places at half-mile intervals where men were telling women to roll over and take their medicine, but she didn't think about it. "Yes, but you *should* have been thinking about it," they all said firmly, down at the Women's Support Group she now belonged to in Minneapolis. Not just B.J. said so. All of them. B.J. said she fervently hoped that now Eleanor was in the Twin Cities she would become sexually active. Eleanor let her talk.

As soon as they were married, Virgil put in a bid for the old District 73 Country School and won it. He dragged it over to their place on the flatbed, laid down a concrete floor for it, and set it down. He never even yanked the old school cupboards and bookshelves off the walls: there were dozens of Elson-Gray readers and some children's storybooks. Eleanor found a book of Japanese fairy tales: she took it up whenever she had a moment. Now Virgil wanted her to recall how he'd be repairing machinery out there in the shop, and he'd call her on the two-way to come out, and how they worked together out there. "Do you remember," he whispered, "how you'd quit whatever you was doing in the house and come on out and help me in the shop?" She remembered: the two-way crackled and growled all the time in the kitchen. She could hear the field hands from Almendus's west half-section swearing because they'd dropped a furrow wheel or a lunchbox out in the plowing somewhere. Then, very loud and close, Virgil's voice would cut in: "Hey, Little Girl, this is Big Red Chief; get your butt out here a minute," and he would go off without waiting for her to answer. He had fixed up both the laundry area and the kitchen for radio reception, so he knew she'd hear him, wherever she was, canning or what. She would go out to the shop, arms crossed across her breasts: if it was cold, running; if it was summer, looking out over the fields past Almendus's place toward Dawson Mills. Virgil was fond of the radio. Sometimes he wanted to make love in the shop; he would lay out the hood drop cloth on the station wagon backseat, which he never did get back into the station wagon. When the wagon finally threw a rod, the backseat stayed in the shop. Each time he was through making love, he said, "This is Big Red Chief; over and out," and gave her head a little slap on the temple.

Eleanor knew she was lucky. All her childhood, her father had gone on every-six-month beating binges. He beat up her

mother, and then he forced her sister. "You don't have to look
so owly," he told Eleanor when she stood dumb, watching.
"Your big sister is a real princess." She was so lucky to be
married to a good man like Virgil, who didn't drink much. It
was boring helping a man in the shop, though. Much of the
time he would say, "Don't go away, little girl; I might need
you." He didn't care that she had quart jars boiling in the pro-
cessor. So she gave his feet a glance (he had dollied himself
underneath someone's Buick now) and she carried the Japanese
fairy tale book over to one of the old schoolroom windows.
Virgil's FARM AND ENGINE REPAIRS sign creaked outside, the corn
tattered in the wind, and Eleanor found a story that she had read
over and over.

"Hey," Virgil shouted from under the Buick he was fixing.
"Get that V-belt and hand it to me." Then he said, "No, dang
it all, not that one—the other one!" Then she would open the
book again.

"Hey, get your ass over here," Virgil cried. "Hand me all
this stuff when I tell you, one by one in order."

She wiped the grease off her hands and went back to the
story. A young Japanese hero had a retinue of servants. Watercolor illustrations showed him mustachioed, with slant eyes and
nearly white skin. All his servants wore thin swords tucked into
their sashes. They looked a little like middle-aged, effeminate
Americans in dressing gowns, who had chosen to arm themselves. Eleanor couldn't keep her eyes off the pictures. The hero
was traveling through Japan, looking for adventure, when he
came to a high, rounded bridge over a river that ran to the sea.
As he began to cross it, he saw that a frightful dragon slept at
the top of its arch. The dragon's scales and horns and raised
back ridge were everything a child would count on when it
came to dragons. No one was around to sneer at a grown woman
reading a child's book when she was supposed to be helping her
husband.

The young Japanese started to step right across the dragon,

and it suddenly reared up. His servants dropped back, aghast, but the hero held his ground. Then the dragon took the form of a beautiful woman, who explained that she was the ruler of a sea kingdom under the bridge. Each night, a centipede of gigantic size slid down from the mountain to the north (she pointed) and ate dozens of her subjects, who were fishes and sea animals. They realized they needed a man—but not an ordinary man. "You can imagine what fright an ordinary man would feel," the sea princess said.

Dusk was falling. She pointed again to the mountain, which now showed only its black profile before the green, darkening sky. Some sort of procession of people carrying lanterns seemed to descend the near slope of the mountain. "Those are not people," the sea princess said. "Those are the eyes of the centipede."

"I will kill it," the young Japanese said simply.

"I think you are brave enough," the princess said. "I took the form of a dragon and placed myself on this bridge, pretending to sleep. You are the only man who hasn't fled at the sight of me."

The hero drew a light-green arrow from the quiver on his shoulder. He sent it at one of the centipede's eyes. That eye went out, but the monster kept coming. He fired another arrow—a pale-pink one this time—but it only put out another eye. Then he recalled a belief of the Japanese people: human saliva is poison to magical enemies. He licked the tip of an arrow the color of a bird's egg and sent it off into the thick dusk. It went true. It put out the creature's foremost eye—and then the princess and the hero were joyous to see all the eyes darken to red, then gray, like worn coals.

The princess clapped. "Wait, O hero!" she cried. She clapped again. Fishes dressed in silk robes like men and women rose from the river. They carried gigantic vases from earlier, greater times. They brought hundreds of years of hand-embroidered silks and linens. They handed everything to the hero's servants to carry.

Then a sea serpent not changed into human form brought a large plain bag. In the watercolor illustration it was light brown, like a gunnysack gone pale. The sea princess said, "The other gifts are for you and your court, since obviously you are a prince. But this bag is for your people. Even if famine comes to your country, your people will never be hungry. This bag full of rice will never empty."

"Then I will carry it myself," he told her. But before raising it to his shoulder, he bowed very low, and the sea princess bowed low back to him. Then she faded.

When the young man returned to his own country, he was known forever as My Lord Bag of Rice.

In the first year of her marriage, Eleanor Grummel read through all the books left in the District 73 schoolhouse. She would hand Virgil what he needed—the snowblower sprocket, the fan belt, the lag screw, or the color-coded vacuum tubing— and then lean against the wall or sometimes sit on the old station wagon backseat and read. She read all the books, but returned over and over to "My Lord Bag of Rice."

Now, eighteen years later, she held Virgil's hand while he whispered to her, his memories blurred by drugs, getting the times wrong, getting the occasions wrong, his eyes weeping from illness and recollection. Eleanor saw herself again standing at the old schoolhouse window, sometimes glancing out at the fields, sometimes studying the illustrations in the fairy-tale book. Now she thought that she had read in an enchanted way, because she had been too unconscious to know she lived in misery.

Twice each day, throughout Virgil's dying, Eleanor drove happily from Masonic, a building of the University of Minnesota hospital system, back to Mrs. Zenobie's boardinghouse in Saint Paul. On the night run, she recited aloud in the car whole passages from the King James translation. Aloud she cried, "And the darkness comprehendeth it not!" or she shouted in the car, "And none shall prevent Him!" She remembered to add "Saith the Lord" after any pronouncements she could remember from Genesis.

August changed to early fall; she still drove with the windows open. The air was dusty and smooth, its blackness so thorough that she felt that it lay all over the Middle West—as if even the Twin Cities, a polite place, hardly made a pinprick of light in all the blackness. Of course the Twin Cities were not really a polite place—Mrs. Zenobie, the landlady at her boardinghouse, was not polite—but politeness was possible.

In the normal course she would have lodged nearer the hospital where Virgil was dying. The university volunteer explained that all the special housing for people like Eleanor happened to be full. Mrs. Zenobie was not the greatest, she explained—and Eleanor would have to drive across to Saint Paul—but the price was reasonable. The volunteer gave Eleanor a map and highlighted her route from I-94 to Newell Avenue, Saint Paul. She urged Eleanor to join a certain Women's Support Group, since she was under stress and was new in the city. Eleanor was allowed to visit her husband any hour of the night or day she liked.

The night runs brought her back to Mrs. Zenobie's at about four in the morning. No matter how quietly Eleanor turned the key and tiptoed past the roomers' coat hooks, Mrs. Zenobie would always wake and come out from behind the Japanese room divider. She slept downstairs, she told Eleanor, because of the crime. If crooks ever realized no one was on the ground floor, especially when it was a woman who ran the household, they would take advantage. And once they robbed a woman, they'd rob her again. The police right now were looking for LeRoy Beske, the lowlife who had owned 1785 Newell, three houses over, and then sold it to someone who never moved in. "You got to learn these things," Mrs. Zenobie told Eleanor, "if you're serious about wanting to start a rooming house. Also I wanted to say I'd be the last not to be grateful you have brought us so many doughnuts from the bakery, but I can't give you anything off the rent for that."

"I didn't expect it," Eleanor said.

"It doesn't matter how many men boarders you got," Mrs. Zenobie said. "It doesn't do any good. Crime is crime."

Mrs. Zenobie had five elderly male boarders, four of whom were not so polite as Eleanor hoped to find for clientele whenever she finally got her own house. Her idea was to have a five o'clock social hour: they would all gather in the living room before dinner and she would give each boarder some wine or cider, so it would be like home. Eleanor herself had never seen a home like the one she had in mind, but the image was clear to her.

Eleanor started up the staircase, exhausted.

"If you're serious about wanting a house," Mrs. Zenobie whispered fiercely up after her, "I heard that 1785 is for sale again now. It'd be big enough." Mrs. Zenobie's eyes glared as steady as bathroom night-lights. "I wouldn't feel you were cutting into my prospects," she said. "There's so many people wanting boardinghouses these days, there's enough for everyone."

Eleanor slept well all that late August and early September. She felt the grateful passion for sleep of people whose lives are a shambles. Only sleep was completely reliable. She dreamed. Every morning, she woke up haunted and mystified by the dreams.

In the mornings, Alicia Fowler, a realtor recommended by B.J. at the Support Group, picked her up. Eleanor felt cared for in Alicia's car. They ignored the big sun-dried thoroughfares—Snelling, Cleveland, Randolph. Alicia knew every house in Saint Paul or Minneapolis and what it likely was worth. Eleanor said, "My idea is three stories, homey, decently built. I can't afford Summit Avenue, but I don't want a dangerous part of town."

After the morning's searches with Alicia, Eleanor took Virgil's car over to the hospital for an hour or so. If Virgil was sleeping, she daydreamed beside his tubings. Once a technician came in to get Virgil ready to wheel down for X-rays. Eleanor realized that whatever the X-rays would teach Virgil's doctor, these trips were not for Virgil's sake but for other patients after Virgil's death. She pointed out that it was painful for Virgil to be moved onto the stretcher table and off again. The technician said he was only following orders. Eleanor did not dare oppose the doctor's orders. After they wheeled Virgil down, she thought of how she should have protected him from that extra pain. Her fist shook as she held his drip stand.

After an hour she left and drove courteously home on Oak and Fulton streets, onto 94, and east toward Saint Paul. She waved to drivers backed up at Erie Street and let them onto the road in front of her. They waved back. She waved to let people from parking lots enter the column of cars. She was delighted to be courteous to strangers. For eighteen years she had shrunk in her seat while Virgil gave the finger to anyone who honked when Virgil crossed lanes. On their few Twin Cities junkets, he pulled ahead two feet into the pedestrian crossing when he had to wait for a stoplight. It forced pedestrians to walk around the front of the car. When a pedestrian gave Virgil a hostile glance, Virgil would gun the engine, which made the pedestrian jump. Eleanor looked out the right-hand window in order not to see Virgil smile. Now she enjoyed driving under the speed limit; she played at imagining other drivers having their lives saved by her carefulness. She even formed a mental image of those in the oncoming traffic saying to themselves, "At least *there's* a car not driven by some natural killer!" as they whipped past on their side of the white line. When Virgil was caught speeding, he would not look up as he passed his driver's license out the window to the officer. While the man asked him a question or told Virgil his computer reading, Virgil steadily stared at the steering wheel and kept both hands rugged on it, as if to drive off. His face looked full and stung with blood. The moment the officer turned away, initialed the citation, and wound up the invariably courteous request to keep it down,

Virgil came to life. He snarled, "I took your number, fellow! If you ever, like *ever,* try to drive through Chippewa or Lac Qui Parle County, I know the right people that'll put you up so high, by the time you hit the ground eagles will have made a nest in your ass!"

Eleanor now went to Saint Swithin's Episcopal Church confirmation class on Tuesdays. There were three men in the group, and an innumerable, changing roster of women—all of them older than Eleanor. One of the youngish men spoke either wrathfully or weakly about one issue or another. Two of the women kept saying, "I'm not sure this is relevant," a remark that caused the young priest to tremble. Eleanor felt at odds with all of them, since her aim in church instruction was not relevance but beauty. She wanted to learn polite ideas, whatever they were. She memorized a good deal of what Father said. Once—only once—she repeated one of the phrases she had memorized. The group looked astonished and then disgusted. She stayed on but only because the group met in a room called the Lady Chapel, where the royal and navy-blue stained-glass windows pleased her.

On Thursdays she had the Women's Support Group. They were people so different from herself that she didn't like to think about it. B.J.—all of them—had been sympathetic when she told them about her father's abuse. When her thoughts grew more and more centered around getting a boardinghouse, they seemed indifferent. Anyone in pain was a priority: in October a woman who had recently been sexually assaulted joined them. After that, Eleanor felt unseen. She knew these women were more intelligent than she was; on the other hand, she felt stung when they wouldn't rejoice with her over having found a house she could buy.

In the week of Virgil's death and the weeks following it, Eleanor had so much to think of that she forgot to tell B.J. and the others that she was widowed at last. When they found out, B.J. threw her arms around Eleanor, crying, "You are so wonderfully centered!"

Eleanor blushed. She felt stupid. People had emotions that meant nothing to her; they used words she never used—"centered" and "on top of your shit."

Eleanor stayed on at Mrs. Zenobie's. There was no social hour before dinner, as Eleanor planned for her own boarding-house, but now and then Mrs. Zenobie's niece brought in a group of Sunday-school students for what was announced as a very, very special occasion. One October Saturday, the children came to explain some small kits to Mrs. Zenobie's boarders. If the boarders would be good enough to assemble these kits, the children would pick them up on Saint Andrew's Day.

Eleanor perked up a little at hearing "Saint Andrew's Feast" since memorizing trivia about saints was a favorite part of her new church life. Each kit was a plastic sandwich bag, in which lay two tongue depressors, a plastic twister, and a plastic baby poinsettia. The idea was to use the twister to attach the tongue depressors at right angles to make a cross, then jam the poinsettia's stem into the twist as well. It made a good Christmas present for shut-ins, and then you could trade the poinsettia for a lily and, presto, you had an Easter symbol, too, which was the kind of thing that shut-ins could relate to.

Eleanor backed around the room divider as discreetly as possible and made for the staircase.

Suddenly a man's voice said, "Oh, no, you don't, Eleanor! No one gets out of this!"—with a laugh. He came out to the hallway where she hovered. "I have seen many cultural atrocities in my life," he said to her—not only not lowering his voice but raising it slightly, and even, as she had heard him do any number of times at the dinner table, adding a slight British inflection—"but I think this one surpasses them all!" It was Jack Lackie, the retired Episcopal priest, a member of Mrs. Zenobie's household.

"The mystery is, what was he really?" Mrs. Zenobie once

said, gouging a used Kleenex into her apron pocket. "Janitor, maybe. Not a priest. You get wise to what people used to be and what they say they used to be. To hear it, I've had boarders who invented the atom bomb, and I've had CIA operatives, and I've had a hundred of President Kennedy's cousins."

Eleanor had felt endeared to Jack Lackie because he never once lifted his trouser cuff to show the ribbing of long underwear. Mrs. Zenobie's other men liked to explain that now that winter had set in, they put on their long underwear, and that was *it* until spring. Two of them shoved their wooden chairs back, bent over, and lifted the bottoms of their trouser legs in case Eleanor didn't believe them. Jack Lackie was the only man not to do it, and Eleanor had made up her mind that she would have him for a boarder in her home when she got it.

Now she smiled at him. It would give a classy tone to the place if someone spoke of "cultural atrocities."

She lay on her bed upstairs, hearing the children's voices singing from below. Under the house, the ground throbbed from a parked Amtrak train on Transfer Street; even the house thrummed gently through the concrete basement and wooden studs. Eleanor smiled in the dark: this was her favorite mood. She felt simple, full of plans, and not confused. It was true that nearly everyone she talked to that day was so different from her they could never be friends. She passed quickly over the idea that she might be lonely the rest of her life. She raced to make image after image of her boardinghouse. There would never, never be any church groups allowed into it. There would be a wood-burning stove in the living room. There would be a wine and cider hour before dinner each night. If anyone sneered or shouted, she would ask that person to leave. There would be an outside barbecue. There would be climbing roses. She would tell Alicia the realtor that she definitely wanted 1785 Newell Avenue.

It seemed like a million years since Big Red Chief's voice crackled at her from the speakers in the farmhouse kitchen. Was it true that you needed to be widowed in order to lead a courteous life? She didn't pause to think that idea through but happily imagined the stained-glass window at 1785 and thought how holy it looked even if it lighted a staircase, not a church. It made her feel holy and unconfused. Months before, Father had said, "It is always a risk to take your soul into real life!" The others nodded, as if wakened and strengthened by his remark. Eleanor made nothing of it, but she memorized it, another graceful phrase, even if "risk" to her meant only the risk of borrowing against her inheritance to buy a three-story house. Her mind drifted back to the house.

On the third Sunday in November, Alicia hurried Eleanor to an office building in downtown Saint Paul, where they crowded into a small room with a conference table and vinyl chairs. There were four other people. Alicia sat close by Eleanor, bending right over the papers in front of her, making sure she signed nothing that wasn't right. A man at the opposite end of the crowded table was being similarly coached by his real estate agent. Presumably he was the owner of 1785 Newell Avenue. Eleanor supposed she would shake hands with him at the end, but for now each avoided the other's eyes. The closing agent's dull, energetic voice kept explaining terms. There was some cloud on the title, but it was cleared. . . . The police had asked that if Ms. Grummel ever saw LeRoy Beske, to call them immediately: he had been seen hanging around several times since he sold the house.

Eleanor was in a dream. She looked affectionately at Alicia's permanented head: it was back-combed and sprayed as stiff as a howitzer shell. If you touched it, surely your hand would come away with tiny cuts. Eleanor had two feelings: affection for this tough person who had helped her get her life's dream, and the memory of her mother, who wore dark glasses when she went to the beauty parlor. Even if she had to cover bruises with pancake, she never missed a hair setting; the time she had three stitches in her right cheek, she postponed her hairdo by

two hours. Eleanor kept signing in exactly the places where
Alicia pointed a Lee press-on nail to show her.

Keys tinkled across the table. Smiles. The men stood up:
people's hands reached across to shake. Then they were back
out into the cold street. Alicia said, "Come on. We'll drive to
Mrs. Zenobie's and walk to your new house."

Eleanor was learning the measured graces of the rich. They
brought each other small but ceremonial presents. Women
brought just a few rosebuds for other women when they had a
meeting together; the Support Group people arrived with news-
paper cones full of flowers to celebrate someone getting her shit
together. Men brought a bottle sometimes—Father had some
sherry for the confirmands at the end. Now Eleanor said, "We'll
drink to the house!" She had a bottle of champagne in the backseat.

The previous owners had left a dining room table and two
chairs. Eleanor opened the champagne. Alicia lifted her glass.
Then they both heard scrabbling in the basement. "Not rats,"
Alicia said quickly and firmly. "I checked that out before. No
rats."

"I'm not afraid of rats," Eleanor said. "I'm a farm girl." She
was about to tell Alicia about how Virgil would lift up a bale
of hay; when the rats burst out she whacked as many as she
could.

"Down we go," Alicia said, rising.

As they moved through the fine old kitchen, Eleanor realized
with surprise that she had paid no attention to the basement. It
was the third floor that had fascinated her: One finished room,
churchlike, with steep eaves going up to the ridgepole, and a
charming dilapidated balcony at the peak end. The other half of
the third floor was not finished; boarders could store their luggage there. The second floor was like all second floors of abused
houses: radiators with paint chipped off, smudgy windows,
deeply checked sills and mullions.

Alicia turned on the basement light. They trotted about the

basement, between the abandoned coalroom and the laundry room, around the monstrous octopus of a furnace, spray-painted aluminum, like ship's equipment. Behind the worktable, there sat against the wall a very thin, old, dirty woman. Her awful eyes gleamed. One skinny hand plucked at her blouse buttons.

Alicia said, "O.K., both together . . ." They raised the woman up. "Nope—she's too weak to stand." Alicia paused.

"Let me," Eleanor said. She bent down, her back to Alicia. All that farmwork. "Just put her on my back." They got the woman upstairs and laid her on the floor in the living room, which had carpeting.

"Police first," Alicia said.

"I'll run to Mrs. Zenobie's," Eleanor said.

Mrs. Zenobie herself frankly listened while Eleanor called 911. She rubbed an elbow and smiled. "You're getting into the problems of running a rooming house even faster than I did! You haven't been there even one night, and already you got a nonpaying-type tenant hiding in the basement! Gosh!"

Eleanor riffled through Mrs. Zenobie's directory. She ordered one chicken-onions-snow-peas-and-rice and gave the address.

"Unsuitable tenants is the second greatest pain next to taxes," Mrs. Zenobie offered.

The police car was already parked at 1785 when Eleanor ran back.

"It's Sunday, so the only social workers are the Primary Interventions. We'll just take her to jail for the night," one of the two young men explained.

Alicia said she had to beat it, since the situation seemed to be under control.

Eleanor said, "I'll keep her for the night." She added, "I run a boardinghouse."

"Doesn't look like one yet," the other young cop said. "We've been kind of keeping a watch on this house. There was a real bad-news type here. This lady probably needs a doctor.

We'll take her, and we'll get a social worker around to you tomorrow."

The policeman looked down at the old woman. "Can you talk, lady?" he said gently.

He waited a second. "O.K. We'll wait for the ambulance." One of them went out to radio.

"This the kind of customer you going to have in this house?" the remaining policeman said with a grin.

There was a knock. Eleanor paid the Oriental foods deliveryman and brought in the little white paper buckets with their wire handles.

The policeman got the idea. He and Eleanor knelt on the floor. "If you can eat, lady, it's the best thing you can do," the officer said. He said to Eleanor, "Show it to her."

Eleanor said, "We're going to help you lean up against the wall." She opened one of the packets, and the old woman suddenly dug her whole hand into the rice. She put a palmful of it into her own face and begun to chew slowly. She reached in again and again.

"She needs chopsticks like I need chopsticks," the young officer said comfortably. Eleanor leaned on her heels. The woman finished all the rice. Eleanor offered her the chicken. "This is going to be a mess," the policeman said. He stood up and ambled into the kitchen. "Someone at least left you some paper towels." Together they wiped the woman's face. Then Eleanor wiped her neck where the Cantonese sauce and a few onions had run down. The ambulance came. The policeman left a number to call if there was any trouble. Eleanor walked over to Mrs. Zenobie's for the last time. Tomorrow night I'll homestead, she thought.

The social worker came the next day. He introduced himself as Rex, from Primary Intervention. Rex told Eleanor that none of the women's shelters had any room for a new person. Eleanor and he sat at the dining room table, while he explained that there used to be an office especially for cases like this woman's.

Now there wasn't the dollars. Rex thought this woman was named Eunice something: she was a victim of the second-to-last owner here, a LeRoy Beske, who'd run a racket diverting old people's welfare checks to himself. Then Rex looked at his hands.

"I don't know how you'd feel about this," he said. "I don't know what kind of house you want to have, but if you could take care of Eunice on a temporary basis, we could offer you the Difficult Care rate. That is, we'd pay you twenty-two dollars a day to feed and shelter her. The hospital says she is O.K. She's just in shock and can't talk. They don't think there is anything organically wrong except she's nearly starved to death. If you wanted to take her in four or five days . . ."

Eleanor said to herself fast, "I could still get five or six courteous people who would have polite conversations at the table. It shouldn't be too hard: it'd still be a house where no one told anyone else to get their butt over here or there."

The truck finally came from Dawson with the furniture. Eleanor bought three more beds from Montgomery Ward. She interviewed prospective tenants. She put Mercein, Mrs. Solstrom, Dick, Carolyn, and George on the second floor. She put Eunice in the room she had imagined for herself, behind the kitchen on the ground floor. She slept on the sofa for several weeks. She kept the third-floor bedroom untenanted until the second floor was filled.

"Here," Mrs. Zenobie said. "They've got that racket on the TV so loud I can't hear myself think. Come in the kitchen."

She watched Eleanor with eyes blazing.

"Have I got this straight?" she said. "You want to trade one of your tenants for one of mine? What kind of crap is that?" She paused. "I don't want to get tough with you. I know you are mourning your husband. But you're in business, too, and you and I are doing business on the same street. So naturally I am looking at everything carefully. Let me just give this back to you, and you tell *me*. You want me to take someone named Mrs. Joanne Solstrom into my house, and then you want Mr. Jack Lackie to move to your house? You're going to pay them one hundred dollars each for the inconvenience?"

Eleanor nodded.

Mrs. Zenobie looked at her fingernails with the finesse of an actress. Since they were cut to just below the quick, there couldn't be much to discover about them. "I never paid any money to have some man move into any house of mine," she remarked.

There are some things you can't explain to some people, Eleanor thought. You can't tell your support group that you're *not* going through "the grief process" for your husband but that you are furious at the State of Minnesota for chipping tax out of your late husband's engine-repair service inventory before you inherited it. You couldn't tell Mrs. Zenobie that you wanted a retired Episcopal priest in your boardinghouse because he talked about history and culture and you did *not* want a perfectly nice woman named Mrs. Solstrom because she sneered during wine and cider hour that if that Tommy Kramer couldn't learn to move his butt out of the pocket, he deserved every sack he got.

"I don't get it," Mrs. Zenobie said. "She pays her rent? She's clean? O.K. But if you think you're going to get any help out of that Lackie, think again. He's retired. He never picked up a leaf in the yard; not around this place he didn't."

Their lives went smoothly through the winter. Eunice still didn't speak, but everyone fed her. Mercein and Dick brought her Whopper burgers, Carolyn brought her doughnuts, George brought her take-out Italian food from a place near his plant. Jack brought her cans of Dinty Moore Beef Stew and helped her stack them up in the unfinished part of the attic. She grew fat. The social worker, Rex, thought it might be months before Eunice could speak again.

She followed Jack everywhere; he talked to her all the time. Eleanor began to feel happy. She moved Eunice to the north end of the second floor: she herself took the downstairs bedroom. Jack arranged his few possessions—his oddly old-fashioned clothes, his complete set of Will and Ariel Durant's *The Story of Civilization,* in the third-floor room. Jack took over laying and lighting the fire in the living room stove that Eleanor bought at an auction on Fulton Street. Each late afternoon, they all watched the dull, comfortable flame through the isinglass while Jack served the wine and cider. Whenever he rose to refill someone's glass, Eunice stood up, too. If he left the room, she followed him. He had to turn directly to her and say, "No" when he wanted to be alone.

The other tenants were grateful that she followed Jack instead of driving them crazy. Eleanor was glad because she needed the hour before dinner to cook, she needed the hour after dinner to plan the next day's work, and she liked to sit alone in the kitchen at night. The dishwasher chugged through its hissing cycles. Eleanor wrote out lists of repairs needed, hardware to buy, meals for the rest of the week. She could hear Jack's voice rising and falling in the living room. He was telling Eunice everything that ever happened in human history.

As the weather warmed, Jack took on some outside chores. He renailed the rose trellis to the house while Eunice passed nails up to him. He sorted through the loose bricks lying in the backyard, dividing wholes from brokens. Whenever he lifted a brick, Eunice picked one up, watching his face. When he set his down, she set hers down. When her hands were free, she ate. There was always food in her jacket pockets—a wrapped ham-and-cheese or Swiss-and-mushroom from Hardee's. Sometimes Jack let her into the third-floor storage area to count her cans of stew and soup. She arranged and rearranged them into pyramids, straight walls, squares. Her eyes lost the terrible glint they had at first. The boarders decided that probably she was only sixty or sixty-five, not eighty or ninety. She bathed, dressed, cleaned her teeth, and followed Jack everywhere.

In March, on a Saturday, it was Eleanor's turn to manage the food shelves at Saint Swithin's. By now she was a confirmed church member.

Just before she left home, someone outside threw something through the first-floor stained-glass window. Glass and wood splinters were scattered all over the base of the stairs. Sharp, normal sunlight broke in. George, Eunice, and Jack had been clearing the breakfast table. Now they stood still. Then Eunice moved toward the mess of glass and smashed sashwork; she bent and picked up a brick. Jack immediately took it from her, in case there were glass shards stuck to it. Eleanor called the police.

"Go ahead," Jack told her. "I'll sweep this up, and George can go outside to see if anybody's around."

Like most people who have done plain labor in their lives, Eleanor could separate events at home from those at the job. All that day she worked hard, instructing volunteers, making quick judgments about clients. She knew now who were the few people who picked up food and sold it later. When they showed up and explained what they wanted, Eleanor looked them right in the face, with a deliberate smile, and said, "I'm so sorry; we're fresh out of that." If the person pointed angrily to where that very item stood on the shelf, Eleanor smiled and said, "I know it looks as if we have it. The funny thing is, we're fresh out."

That afternoon, she was happy to get out of her car and start up the sidewalk to her boardinghouse. Since it was still March, Jack would have lighted a fire, and they could all gather as usual and speculate about who had broken their stained-glass window.

Her neighbor from across the street called, "Big trouble, huh, Eleanor?"

He was coming after her to talk. "In a way, I'm glad that happened, Eleanor," he said in a kind tone. "I know it doesn't seem like the right thing to say, but at least now that guy'll get what's coming to him."

Eleanor said slowly, "LeRoy Beske, you mean."

"That creep," the neighbor said. "Hanging around here. Trouble whenever he shows up. I'm sorry it had to happen at your place, Eleanor, but all of us along the street feel relieved." He paused. "Cops came, of course," he said. "They wanted to talk to you and said they'd be back around now or so."

Then a last word from the neighbor: "That Jack Lackie, that tenant of yours! I'll say one thing for him: If a job needs doing, he does it!"

Eleanor looked and saw that the paper toweling she had suggested Jack stuff into the broken window wasn't there. The whole window was reglazed, although only in clear glass now.

Inside the house, the living room was empty and dark.

"Hello?" Eleanor called up the staircase.

"Hello!" Jack called down, in an odd tone.

Eleanor turned back to the door, since someone had rung the bell. It was two policemen Eleanor remembered from months before.

"Finally you got home," one of them said. "We've knocked and rung your bell, but no one would let us in."

Both policemen came right in.

"I hated losing that stained-glass window," Eleanor told them.

"That's the last window Beske'll bust in a long time," one man told her. The other loped over to the staircase and called upstairs: "Everybody down! Police!"

"Well," Eleanor said, preening a little. "I think it is very nice of you men to be so concerned about a broken window."

Then they told her what had happened. LeRoy Beske had thrown the brick through her window, all right. Then he had hung around, and the boarders had seen him go around to the side of the house. They heard a sharp cry. Dick and George ran outside and found Beske bleeding severely from a head wound.

A blood-splashed brick lay near him. They glanced around a little—and then upward at the little balcony off Jack's third-story room. There was no one there. Both men hurried into the house to call the police. They both noticed that neither Jack nor Eunice was in the living room, where the other boarders began to huddle, overhearing the telephone call to 911.

Eleanor thought to herself, her boardinghouse, her polite structure, had fallen into violence just as quickly as any other household in a crime-filled country. The man she had designated to be the cultural leader had assaulted someone right in her own side yard.

One after another, the boarders denied any knowledge. Jack's turn came. Eleanor nearly shuddered. His voice denied knowledge just as flatly as the others' voices had.

"Now this lady: your name is . . .?" The policemen were now looking at Eunice. She was forty pounds heavier than when they had seen her three months earlier.

George said, "That's Eunice. We can pretty much answer for her, officer."

The officer said, "She'll have to speak for herself. Eunice," he said, "what did you see, and where were you?"

Eunice opened her mouth. Her voice croaked and squealed like equipment long unused; phlegm caught in her throat and stopped a vowel now and then, but Eunice talked. When she started in, Eleanor remembered "My Lord Bag of Rice" and how the hero helped the sea princess. For the moment, Eleanor forgot that her reason for having Jack in her boardinghouse was that he should provide cultivated conversation. Now she believed that she had intuitively spotted Jack as a kind figure who would stand guard when they needed him. She thought: Well, well! Now he'd done it. So she had been canny. Her mind felt large and nervous.

Eunice was not ratting on Jack. Eunice said, "In the beginning the human race needed strong leaders. The Jews in Egypt needed a leader to get them out. When medieval farmers had their lands stolen by the church or the state or by their landlords, they needed brave people to get them their freeholds."

She kept talking. When Eunice got to the Reformation, she switched to Chinese history. She explained that the Chinese invented watertight doors for ships, so that no enemy could rake through the entire hold and sink a ship. Any leader knew it was devastating for a man to be trapped in a watertight compartment with the sea pouring in. Nonetheless, a leader told men on the other sides to secure the watertight doors. They heard the doomed man's screams, but the leader could save the rest. A leader could do desperate acts while others froze.

Then there was a brief pause, in which Eleanor could see that Eunice was going to switch to another culture. She explained how painful it was to learn that the world was not terracentric—so painful a truth thousands couldn't bear it.

"O.K, lady, O.K.," one policeman said.

"For now, that's enough," the other said to Eleanor. "You all have your dinner. We'll come back tomorrow, and anyway they will know by then if LeRoy Beske is going to live or not."

Before the door had closed behind them, Eunice had begun again. She explained that in every age of bullies, a leader shows up to give the people respite. She told them about John Ball, a sixteenth-century agricultural reformer. She explained the odal law of Norway. Jack declined to have wine with the others, and Eunice followed him upstairs, telling him about how Captain Cook used psychology to induce his men to eat sauerkraut. It saved them from scurvy.

Those down below could still hear her hoarse, unaccustomed voice, less distinct, as she and Jack rounded the landing and started up the reverse flight. They heard her close the door of her room. Jack's steps continued up on the third-floor stairs. Then they heard Eunice speaking to herself in her room.

Eleanor lighted the stove, listening to the boarders' various exclamations. Gradually they told each other their versions over and over, more and more quietly. After a while, Eleanor put

the crock pot of stew on the dining room table. She called to
Jack and Eunice. Everyone sat quietly, whispering now and
then—"Would you please pass the rolls?" "Would you send the
carrot sticks down here?"—with a good deal of glancing at
Eunice.

Her face was full of color. She looked fifty now, not sixty.
She kept facing Jack and telling that nineteenth-century Chinese
grandmothers were certainly sorry to see their granddaughters'
feet bound the first time. She described how the mothers and
daughters cried as they removed their clogs at night, unwinding
the bloodied cloths from their toes—yet they, more than the
men, made certain the practice was kept up.

One by one the boarders finished eating, nodded to Eleanor,
and left the room. Eleanor and Jack and Eunice remained at the
cluttered table.

At last Jack rose. Eunice followed him immediately, in her
usual way. She was explaining what the Marines did in Mexico
in 1916. Eleanor set the dishwasher growling over its first load.
When she went upstairs, she heard Eunice, alone in her room
behind her door, saying that the Michigan National Guard
helped Fisher Body plant number 1 defeat union workers in
1937. Eunice's voice, getting exercise, sounded smoother now.
Eleanor paused on the landing, decided to go back downstairs
to bed, then noticed Jack sitting on a stair on the flight above.

"You're listening," she whispered to him, going up a few
steps. They regarded each other in the weak night-light.

"How can I help it!" he said in a whispered laugh. "Amazing!
Amazing!"

Eleanor said, "She's not so amazing! It isn't her! *You're* the
one that's amazing!" She didn't mind if her enormous happiness
showed in her whisper. She felt out of her class, somehow—
but this much she knew: it is amazing when a man uses all that
violence that's in men to help people instead of just pushing
people around! Virgil would never have dropped a brick on a
friend's enemy. Her father never defended anyone. She realized

that sometime between dinner and this minute, she had decided to lie for Jack if she had to. She would say what was necessary to keep the police from cornering him. It would be something new for her: she had not even been able to prevail on the X-ray technicians to leave poor Virgil in peace. She had underestimated Jack, admiring only his ability to talk courteously.

Now she whispered, "You have actually saved her life!"

He said, "You don't even know what happened."

Eleanor ignored that idiotic modesty and whispered, "What's more, she half saved yours, too. When she rattled on and on all that history to the police, they obviously decided she was out of her head, and they got up and went home! Of course," Eleanor added, feeling very sage, the way bystanders do when they second-guess the police, "they had been looking for that awful LeRoy Beske for a long time, anyway."

"She didn't save my life, either," Jack now said.

Behind her door Eunice was moving away from Max Planck and introducing Marilyn French and Ruth Bleier.

Jack said from his stair, slightly above Eleanor's, "I want you to listen now. I did not—repeat: did not—drop or throw a brick onto LeRoy Beske from that balcony. You know who goes around this house carrying cans of beef stew and books and bricks."

Eleanor was still. "I don't believe you," she said then.

Jack said, "LeRoy Beske swiped her welfare check for over two years. At the end, he hid her and then nearly starved her to death and dumped her in your basement when he couldn't figure out anything more convenient. She was mad at him. Then he made a mistake. He was drunk when he came around here this morning. For the fun of it, he tossed a brick through your window. He didn't figure Eunice right—she was on the balcony when he ambled by a few hours later. He shouted, 'Hi, little girl!' to her when he saw her. People on the other side of the house heard him. He probably didn't recognize her. He shouted, 'Hi, princess!' She had a brick with her, because she and I were going to build the barbecue today. She was so mad she got off a fast, accurate shot. Anyway," Jack finished up in a satisfied, brutal way, "she got him good."

He whispered down at Eleanor, "Another thing. I am not a retired priest. I am a retired janitor. What you have here is a retired janitor who has read a lot of history."

By now Eunice's voice had almost the lilt and ease of ordinary women's voices. She said that Eskimos' teeth had caries from eating American-made candy bars. She said Eskimos were listening to reggae up there, on the ice floes. She described the hole widening in the Antarctica ozone.

Eleanor and Jack sat on for a few minutes. Eleanor imagined the Eskimos looking out over the ice-filled water. She also remembered the watercolor illustration of the hero with his huge bag of rice: It weighed on one shoulder; he was looking out over water; his robe was painted in baby colors—pink and light blue and dusty yellow—and the Sea of Japan was a pale green, a shade you might choose for a child's nursery.

The Ex–Class Agent

BUDGE HARLEY had always recognized the good of letter writing. At ten years old he knew a note saying, "Dear Mother: Everything is going fine, but please send fifteen dollars by return for new cleats," brought the fifteen or better—but only relayed through Mrs. Harley's bookkeeper-cum-manager in Stamford. If he did her a leisurely account of some Calley Academy snafu, on the other hand, his mother would actually write him herself. If nothing better offered, he would tell her about the Head's latest threats to the lower-middle class—they would have to write two history papers about nineteenth-century Europe and Russia instead of one, all because of a trivial if carefully planned misbehavior by the whole class.

Actual disgrace was better grist for letters: in 1942 Budge's roommate got not only expelled from Calley but "expunged from the Academy records" for making a snow statue on the Alumni House lawn during Parents' Weekend. It faithfully depicted a pair of parents in flagrante. At the end of Budge's upper-middler year, a girl's mother showed up at three o'clock in the

afternoon, drunk, it was thought, and explained in a loud midwestern accent that if she was pulling her daughter out of Calley
before the girl finished her senior year, it was no one's goddamned business but her own. The four or five upper-middlers
and seniors standing around smiled at her dimly and eased on
out of the Tiffin Room. The Head wouldn't even see her, but
sent the Academy driver to pick her up and drive her all the
way in to the North Station. It was days before anyone told
Coreen, the daughter, a kind of colorless girl, that her mother
had shown up and behaved very non–de rigueur. Budge described the whole thing to his mother. "Jesus," she wrote back
appreciatively.

Four days for Budge's letters to get over, four for hers to
get back, nearly weightless in their skimpy envelopes, *Mit Luft-
post* and *Par Avion*. In return for his little life dramas, she told
him about Cau. She could make a Moral Rearmament testi-
monial sound like first-rate faux pas at a really out-of-control
cocktail party.

The thing was, Budge told himself even at twelve, fourteen,
sixteen, not to get carried away about some earnest subject. You
needed balance and humor. He was the best tackle in Calley's
"royal-blue line"—but he didn't write his mother about how
much he wanted to smash Middlesex in his last fall at the school.
He told her instead about the Massachusetts sky in October.
After practice, when the sun lay cold and orange on the bare
treetops, Budge hunched home from the field, pretending he
didn't have a warm dormitory to go to. He pretended that if
he wanted dinner that night he'd have to steal or beg for it, and
finally he pretended he hadn't any bed with both *Nineteenth-
Century Europe* and *Dave Darrin's First Year at Annapolis* waiting
for him. He would sleep in the gutter that night, and Calley
boys in suntans or flannels would trot by, uncaring. At the
dormitory door, he dropped the pretending. There it all was!
Warmth for the heroic, exercised body and the bright dinner
tables, master and eight boys and girls at each, where sometimes

the conversations were funny and surprising. He never gave his mother anything to have conscience pangs or worry about.

Years later, even the dove-gray V-mail photostats his mother got from Somewhere in Africa and then Somewhere in Italy read as philosophically and incidentally as nineteenth-century walking-tour pamphlets. Anzio beachhead, in Budge's telling, was a curious place where an army doctor fortunately took out his appendix, so he was not with his unit when it tried to ascend the slopes the Germans didn't want Americans to ascend. The whole letter sounded like one more amusing My Operation story.

The name "Budge" had started at Calley. The *Daily* noted gratefully in its November 14, 1942, issue that Harley seemed to be everywhere, blocking every disheveled Exeter player, messing up all the plays, and giving no ground on defense, either. They called him "No-Budge"; it shortened to "Budge" and stuck. Even Millie, through their courtship, called him Budge. When he returned to Calley at age forty-one to be Assistant Director of Development, Budge as name and memory was solid gold. His assistant, Kim, and even Austin, the bonehead on the computer, called him Budge in person and as a matter of policy on letters going out to alumni/ae.

At fifty-eight, Budge still liked letters so much that he and Millie exchanged notes magnetized to the refrigerator. Hers of this morning, formally placed and dated in their regular tongue-in-cheek tone:

CALLEY, 7 OCTOBER 1982: PLEASE MAKE NO PASSES AT MID-WEST BEAUTIES STOP HURRY HOME STOP FASTEN YOUR SEAT BELT WHEN THEY TELL YOU TO STOP I LOVE YOU (SIGNED) MILL P.S. IF I WERE YOU I WOULDN'T EVEN MENTION TO THE TWIN CITIES GROUP THAT THE RUMOR THAT CALLEY IS GETTING TRILATERAL COMMISSION MONEY AND THEREFORE DOESN'T NEED ITS ALUMNI IS FALSE. I WOULDN'T EVEN BRING IT UP AT ALL LOVE MILL

Budge strode across the Common to the Development building, half noting the dutifully chalked KICK HARVARD FRESHMEN ON SATURDAY and half trying to think up some wiseacre response for Millie. If he mailed it from Saint Paul, he would beat the letter home, and if he had come up with something kind of sweet and funny and dumb, they would have a nice moment over it.

Budge liked his work in Development. He was not an Old Boy trying to hang French oil paintings in the computer rooms so it would all seem more like the Academy one knew as a kid. He was an Old Boy who liked the actual work. He liked rethinking the givens from time to time, to make sure that he and his team—Kim and Austin—weren't missing any marvelous chances for innovation.

He enjoyed the briefing for Minneapolis–Saint Paul, a two-day job. No one in his right mind liked Logan Airport—at least, confused as it was in 1982—but Budge did. He liked the ratty, old-fashioned Callahan Tunnel because it had classic tunnel ambience. He liked setting spirited dollar goals for the Minnesota-Iowa-Wisconsin alumni, letting them make their sarcastic remarks about his Soviet-taskmaster's-quota style. He noted they were invariably charmed into making the kid-hours and alumnus-dollar quotas anyway.

Budge did each geographical section of alumni every third year. The interval meant that enough members of any local alumni group were the same to keep continuity, but the intervening two years would provide enough statistical and gossip changes at the Academy so that Budge could bring them fresh news. His briefing team kept him ready with affectionate miscellany.

"All set for gen?" Kim said, smiling. She was waiting for him beside his desk. He saw she had the Calley movie in its carrying case, standing by her ankle. They started their routine.

Kim told him a little about each sheet, passed it over; Budge asked a question or commented, and laid it facedown in his briefcase. Later, on the 727, he would reverse the whole pile so everything came up in the right order. The top sheet had a very few "gross" figures on it. The next page gave what he and Kim called "comparison-shopper figures." They proved to Minneapolis–Saint Paul alumni/ae that their group always gave more than the national average. Whenever the Minneapolis–Saint Paul alumni/ae were less generous than the national average, Kim and Austin between them would come up with some other kind of finding—such as the per-classmate-head-over-the-last-ten-years giving record. The third sheet was gossip—selected bios on individual local alumni or alumnae. All the rest of the packet was rafts of the pale-green-and-white printouts of five-year giving records. Finally, there was a memo sheet, reminding Budge to check projection equipment, silver taping, and so forth.

"Almost all the Twin Cities news is good news this time," Kim told him. "Total count of givers up two. Eighty-three alumni—seventy-four men and nine women. Plus fifty-six more in the Minnesota-Iowa-Wisconsin grouping. There is one new couple since you were there three years ago: the Minzeskis. Of the whole group, only four are Inactives and only two are DCs. DC was the Calley Academy abbreviation for Don't Contact—people who not only didn't want to be asked for money but didn't want to be asked for family or job news, either. Kim handed him the top sheets and began picking up on her page three material. "Budge, do you remember Eddie Goodnough, class of 1912? Last time you visited him in the Episcopal Church Home on Feronia Avenue? He's died in the last four or five months. Here's your map—green marker is the fast route from the airport rental to the Minnikahda Club, where the dinner is. That purple circle marks Lee Framweller's house, president of the area association, and the Framwellers want you to stay with them again." She handed Budge the map. "Your car's Avis this time. Lee's wife's name is Teekie. And, Budge, don't ask the Framwellers about their kids unless they bring it up. Since you were there last, the Admissions Office has turned down their second kid for Calley. Lee Framweller dropped his usual one-thousand-a-year gift to ten dollars, and I think the ten is just out of good manners."

Kim read rapidly a note to herself, then unclipped a sheet from it to give Budge. "Your Divorced Women project paid off, Budge. You remember, you had nine women in the Twin Cities area, one remarried. Here's the sheet from three years ago, showing their then-employment if any, their giving records for the five years previous to the divorces, and the husbands' incomes—especially Bob what's-his-name at Honeywell, whom we figured at sixty-eight thousand and up, likely up. It all went the way you said: the significant drop in each divorced woman's giving and then, after a year, her getting the level right back up to what it was before, even though she isn't making anywhere near so much money as the ex-husband in every case. You mentioned sense of pride or continuity: well, you were right—or whatever you told them last time you were out there was right."

Budge remembered what he had told them. He had gone around during the cash bar, carefully mentioning to each of the women a figure he knew she couldn't afford to give. For example, Bunny Kirk made $13,000 if she made that. That meant $25 from her would be fine—$50 handsome. What Budge had told her, though, was that the Academy depended on the executive-level people like her to come through with the big hundred-dollar annuals. He had said he only wished it *were* true that every little bit counted, but alas, every little bit didn't, and the managers, the executives, were going to have to come through for the school—unpopular as the idea might sound. He had seen a light in her eye—and from what Kim showed him now, he had read Bunny, and the other eight, right.

"Now just one more curious thing," Kim said. She passed Budge a last sheet of typing, with a photocopy of a letter on Calley stationery attached. "We've never had anything just like this before—not since I've been on the job. I thought you'd be especially interested, because it has to do with an alumna in your class. Did you ever know Coreen Sorel? She's been a Don't Contact since 1952, and now suddenly, starting last year, she is a top-notch class agent. All through 1980 I had been stuffing the Class Notes with pleas for someone to become class agent, because the previous one burned out. Suddenly this woman volunteered—like a windfall. She never said why she was DC all these years, or why she suddenly was willing to work. Frankly, I didn't expect much. But then she got off two very good letters. Here's the recent one."

Dear Classmates:

As I take on the job of class agent, I am struck by the fact that we are all people in our late fifties. We must know our minds by now. One reason we were ever sent to a private, liberal arts school in the first place was so that we would turn out to be people who decide their own values. There'd be no sense to good schools if their middle-aged graduates could be made to change their minds just because some class agent did a booster pitch.

It went on to ask, not for changes of heart, but for very small checks from alumni/ae who had not been giving. It pointed out that the per capita giving was what corporations looked at. It mentioned Calley as a kind of armed keep against an invasion of junk values. It suggested that liberal arts education was a flag flying for excellence and mercy both. The letter didn't mention that she had actually not graduated with the class.

Budge liked the letter, but it crossed his mind that his mother would have found it very earnest indeed and would have said "Jesus!" politely and maybe have asked her bookkeeper to send a check or maybe have forgotten it.

"She got her results," Kim said, seeing Budge had read to the bottom. "Nineteen forty-two went from three percent to forty-one percent outright giving and another six percent pledg-

ing. And she picked up all three Lybunts in the class." Lybunts
were alumni who gave Last Year But Not This. Sorel brought
the 1942 figure up from bottom to third from the top in per
capita, and eleventh in dollar figures, not counting Old Guard
and bequests. Kim said, "I don't know what you have for a
time-line in the Twin Cities, Budge, but in case you have time,
I fixed this up."

She was holding a map of Saint Paul and environs between
them, showing him a blue-marker-indicated route northbound
to White Bear Lake on I-35E. "Sorel has an RFD address, so
you will have to ask locally. No one else in the Twin Cities area
knows her. Not after all those years as a Don't Contact, I suppose. And she only had one year at the school, too—upper-
middler."

Budge saw in his mind's eye a reddish-haired, pale girl,
whom everyone sneered at a little for raising her hand all the
time in European History II. Now she would be his age. He
rose, snapped the briefcase shut, and bent for the Calley movie.
"Sorel, the mystery woman!" he said with a grin for Kim. "I
will find her out—Come out, come out, wherever you are, angel
of White Bear Lake!—and I will tell her of our undying gratitude, and I will get her back."

Kim smiled. "And tell us what she's like."

Before the 727 captain told everyone he was starting his
descent for the Twin Cities area, Budge had memorized what
he had to know absolutely by heart and was more or less on
top of ten or eleven other details about Minnesota–Iowa–
Wisconsin alumni/ae. He had to remember, for example, that
not only had Lee Framweller's youngest not made it into Calley,
but a daughter of George and Amy Williams' had OD'd in her
cluster dorm at the school. It meant watching tone, especially
if he caught them to talk to during cash bar. As for Lee Framweller's son, Budge always made a point of never calling up
Admissions to find out why such and such an alumnus's kid
didn't get in. He needed to be able to tell parents, at cash bars

and club dinners all over the United States: "Gosh, I haven't the vaguest. We are pretty committed to letting the Admissions do their thinking without any pressure from us. We *have* to leave them to it—well, you can see how bent out of shape things would get if the Development Office thought it could lean on the Admissions Office." He didn't mention that on the occasions when the Development office *did* feel strongly, it pressured the Admissions people with all the delicacy of a boa constrictor.

As Budge took his Avis out onto 494, he had his usual delight in being lost in the universe. It happened for him when he got into a rental car. He was no longer on the manifest of Northwest Airlines Flight Number 51 and he was not yet being shepherded around by President-of-the-Local Framweller. Happily married, employed, educated men don't get lost in the universe much: he felt heightened, if vague, feelings. He didn't want to identify them: he was content simply to have them. Today—this time— he was especially pleased because there was one genuinely un- usual element in tomorrow's work: looking up Coreen Sorel. Not only did Budge never get lost much in the universe, but he got few surprises. Planners and public relations people tend to think up everything that will happen ahead of time: it was the very nature of his work that it seldom surprised him. Very occasionally something unusual turned up: a member of Calley's Old Boy skinflint contingent (people who went to alumni din- ners, sang loudly, but never donated) might give Budge a check afterward—but it was rare. Bequests usually came from the people Budge and Kim and Austin hoped would make bequests. Large gifts came from people Budge and Kim identified and then focused on. As for the small donations, the rule seldom varied: good letters from class agents brought in good per capita participation; indifferent letters accomplished less. In all his years of fund-raising, Budge rarely came across a long-standing Don't Contact who suddenly volunteered and turned out to be a natural—and then, stranger still, quit again.

Budge's work at the Minnikahda Club had two parts: first, the cash bar before dinner, with its conversations; and second, his formal talk during dessert, and introduction of the new Calley Academy movie. Work started—being cheerfully lost in the universe ended, that is—the moment he made first contact with anyone from the school. This evening it happened in the classy, scary little ironwork elevator of the Minnikahda Club, because Lee Framweller got into it with him. The elevator ride merged into the social hour. Budge tried to get around to most of the Calley people, remembering, when he could, Significant Others, as well. People in the recent classes brought in the most Significant Others—who were fine with Budge and Kim if they stayed the same. It was the turnover, with the unfamiliar faces and names, that kept providing what Austin called low-resolution information. At a Calley evening, Significant Others generally got through with lots to drink. Budge listened to a fairly acceptable story about what happened when Nancy Reagan applied for AFDC help from a Polish welfare worker. He gradually looked up, and found, five of the divorced women identified three years before and thanked them for sustaining their loyalty to the school. At one point he bought a drink for Lee Framweller's wife, Teekie, asked her very lightly how the boys were doing, and got such a fast, glittery smile—"Oh, just fine, thanks!"—that he knew to stay off the subject. It was the glittery smile of hundreds of alumni whose kids never made it to Calley, or did and flunked out, and went to the Bay Area for a life of dope and macrobiotic diet and Shintoism or whatever was going.

All the while, Budge kept track of technical minutiae. The projector was now up, under the great royal-blue banner reading THE CALLEY CONNECTION. Drop cords O.K., and he took two minutes to give Ferd Hancock a voice-level test-out and helped him with silver taping. He fell into conversation with two old women. They were talking about girls' basketball rules in 1934, comparing them to what they called the "boys' rules" now used

at Calley. They were neat, pretty women: the one with silver
hair suddenly reminded Budge of his mother; Budge egged her
on in her anecdotes. Like his mother, she warmed to the light
touch: she told him how Miss Hall's beat the hell out of Calley's
intramural "Griffin" team one year. Budge had another drink
someone handed him, remembered that Eddie Goodnough was
now dead and that we all pass through life as a sparrow flies
through a banquet hall. In Budge's day, the Head doubled as
history teacher. He would read aloud from Bede: *Your Majesty,
when we compare the present life of man on earth with that time of
which we have no knowledge, it seems to me like the swift flight of a
single sparrow through the long hall where you sit at dinner with your
thanes and councillors on a winter's night. The sparrow is safe while
he is inside, but after a few moments of the fire's comfort, he vanishes
into the wintry world of rain or storms raging. Therefore, if this new
teaching brings any certain knowledge, it seems only right that we
should follow it. . . .*

Budge asked someone to point out the new couple in town—
the Minzeskis.

The dinner itself: Seventy-five people took their Lytton-
photocopied sheets and belted out the Calley football song. By
now some of the lit-up Significant Others who could read music
were louder and surer, at least on the refrain, than the alumni.
Budge made a note to tell Millie that—not meaning to feed into
the great maw of American cynicism, but the fact was, one good
non-alumna or non-alumnus with two martinis who could read
music was really worth ten loyal monotones anytime. "O Calley, may your blue line wave," they shouted. "Keep rolling
over the red and gray," they sang in voices from twenty-year-
olds' to the Old Guard classes'. "O Alma Mater, our school for
aye!"

Then everyone attended to the lamb chops and a Pinot Noir
that was better than the genuine *vin inférieur* that the Detroit
alumni had ordered up two weeks before. Lee Framweller announced the evening's order of events. He made the parents of

the "deserving Calley senior" who won the twenty-five-dollar book award rise and be applauded. He introduced Budge. "Budge Harley," Framweller told them cheerfully, "despite whatever else he *says* he's come to visit us about, is basically here to lift all our pockets, so watch yourself, fellows."

"Fellows and women!" shouted a feminine voice from the rear.

Framweller bowed and grinned. "Watch yourselves, fellows and women! Budge doesn't care which sex the money comes from, just so it comes!"

By the time everyone had stopped clapping, Budge had his notes laid out the way he wanted them. "Right away," he said, "let me tell you a couple of new items before I forget. First things first. Dusty Sturgis, of Hopkins, Minnesota, threw the darndest Hail Mary I have ever heard of with just possibly the exception of Kramer's pass to Ahmad Rashad in the last second of the Cleveland game a couple of years ago. Sturgis's pass, in the last four seconds againt Exeter, put Calley out in front twenty-eight to twenty-one." Budge waited for the particularly aggressive clapping and shouting from a rear table, probably full of people from Hopkins and Golden Valley, to quiet down and then went on. "One other football update for you. Bill Minzeski's ankle is O.K. again, so he is going to be able to play against Harvard freshmen day after tomorrow. The Minzeskis are fairly new in the Twin Cities area. Just in case you haven't all met them, could I ask Jill and Clay to stand up a second?" The Minzeskis rose together, swiftly, smiling—all set since Budge had warned them about it during the cash bar.

"Now, for those of you who have other things to do in life besides follow Calley football stats, let me just tell you that Bill Minzeski is not just a blessing to the royal-blue team. His recent paper on the American Class System, in which he likened some of our attitudes to those of mid-nineteenth-century European attitudes, won the Rogers Award this year, for Excellence in Ethical Thought."

Budge then went to the Comparative Shopper. Minnesota had the finest giving record of any state. He apologized to all Wisconsin-Iowa alumni/ae present but told them they knew, of course, how to fix the situation. He explained that prep schools, unlike colleges, could never become a recognized educational issue to the American people at large. People didn't go off to World War II thinking that when they got home they would use the G.I. Bill to go to prep school. Small engine-repair shop owners did not dream of sending their daughters to Walnut Hill or Calley. From the point of view of development, then, prep schools were perceived as snobs howling for funds they had too much of already. Therefore, alumni support was everything— everything! Thanks to each of you, Budge went on, noting that those present who never gave anything were smiling as widely and receiving his thanks as personally as the regular donors were. He supposed that such people actually believed, at the moment, that somehow they *had* given, and therefore deserved commendation. They had to pay for their dinners at the Minnikahda, anyway.

"Now we have a terrific movie to show you," Budge said. "Did any of you see *The World According to Garp?*" Most hands went up, and people smiled. Budge smiled back. "Well, let me tell you about this Calley movie. About two years ago, we decided to make it. The Development staff identified a Visiting Committee of alumni, and they worked out the general design for the film. Right away I had what I thought was a super-wonderful idea about how the film ought to start: We'd have a good-looking baby being tossed in the air, the way the Garp movie had, against a royal-blue sky—you know, royal-blue for Calley—and then after the audience had looked at the baby for a couple of minutes behind the credits, a voice would say, 'Yeah, gee, he's cute' or 'Yeah, gee, she's cute!' and the voice would go on: 'But what about fourteen years up the road?' and then you would hear the Calley song and we'd have some character generation for the credits, and the scene would switch to a really

nice-looking boy or girl standing in the Calley Gallery, looking
at paintings of blue sky, and everyone would see that the nice-
looking baby had grown into this really nice Calley kid that
liked art. Well"—and here Budge held his arms out, palms up,
for them—"since we are mixed company here, I won't share
with you what the Visiting Committee on the film said about
my idea. Enough said, they turned it down. But I have to admit
they did come up with a lovely movie. I hope you enjoy it as
much as I do!"

Budge sat down beside Teekie Framweller, who was operating the projector. Someone in the dark slapped Budge's
shoulder. Other voices said, "Nice talk, Harley," and Budge
twisted his neck each time to turn a smile to whoever it was
who had spoken. Since he had shown the movie in Baton Rouge,
San Mateo, Dallas, and Detroit, he watched only absentmindedly. Sensitive-faced boys pulled Stroke and Number Seven oars
on the Cam, nice view of the Backs. No voice-mention that the
Cambridge boys humiliated the Calley crew that day. Sensitive-
faced girls rapidly drew the curves of a man's bent back in the
Calley Senior Life class. Sensitive-faced teachers conferred about
a student. Sensitive-faced Admissions people sat around an oval
table, discussing just how badly prepared for Calley a certain
inner-city kid was, and could he still make it through, and would
Calley Academy work out for that kid the way it wanted to.
The camera moved in over the Admissions people's shoulders
and showed the boy's application materials. Finally one of the
Admissions officers said in a big, frank voice, "Oh, the hell with
it, people! Look. He is obviously a terrific guy! I love him! He
doesn't play football. He doesn't play hockey! He never even
got a yellow in the one hundred meter! But he is crazy about
reading. He doesn't know five cents' worth of English usage,
but he can express feelings about his own life and society, as he
judges it, like nobody's business! We've been round and round
about all his nonqualifications. But the fact is we all want him,
and we know it. Let's take him!" Then all the other Admissions

people around the table (the camera panned around the table) all got that dawning smile which actors do better than real staff (which was why the Visiting Committee on the film opted for actors instead of Calley Admissions staff). The camera then went straight to the kid's photo again, lying on the table—a terrific-looking humorous-faced kid, black, kind of pudgy, sensitive— and then the photo came to life, and there was the kid, in what was obviously Creighton Slums (more formally, Calley's Creighton Hall Dormitory), holding forth in a bull session about how just because Shakespeare talked about the poor, it didn't mean Shakespeare gave a goddamn what happened to the poor. Three white girls and two white boys were listening to him, impatient to rebut.

Near the end of the film, the Headmaster said straight into the camera, "The thing is, Calley Academy is a project that works. The question is: What makes Calley work so well? What's going to make it work in 1982 and what's going to make it work in 1992?" Budge could feel nearly physically the roomful of Minnesotans sag a little as they anticipated the pitch (alumni/ae support makes Calley work!)—but this is where the movie had a better idea. The scene suddenly jumped to a football locker room, but it was not the Calley football locker room. Sitting on the benches were boys in white pants and red jerseys, their white helmets on their knees. A coach was giving them the final word before they went out for the first quarter. "Guys—just one final remark to you. Remember this peculiar thing about Calley. If you want to beat Calley today or any day, you're going to have to beat the butt off the whole team of them, because that's how they play. They may have the good quarter-back, all right, but we've studied his weakness and you all know how to play him. They may have the one terrific tight end and the one terrific defensive linebacker. But that isn't what their game's based on. They're not using the star system. Calley plays team, team, team, all the way—so listen, you guys—" and the camera, POV EXETER PLAYERS, jogged out of the locker room, camera jiggling as if resting on a boy's pads, across the street, past the Exeter lacrosse field, finally into the football field. The camera swiveled, the way the eyes of a curious, excited young player might: it looked between smeary bars, the way young eyes looked out from behind the face mask, and what it saw was Calley kids, players and cheerers. SOUND TRACK, tremendous cheering; CAMERA, still POV EXETER PLAYERS, panned Calley Academy shouting and smiling; freeze-frame, and "THE END—WHICH IS ALWAYS THE BEGINNING" came up, generated across the blue banners. Budge thought, for the dozenth time, O.K. Good flick. Good audience tonight, too. Write Millie about those two old basketball ladies, forwards against Miss Hall's, and tomorrow drive out to White Bear Lake to see that Coreen Sorel, and Northwest Flight 42 with time to spare.

Next morning, Budge drove north through suburban ticky-tacky and some still-rural, some new country places. The aspens were yellow, the maples brilliant. He had not called Coreen Sorel ahead and knew perfectly well why he hadn't: he had the PR man's inveterate hope of a surprise once in a while. He knew Coreen couldn't be mysteriously beautiful unless she had monumentally changed after the age of seventeen, but she might be mysteriously rich or talented at something. Any mystery would be nice, because he was tired from staying "up" for the job throughout the late afternoon and evening yesterday. Budge didn't need major adventures: he was happy in home and job. What he needed was minor adventure, if any offered itself.

A Union 76 dealer told him how to find the Sorel place, at the junction of two township roads. It was a three-story farmhouse on high ground, overlooking a grove of oaks. Disused pasture went farther up the hill behind it. The house had been built with an unusually steep, classical-looking roof—like the roofs of houses on Christmas cards. It had two chimneys in the old way, and the third-floor peak had a floor-to-ridgepole window. Downstairs, a trio of windows, with real mullions, were opened to the warm fall day.

Yet what a sad-looking place it was! The house needed paint. A roof gutter hung free off one end's mooring. The lawn, despite its commanding size, was parked over and ruined by broken machinery. Four lawn mowers and some larger machine lay tipped over, and a pickup door leaned against an upside-down snowmobile with no treads. A badly lettered sign read SMALL ENGINE REPAIR. ASK FOR WAYLAND. The nasty-looking pickup by the mailbox had the inevitable sunshield over its rear window: deer leapt a silver stream beneath a flocked-gold sunset or moon-set, whatever the case. The deer were kelly green, with baby-blue and silver highlights.

On the lawn, close under the downstairs casement windows, stood two high-impact plastic deer, painted with fawns' spots although both animals were fully antlered. Whoever had mowed the lawn had saved time by not moving machinery or the deer: higher, messy grass straggled between the skinny legs and the Lawn Boy green.

There were teenaged kids everywhere: lying on the lawn, two sitting on the pickup cab roof, one leaning comfortably against the truck door that was already leaning against the snow-mobile. Budge nodded and smiled at the kids on the pickup roof, but they looked through him. As he walked up to the house, he heard himself saying "Hi" in the energetic, crow-eating way city people use to greet country people's large and probably vicious dogs. All his life Budge had called German shepherds "Old Fellow" and "Old Man" when he was scared stiff of them. As he got near the busted screen door he had the impression Coreen Sorel had been mugged, her house broken into by a teenaged gang, and the robbers never meant to leave the premises. They were taking over.

Someone had put a fist through the screen, but the bell worked, and a cleaning lady came to answer. She regarded him

cautiously, from under wispy reddish hair and a wide forehead
with a very bad bruise on it. She held a crescent wrench in one
hand; her flowered apron's pockets bulged with screwdriver,
wooden ruler, one angle of a square. She chinked with all her
kit.

Budge smiled and said, "I can tell I've pulled you right away
from the middle of a major job—sorry! I am looking for Coreen
Sorel, if she's around?"

As soon as he spoke he realized this was Coreen—of course.
This was the mysterious class agent, ex–Don't Contact, and this
run-down place and these horrible kids and this horrible screen
door she now opened were the gear of her life. Budge felt ag-
grieved and, in the next second, grateful: she *was* a mystery,
after all. He followed her gingerly into a shadowy hall. He nearly
tiptoed after her. They both knew why he had come, but she
hadn't immediately sent him away, so he was encouraged.

Sorel took him to a spacious, nearly empty room, filled with
sunlight from the three casement windows. But the only furniture was a large, chipped dining room table and a good many
tubular-aluminum chairs with vinyl cushions, one of which had
been slashed. From the window came two boys' voices, very
loud and angry, using foul language. Across the road, the oaks
were going to bronze, and their leaves hung already in curly
clusters, glinting beautifully as pirates' coin. Budge had a split
second of pathos: What a mess, he thought, the poor make of
things! How differently grade-school storybooks presented the
poor, in their hollyhock-cornered cottages: Over their wooden
bowls and spoons, their clean rounds of pale cheese, and with
Canterbury bells popping half into the windows, the poor talked
about kind facts; there were no teenagers' obscenities or plastic
deer. In literature, the poor have a beautiful relationship with
nature; in north White Bear Lake, Minnesota, the lawnful of
busted junk, the house with its linoleum floors, the lawn stat-
ues—which now, Budge could see out the windows, stood

mounted one on the other—were all tilted in enmity against the planet, somehow.

Budge smiled at Coreen. Whatever his inward moral shock, he kept a cordial presence. He explained his business. He praised her smooth, strongly felt letters on behalf of Calley Academy. He told her he remembered her from the upper-middler year at school. He led her toward telling him about herself—but indirectly—so that at no point need she explain that she was poor.

The kids were not hers, she told him. She ran a foster house. "I'd like to introduce you to my mother," she said.

Budge glanced around in total surprise. In a corner behind the doorway through which he had entered sat a very old woman, carefully dressed in fuchsia.

"I wondered when you was going to introduce me!" she shouted. "One thing about Coreen—the manners of these kids must be rubbing off on her. I taught her manners one time." All this she said looking at Coreen, not Budge.

"How do you do, Mrs. Sorel."

"Coreen doesn't care about their manners is one thing," the old woman said. "If she likes them O.K. she doesn't care if they bust her in the face. I wonder if you noticed her forehead—but don't try saying anything against that rotten kid: she won't listen to you. 'Wayland will turn out, Wayland will turn out,' is all she says. Well, if you ask me, Wayland's just plainly no good."

Now Coreen went to the window and leaned so she could see to one side. "Wayland!" she shouted. "You come get those deer back down so they're decent, and then finish up your detail or I'll give you another one!"

A tall boy showed outside. He took the top deer off its mate, gave a grin that wasn't really so much insolent, Budge thought, as aimless, and ambled off.

"The social worker came by and said them kids aren't supposed to hit anyone, or back they go to the judge," the old woman commented. "It isn't what I brought this girl up to, I can tell you." She made a tiny fist of one hand and regarded the knuckles on it, in a thoughtful way.

"Tell you what," Coreen said pleasantly, returning from the window. "The kids have so much going on outside, we'll never be able to hear ourselves think in here. Would you like a glass of sherry? Good! I'll take you up to my space."

Budge winced at "space" but not at leaving the brutal mother and not at the sherry. If I had the mother, he said to himself, I expect I would be into the sherry by nine each morning, and here it is already eleven.

"Teachers' in-service," Coreen said over her shoulder to him, "is why the kids are all around today." She led him up a linoleum-covered staircase. Even its risers carried their nicked layer of nasturtiums attached to English ivy and arranged in diamonds. That particular linoleum or wallpaper design was another thing of the 1930s, like crime, Budge would have written his mother if she'd still been alive: just awful, but nothing in the 1930s ever seems to go away. On the second-floor landing, someone had half buried a gum wrapper in a pot of cyclamen. At the third, Coreen took a huge bunch of keys from her apron pocket and unlocked three separate locks. She swung the door inward and said, "Peace and quiet!" to Budge.

A high apartment ran the whole length of the house; its ivory eaves went straight to the ridgepole. Reproductions of Millet and Corot hung in brave, gold-sprayed frames. At the south end, Budge saw the long, narrow window going from floor to ceiling that he had noticed from the outside. It let in sunlight without tracery. Before it stood a rolltop desk. There was a black-velvet-covered cot and a small cabinet, three comfortable, nearly threadbare chairs. Budge wandered around the bookshelves, glancing. He had a look at the Dürer print of the Prodigal Son woodcut and a boring but very *echt* brass rubbing from Thaxted Church. A beautiful watercolor by someone he didn't know showed a black merchant ship moored in a whity, dreamy harbor at San Cristobal. Coreen had a bottle of Manzanilla out

·

of the little cabinet and was handing Budge a glass. Budge sat in the deep chair near him, with his feet on the Belgian woolen carpet, an imitation Sarouk, and he glanced from *The Gleaners*, lighted by the steep sunlight, to Coreen Sorel.

"What an amazing, wonderful place you have here," he cried.

"I love it."

"I think it is absolutely amazing!" he exclaimed again. "You've made yourself a marvelous island here—well, better than that! It is nearly symbolic! When you think about it! The best of nature"—he gestured with his glass toward the handsome window full of sunlight—"and the best of art. And the books! The wonderful peace and privacy of all this! And that great rolltop!"

The rolltop was a little lifesaver to Budge, because he did admire it, whereas he had had to wince his way through calling the reproductions "the best of art." He was already saving up details for Millie—this pleasant room, so surprising a switch from the bleak props of this woman's life. "If you were thinking of a 'midwest beauty,' " he would tell Millie, "read pathos and guts for beauty! And the mother! Now I remember her from 1941! Carrying on in her horrible way, right across the hall from the mailboxes at Calley!" He would tell Millie that maybe a sense of place is what makes us civilized: here was this woman of no particular personality, so far as he could tell—but she had a sense of place. Maybe it was a sense of place that was making her a class agent: she wanted to keep Calley Academy as a good *place*.

He drank his sherry, gathering himself to draw her out a little. Midway through their second sherry, while she was explaining how she had always wanted to run a foster home—it had always seemed like a cozy idea to her: a dream, even—Budge brought out a pleasant comment. He told her what she had gone and done—did she realize?

"No; what?" she said, a little ironically. He rather loved her a little for trying to look ironic in her horrible apron with the carpenter's square still hanging out the pocket of it.

"Well, corny as it may sound, you have preserved civilization in one place, *intact,* just the way monks did it during the Dark Ages. Do you recall the Head's course in European history?"

To Budge's surprise, she burst out at him: "Do I ever!" Her tone was actually joyful—nearly girlish.

He went on, "It is something like your situation. Bigger scope, but same idea. Outside, what do you have? The great empire all going to pieces, nothing but brigands, muggings, or whatever medieval people called muggings, and then inside, the best of art, the best of peaceful surroundings, preserved—and if the monks didn't originate art themselves, at least they copied it."

Her reaction was a little flat. He'd thought he'd phrased that rather neatly! Oh, well!

"I am dying of curiosity, of course," he told her conversationally. "All those years you were a Don't Contact—and then, one of our best class agents!" He would hold off coming to the point, in the hope of bringing her back into the fold without having to ask.

"How did that dreadful woman finally see the light?" she said with a laugh.

He thought she was so wonderful to make her jokes in her dingy clothes.

"I had only one year at Calley," she told him. "It was a fluke I got even that. My mother was what we now call a 'single parent.' Then, I expect, we called it a 'poor widow.' But she had a nice cousin: a funny, burly sort of woman from Lawrence—the one in Massachusetts. I remember her because she had one of those permanents where the hairdresser starts from scratch—with no reference to what the client's needs or wants may be at all! She was a rough woman, married to a rude, horrible man, I remember—but she had heard of Calley, perhaps because it is so close. Somehow she got it into her head that sooner or later one of our family had a right to go to such a place. Anyway, she gave my mother enough money for me to have two years there. I would have to skimp all the frills; they prepared me for that. I was the only person I know who never once took a taxi from the South Station to the North Station. I expected to be miserable all the time. I knew my clothes would be too few or dead wrong—and they were. The other kids came from day schools. They had listened to Mozart. They knew the very moment the second theme was introduced in the sonata-form movement. I remember feeling the gummy, webbed seat of that Boston and Maine train the first time—I remember we were passing Ballardvale, where the track is rather high over the terrain—and thinking: This will be a miserable experience, but I will get a wonderful education out of it. So I was very surprised—within a week—to find myself completely happy there!" She stopped, perhaps with a sudden feeling that all this was no longer appropriate, since she had backed out of raising money for Calley.

"Oh, please go on," Budge said.

"It was the classes. The classes," Coreen Sorel said. "Only ten of us, sometimes eleven, asking questions, not needing to act dumb as I'd had to in high school, not needing to feel scorn if I showed interest—and the masters and instructors being so interested in our remarks. Never in my life until then—and never since in anything like that same way—never has someone routinely, repeatedly, said, 'Coreen, what is the idea this author is trying to show? And what do you think of it?' Then the masters would follow up with, 'Good! You got it! What makes you think that's what Blake was trying to say?' Other people's hands would be waving—we all wanted to get into it. The teacher himself was moved. Never before, never since," Coreen repeated as if a little dazed. "Blake, too! My high school gave me Longfellow! But at Calley, at sixteen, we had Blake on chimney sweeps!"

Budge closed his eyes. "Wait a sec!" he said. "Here it is:

'And so Tom awoke; and we rose in the dark, / And got with our bags & our brushes to work. / Tho' the morning was cold, Tom was happy & warm: / So if all do their duty they need not fear harm.' "

"That's it," Coreen said. She didn't seem impressed by his ability to remember these lines. "But the spring vacation of my first year, my mother asked me to come into the kitchen to talk about something serious. I remember how clearly she said, 'I want your opinion on it, too.' Now, that was always bad news, when she wanted my opinion on something! In our household there were no *issues* for shared decisionmaking—as we say in social work. There were only necessities. But my mother had some idea of *manners*. As you saw downstairs. It was manners to ask for someone else's opinion. I expect you could say that Ag Secretary Block has very good manners with midwestern farmers. There we sat then, she and I, with our elbows on the yellow oilcloth, my shoulder near the cord hanging down from the Four Roses promotion electric clock. As long as the clock was plugged in, the lighted roses covered its noisy motor. I remember looking up at the lighted roses, and listening to the thrum of the clock, and thinking: Something good is about to be taken away from me.

"My mother wanted to know if I would mind not having the second—my senior—year at Calley. If I would finish at public high school, we would be a thousand dollars ahead, and frankly she could not see what difference the fancy school out East made, anyway.

"I expect I looked horrified, because she said fast and loud, 'Thanks to Thomas Jefferson, we have a perfectly good education for every American citizen without added cost—so why dish out a thousand dollars to some—'

"I remember thinking of Mr. Sweeney—"

"Mr. Sweeney!" cried Budge. "English Three!"

Coreen smiled and went on: "I remember him leaning over the front row of our little class and saying, 'Do you see how different it is to visualize a little boy's hair being shaved off so he can work all day with soot on his head in people's chimneys—how different that mental image is from talking about "child labor"?' Then I remember he'd return to his desk and go hulking around it and say, 'Blake had various angers—but the biggest anger he had was against adults for cruelty to children!'

"I had a last straw of hope with my mother. I asked her what about her cousin who gave the money specifically so I could go to Calley? How would she feel if my mother pocketed that for something else?

"Mother gave me the tired, virtuous look that means you are going to be absolutely done in. I don't know just how men do that to one another—but *women* do it by looking tired and virtuous; watch it when you see that look. It means rattlesnake bite in the next second. She told me that her cousin said it was up to me. Me, Coreen. Whatever I decided.

"And so I asked for the senior year at Calley. 'All right, if that is how you feel despite all I've pointed out to you,' she said. I stuck. Then she forgot the whole discussion. One day she went east and pulled me out of the school. Maybe you knew that." Coreen gave Budge a fast look.

"I heard about it," he said.

"Sometimes, during that senior year back home, I would hunt up my Calley English anthology and try to explain something of Blake to my mother. We would be sitting eating supper. I never could get her to stop eating while I read to her. I remember once thinking: If I could just get that arm to stop taking food onto the fork, up into the air, over into the mouth, back down for more. Up into the air, over into the mouth, back down for more. No matter what I read! I was doing the one about Jerusalem in England's green and pleasant land, and I remember saying, 'Wait, Mama! Don't eat!' but do you know, that arm, she lifted by main force, from underneath my hand—by main force, despite me, she kept eating! She never broke her rhythm once."

Budge accepted a top-off to his sherry.

Coreen Sorel told him she took Social Work at Minnesota and read the Calley alumni magazine Class Notes for 1942 until she couldn't stand it anymore. Everyone except her was finding work in New York or Europe! Somebody even went to Russia on a grant! Russia! She had wanted to go ever since the Head's Europe and Russia course. And the thing was, Calley graduates reported "bumping into so-and-so at Saint Peter's Square" or "bumping into so-and-so on the Charles Bridge in Prague!" Coreen Sorel never "bumped into" anyone. Her life had no Strand or Filene's Basement or watering places of Europe. She asked to be taken off the mailing list.

"Life has its own distractions, though," she said. "I always wanted to run a foster home, so I began to do it. A thousand years went by then, and I expect I never thought of Calley at all. Nor of William Blake."

"Then," Budge said—noticing that his voice sounded very significant and sanctimonious, which meant he had had too much sherry. He roused himself. "Then why did you get in touch with us at last?"

"It was the government funding cuts," she said. "It's a technical thing. We used to send very disturbed kids to treatment centers. Eighty-five dollars a day per kid. Foster homes pay only ten or twelve dollars a day—unless there is a 'Difficult Care' clause written in for a kid. Like this kid Wayland you heard my mother complain about—who gave me a sock in the head the other day. Wayland is 'Difficult Care,' so I get twenty-one dollars a day for him. Well, when the present administration brought in all the funding cuts, the social workers started sending disturbed kids to foster homes instead of to residential treatment centers, because they hadn't enough money.

"Somewhere in the middle of those funding cuts I began to remember discussions at Calley. I began to think of how literature—Blake is what I remembered, specifically—makes you have a mental image of the people in bad luck. So I thought:

We mustn't let the schools go—where people are taught to make those mental images. We mustn't not support those schools! So I wrote."

She paused again, looking around her private room. "But I stopped, didn't I," she said.

Budge waited. If she committed herself to a reason, he could then perhaps talk her out of it.

"In two weeks this room will be a bedroom for four more kids," she said.

Budge was shocked. He managed to wonder aloud, "Your beautiful private place!"—and his admiration for it, now that it was to be lost, was one hundred percent genuine and pained.

"You know how it goes," she said with forced cheer.

"How does it go?" Budge said.

"Oh, they figured me O.K.," she said. "They said if I could get the extra kids in, it'd make a life-or-death difference to them. All they had to do was tell me about the homes they came from and the fathers of two of them . . . so out goes the rolltop desk!" she looked at him squarely.

"I gave up on Calley. What a dream it was, though! The idea that a prep-school education could change anything! What a dumbbell I was! I mean—what interest could anybody at Calley have in what I'm doing? Nothing personal against you, of course."

Budge shrank. He was at something of a loss—but still he was sure he could think of the right way to bring Coreen Sorel around.

After a while, Budge rose. Coreen took him down the staircase. Next week I go to Mobile, he thought—then Charleston, Tryon, and Atlanta. Two weeks after that I go to Portland, Kennewick, and Spokane. Next year, Detroit, Buffalo, and Cleveland again. I ought to get this class agent tied back in.

All the way down the staircase he told her how much he admired her hanging on to her civilization as long as she had—despite all the difficulties. He would never forget, he told her (deciding not to hug by way of parting), sitting with her, looking at *The Gleaners,* looking at that wonderful apartment, and listening to her tremendously courageous story.

She didn't seem so charmed as he, but he said to himself firmly: It is my fault. I am the one had three sherries. Maybe she had only two. Or she may simply have more tepid feelings. After all, the print was Millet, not Michelangelo, for cat's sake.

He was not even out the broken screen door before he overheard her voice raised. "Wayland? Come in here, Wayland!"

Budge stood for a moment outside the house front, looking down over the horrible lawn, taking in again the loveliness of the oak glade past it. He tried to identify just what he was thinking, when suddenly he heard voices, very clearly, straight behind him—no doubt from inside, coming out the open casement.

"Wayland, sit down," Coreen's voice said sternly. "Mother, you are going to have either to leave or to be absolutely quiet."

"Well, of all the—" came the old woman's snarl.

"Shut up, Mother," Coreen's voice said. "Listen, Wayland. You listen to me very closely now."

"Jeez, Coreen, I been listening," said Wayland's voice.

"Now, here's what you do, Wayland. You stop acting crazy. You stop losing your temper and slugging people. You stop not having a job. You go out and get a job—and I don't mean some deal with a pickup some friend puts you onto. I mean a real job. Sane people have to have money. Are you listening, Wayland?"

"Jeez, Coreen."

"You know the reason you have to do this—stop acting crazy and get a job and get money? It's because there isn't anyone anywhere in the world who cares whether you go on acting crazy and poor all your life or not. You understand that, Wayland?"

"Jesus, Coreen!"

The old woman's voice came from farther back: "If you

can't get that boy to stop cussing, you better throw him out!"

"Mother, you shut up or I will carry you into the yard personally. Now listen, Wayland. People always think some big kind rich cultivated person somewhere would be looking out for them if only that big kind rich cultivated person knew of their sufferings! I remember this one history class I took at a school I once went to. The Russian peasants—They were like you, Wayland. Poor and forever drinking, having quarrels with their parents and their foster parents and everyone else, picking up a club and hitting someone, and howling around the house. Well, these peasants always had the idea that if they could just get hold of the czar—that's the king, see—if they could just get hold of the czar and show him what they were going through— how poor their hovels were, how poisoned the wells were, how the bailiffs were cheating them, how the bailiffs tricked them into working even longer hours—then the czar would make it right. The czar would be touched! That's how much they knew! They never got it through their heads that the czar was a happy man. The nobles, who were oppressing the peasants, were the czar's family friends, after all. They were his Old Boy network. They danced with each other's cousins. They met each other by accident when they traveled in Europe. Look—there'd they be, sitting around feeding pigeons at Nelson's Column, and some-body would come up in a fur coat just like yours and slap you on the back and shout, 'By God, look who's here? It's Ivan Dmitrivich! Hey, Vanya, hot enough for you?' if they were all sweating in their fur coats.

"Now listen, Wayland," Coreen said, "You tell *me:* would people like that, jet set types, would they care whether a few thousands of peasants were starving or not? Nobody else cares whether you go on acting crazy and being poor and end up in Attica or Sandstone or Comstock! Listening, Wayland?"

"I *been* listening, Coreen."

"O.K. Here is what you do, then . . . " and her voice dropped. Budge knew the change in tone meant some practical

program was being laid out for Wayland. The moment of rhetoric was over.

He thought of his own mother, whose voice had never become stentorian about anything, whose humor and light touch
had never failed her. He thought of how Coreen Sorel had made
an island of civilization out of that third-story apartment and
kept it a pinnacle above all this junk-laden grass and the awful
house. Now, he realized, his conversation with her had been
another island. He was glad he had come, however saddened
he felt: he had given her another island—an island in *time,* that
is, in which their conversation had got clear of this vulgar, sad,
common, inevitable roughness. Coreen had got her chance to
talk about the Blake poetry, for instance. He was glad he had
known a stanza or two to respond with.

So he made his way rather tenderly away from the house.
He passed some smashed machinery, picked his way over a little
pile of lightly rusting C-clamps. He noted that the high-impact
plastic deer again had all eight feet on the ground, no longer in
the posture of love. In a moment he had passed all the failed
tools and props of the ex–class agent's life. He let himself into
the little rental car as if he'd been bruised.

In five minutes, though, because the October morning was
so beautiful and he had an appreciation of countrysides anywhere, he was himself again.

After the Baptism

THE BENTY FAMILY had a beautiful baptism for their baby—when a good deal might have gone wrong. It is hard to run any baptism these days: of all the fifty-odd Episcopalians in Saint Aidan's Church, not to mention the two Lutheran grandparents, who really believes much of what the young priest says? No one with an IQ over one hundred actually supposes that "baptism could never be more truly, truly relevant than it is right now, in our day and age." People may get a kick out of the rhetoric, but that doesn't mean they believe it. If Bill Benty, Senior, the baby's grandfather, tried any of that proclaiming style of Father Geoffrey, if he tried anything like that just once over at the plant, he'd be laughed out to the fence in two minutes.

At least Father Geoffrey was long enough out of seminary now so he'd left off pronouncing Holy Ghost Ha-oly Gha-ost. His delivery was clear and manly. When he took the baby from her godparents, he took hold of her in a no-nonsense way: her mussed, beautiful white skirts billowed over his arm like sail being carried to the water. But the man was vapid. A frank, charming midwestern accent can't bring dead ideas to life. He had been charming about agreeing on the 1928 baptism service, instead of the 1979. Bill's wife, Lois, loved the beautiful old phrasing. Beautiful it was, too, Bill thought now, but on the other hand, how could any realistic person ask those particular three godparents "to renounce the vain pomp and glory of the world"? Where would that crew get any glory from in the first place?

The middle-aged godparent was Bill's long-lost first cousin, Molly Wells. Thirty-odd years ago she had run away to North Carolina to marry. After almost no correspondence in all those years, Molly had shown up widowed—a thin, sad woman with white hair done in what Lois called your bottom-line, body-wave-only permanent. Neither Bill nor Lois had met her husband. Bill had mailed her Dittoed, and later photocopied, Christmas letters, as he did to all his relations, giving news of Lois's work in Episcopal Community Services and whatever of interest there was to say about the chemical plant, and young Will's graduations and accomplishments—Breck School, Reed, the Harvard B School, his first marriage, his job with the arts organization before the snafu, his marriage to Cheryl. Molly and her husband had no children, and her responses to the Bentys' news were scarcely more than southern-lady thank-you notes.

Then in July of this long, very hot summer, she announced she was now widowed and would visit. Here she was, a house-guest who kept to her room, considerate enough not to dampen their family joking with her grief. Today, for the baptism, she wore a two-piece pink dress, gloves, and a straw-brimmed hat. Since one expects a young face under a broad-brimmed hat, Bill had had a moment's quake to see Molly, when she came down the staircase that morning. Molly had frankly told them she had not darkened the doorway of a church in thirty years but she would not disgrace them.

The other godparents were an oldish young couple whom Will dug up from his remaining high-school acquaintance. Bill had warned Will that you had to give these things time: when a man has been caught embezzling he must allow his friends months, even a year, to keep saying how sorry they are, but the fact is, they can't really ever look at him the same way again. For a good two or three years they will still mention to people that he was caught embezzling or whatever, but in fact they have no rancor left themselves. In about five years, they will again be affectionate friends but never as in the first place. It was only a question of having the sense not to ask them for help getting a job the first two years—and then simply to wait.

Probably Will was lucky to have found this couple, Chad and Jodi Plathe, to stand up for his baby. They were not Episcopalians. They were meditators, and if not actually organic farmers, at least organic eaters. When Will and Cheryl brought them over to Bill and Lois's for dinner earlier in the month, it had been fun to goad them. Each time Chad mentioned an interest of theirs, Bill had said, "Oh, then it follows you must be into organic eating." Or "Oh, then it follows you must be into horoscopes." "Into Sufi dancing, I bet." They were—into all the philosophies he brought up. They looked at him, puzzled, and young Will said, "Very witty, Dad—oh, witty." Once Chad said something hostile back, Bill forgave him everything. In one sense, Bill had rather listen to a non-Christian fallen-away Bay Area Buddhist who is man enough to take offense, at least, than to this Father Geoffrey, with his everlasting love for everything and everybody.

Now Chad and Jodi stood at the font, their backs to the grandparents in the first row and all the congregation in the next rows. They wore their eternal blue jeans, with the tops of plastic sandwich bags sticking out of the back pockets. They wore

1960s-style rebozos with earth-tone embroidery and rust-colored sewn-on doves. Their shoulder-length hair was shiny and combed. At least, Bill thought comfortably, very little evil in the world was generated by vegetarians. He saved up that idea to tell Chad if the conversation dragged at dinner.

Early that morning, Bill had taken his coffee happily out into the little back-kitchen screened porch. The wind was down, and the ivy's thousands of little claws held the screens peacefully. Like all true householders, Bill liked being up while others slept. His wide lawn lay shadowed under four elms the city hadn't had to take down yet. The grass showed a pale gleam of dew and looked more beautiful than it really was. Across the avenue, where the large grounds of Benty Chem started, Bill had ordered a landscaping outfit to put in generous groupings of fine high bushes and hundreds of perennials. He ordered them planted on both sides of the fence. Now that it was August, and everything had taken hold, the grounds looked lavender and gentle.

"You can't make a chemical factory look like an Englishman's estate," Lois had told him last week. "But, darling, darn near! Darn near! If only the protesters would wear battered stovepipe hats and black scarves!"

Bill told her that he had heard at a Saint Aidan's Vestry meeting that the protesting or peace-demonstrating community of the Twin Cities definitely regarded Benty Chem as a lot more beautiful place to work around than any one of Honeywell's layouts. "And they should know," Bill added with satisfaction.

At seven-thirty, the usual Sunday contingent of protesters weren't on the job yet. It was generally Sue Ann and Mary, or Sue Ann and Drew, on Sundays. Bill learned their first names automatically, as he learned the first names of new janitorial staff at Benty Chem. Now he gathered himself, got into the car, and was out at Northwest Cargo Recovery on Thirty-fourth Street in good time. He signed for the lobsters. They were moving around a little, safe, greenish-black, in their plastic carrying case.

"Hi, fellows and girls!" he said good-naturedly to them. He felt the luggage people smiling at him from behind their counter. Bill knew he was more spontaneous and humorous than most people they dealt with. "For my first grandchild's baptism!" he told them.

When he got home, the caterers had come. Lois was fingering along the bookcases, looking for the extra 1928 prayer books. Molly sat, cool in her silk two-piece dress. "I do believe it's threatening rain," she said in her partly southern accent. "Oh, and rain is just so much needed by our farmers." Her "our farmers" sounded false, feudal even, but Bill said, "Darn right, Molly!"

Now he relaxed in church. He flung an arm around the bench end, a little figure carved in shallow relief. Some Episcopalian in Bill's dad's generation had brought six of these carvings from Norfolk. They all cracked during their first winter of American central heating. Bill and a couple of other vestrymen glued the cracks and set vises; then they mortised in hardwood tholes against the grain, to make them safe forever. Each bench end was a small monk, with robe, hood, and cinch. The medieval sculptor had made the little monks hold their glossy wooden hands up, nearly touching their noses, in prayer. The faces had no particular expression.

Bill sat more informally than other people in Saint Aidan's. He had the peaceful slouch of those who are on the inside, the ones who know the workings behind some occasion, like cooks for a feast, or vestrymen for a service, or grandfathers for a baptism. Bill had done a lot of work and thinking to make this baptism successful, so now his face was pleasant and relaxed. He was aware of the Oppedahls next to him, the baby's other grandparents, sweating out the Episcopal service that they disliked. He thought they were darn good sports. He leaned across Lois at one point and whispered to Merv Oppedahl that a strong Scotch awaited the stalwart fellow that got through all the Smells and Bells. Merv's face broke into a grin, and he made a thumbs-up with the hand that wasn't holding Doreen's hand.

All summer the wretched farmers' topsoil had been lifting and lifting, then moving into the suburbs, even into Saint Paul itself. Grit stuck to people's foreheads and screens, even to the woven metal of their fences. But inside Saint Aidan's, the air was high and cool; the clerestory windows, thank heavens, were not the usual dark- and royal-blue and dark-rose stained-glass imitations of Continental cathedral windows—full of symbols of lions for Saint Mark and eagles for Saint John, which a whole generation of Episcopalians didn't know anything about, anyway. Besides, they made churches dark. Saint Aidan's had a good deal of clear glass, and enough gold-stained windows so that all the vaulting looked rather gold and light. It was an oddly watery look. In fact, the church reminded Bill of the insides of the overturned canoe of his childhood. It had been made of varnished ribs and strakes; when the boys turned it over and dove down to come up inside it, madly treading water, they felt transformed by that watery arching. It was a spooky yellow-dark. No matter that at ten their voices must still have been unchanged; they shouted all the rhetoric and bits of poems they knew. They made everything pontifical. They made dire prophecies. They felt portentous about death, even. Not the sissy, capon death they taught you about at Cass Lake Episcopal Camp, but the death that would get you if a giant pried your fists off the thwarts and shoved you down.

Now Father Geoffrey was done with the godparents. He put his thumb into the palm oil and pressed it onto the baby's forehead. Then he cried in a full voice, "I pronounce you, Molly Oppedahl Benty, safe in our Lord Jesus Christ forever!" Tears made some people's eyes brittle. They all sang "Love divine, all loves excel-l-l-ling . . ." using the Hyfrodol tune. Then it was noon, and they could leave.

Everyone tottered across the white, spiky gravel of the parking lot. They called out unnecessary friendly words from car to car. "See you at the Bentys' in five minutes, then!" and "Beautiful service, wasn't it?" "Anyone need a ride? We can certainly take two more!"

The cars full of guests drove companionably across the tacky suburb. People felt happy in different ways, but all of them felt more blessed than the people they passed. They may have been to a sacrament that they didn't much believe in, but they at least had been to one. Ten years before, all these streets had been shadowy under the elms. Now, though spindly maple saplings stood guyed in their steel-mesh cages, the town showed itself dispirited in its lidless houses that human beings build and live in. The open garages, with here and there a man pottering about, looked more inviting than the houses. The men tinkered in the hot shadow, handling gigantic mowing and spraying equipment parked there. No one could imagine a passion happening in the houses—not even a mild mid-life crisis. Not even a hobby, past an assembled kit.

Another reason everyone felt contented was that all their troubles with one another had been worked out the week before. Unbeatable, humane, wise, experienced administrator that he was, Bill explained to Lois, he had done the best possible thing to guarantee them all a great baptism Sunday by having Will and Cheryl (and little Molly) over to dinner the week before. There were always tensions about religious occasions. The tensions are all the worse when most of the religion is gone while the custom lives on. Each detail of the custom—what's in good taste and what's the way we've always done it before—is a bloodletting issue. Now, there were two things to do about bloodletting issues, Bill told Lois.

"Yes, dear?" she said with a smile.

"If the issues can be solved to anyone's satisfaction, just solve them. But if they can't be solved at all, have the big fight about them a week ahead. Then everybody is sick of fighting by the time you have the occasion itself."

Lois said, "Makes sense. What can't be solved, though?"

He gave her a look. "Our son and our daughter-in-law are not very happily married. They started a baby two months before they married. And you and I will always just have to hope that it was Will's idea to marry Cheryl and not Merv Oppedahl's idea at the end of a magnum. Next: Cheryl wanted the baby to be named Chereen—a combo of Cheryl, for herself, and Doreen, for her mother. Our son thinks Chereen is a disgusting idea. Next: Cheryl puts a descant onto any hymn we sing, including—if I remember correctly, and I am afraid I will never forget—onto 'Jesu, Joy of Man's Desiring' and Beethoven's Ninth, whatever that one is."

" 'Hymn to Joy,' " Lois said.

" 'Hymn to Joy,' " Bill said. "Next: The Oppedahls are probably not very happy that their daughter has married someone who did two years at Sandstone Federal Prison for embezzlement. Next: You and I are not happy about Will's marrying Cheryl. She is tasteless. He is mean to her. Are you with me so far? Then next is the choice of godparents. Good grief! It is nice that Will wants to honor his second cousin Molly Wells by asking her to stand godparent, but she hasn't gone to church in thirty years. And Cheryl wanted a young couple, not an old great-aunt, for her baby's sponsors. It is obvious Will chose Molly because she gave them seventeen thousand dollars by way of a nest egg. Very handsome thing to do. *Very* handsome, considering Will's record."

Lois said, "Oh, dear, must you?"

"All these things are on people's minds. It's best to have it all out ahead of time. Just because a rich aunt gives someone money is not a reason for having her stand godmother—especially when the baby's mother obviously doesn't want it. Next: The Oppedahls aren't going to be comfortable with the Episcopal Church service, but they'd be a sight *more* comfortable if we used the modern lauguage of 1979—but the baby's grandmother on the other side wants 1928."

Lois said, "Oh, dear. I thought *I* was going to come out of this clean."

Bill laughed, "No one comes out of a family fight clean. Next: Mrs. Oppedahl is a horrible cold fish who doesn't like anybody. She doesn't even like her own daughter very well. In fact—poor Cheryl! Do you know what she told me? She told me the first time she ever felt popular, as she put it, was at Lutheran Bible camp, when all the girls discovered she could harmonize to the hymns. Suddenly it made her part of the group. When they all got back from camp, the girls talked about her as if she were someone that counted, and the boys picked up on it. She was O.K. in high school after that. She told me that just that one Lutheran Bible Camp gave her more nourishment—her word—than she'd ever got from her parents."

"You're a wonder, dear," Lois said. "What about the other godparents?"

"The holistic birdseed-eaters? They know perfectly well that the only reason Will chose them was to override any chance of Cheryl's having some couple *she'd* choose. They know that I think their knee-jerk Gaya stuff is silly, and they will feel awkward about the service. I don't know what to do about them."

Lois said, "We will have lobsters. That's not meat! Then they won't bring their plastic bags of whatever."

"Boiled live lobster. Great idea. They will eat it or I will shove it down their throats," Bill said. "I will offend Doreen Oppedahl by offering Merv a strong drink. It'll buck him up, and she's hopeless, anyway."

"Have we thought of everything?" Lois said.

Bill turned serious a moment. "I am going to tell Will he can't speak cruelly to his wife in my house."

Lois said, "Well, poor Will! Do you remember how when we were all somewhere, at someone's house, suddenly there was Cheryl telling everyone how she and Will met because they were

both at the microfiche in the public library together and they
both felt sick from the fiche?"

"Nothing wrong with that," Bill said. "Microfiche does
make people feel like throwing up."

"But she went on and on about how nausea had brought
them together!"

Bill said, "I remember. Will told her to shut up, too, right
in front of everyone."

The week before the baptism, therefore, Will and Cheryl and
little Molly joined Bill, Lois, and their cousin Molly Wells for
dinner. They aired grievances, just as Bill had planned. Then
he glanced out the window and said to his son, "Come on out
and help me with the protesters, Will."

Everyone looked out. The usual Sunday protesters had been
on the opposite sidewalk, near the plant fence. They looked
flagged from the heat, but determined. Bill saw it was Sue Ann
and Polly this time. They had their signs turned so they could
be read from the Benty house. IT IS HARD TO BE PROUD OF CHEM-
ICAL WARFARE was the message for that Sunday. Now the two
young people had moved to this side of the avenue, doing the
westward reach of their loop on the public sidewalk but taking
the eastward reach on Bill and Lois's lawn.

"Not on my lawn they don't," Bill said, smiling equably at
the others. "We'll be right back."

Father and son went to the lawn edge and stood side by side,
waiting for the protesters to come up abreast of where they
were. The women, in the house, could see their backs but
couldn't hear what was said. Presently they realized nothing
violent seemed likely. They made out the protesters smiling,
and Bill turned slightly, apparently calling a parting shot of some
civil kind to them. The protesters moved back over to the Benty
Chemical side of the street, and Will and Bill came across the
lawn toward the house.

Bill had used that time to speak to his son. "I can't stop you from treating your wife rudely in your own home. But in mine, Will, don't you ever swear at her again. And don't tell her to shut up. And stop saying 'For Christ's sake, Cheryl.' "

"Dad—my life is going to be some kind of hell."

"I bet it might," Bill said in a speculative tone. "It well might." Just then the sign-bearers came up to them. One said, "Good afternoon, Mr. Benty," to Bill. The other of them said in a very pleasant tone, "There must be some other way human beings can make money besides on contracts for spreading nerve diseases that cause victims five or six hours of agony," and they made to pass on.

"Off the lawn, friends," Bill said levelly. "Sidewalk's public, lawn's private."

"Agony is another word for torture," the first protester said, but they immediately crossed the street.

As Bill and Will came back to the house, Bill said in a low voice, "Go for the pleasant moments, son. Whenever you can."

All the difficult conversations took place that could take place: all the permanent grievances—Will's and Cheryl's unhappiness—were hinted at. People felt that they had expressed themselves a little. By the end of the day, they felt gritty and exhausted.

A blessed week passed, and now the baptism party was going off well. The caterers had come, with their white Styrofoam trays. They set out sauces and laid the champagne crooked into its pails of ice. They dropped the lobsters into boiling water. There was lemon mayonnaise and drawn butter, a platter of dark-meat turkey—damper, better than white meat, Lois Benty and the caterers agreed. It is true that as she made her way around the Bentys' dining room table, loading her plate, Doreen Oppedahl whispered to her husband, "It'd never occur to me, I can tell you, to serve dark meat on a company occasion," and Merv whispered back, "No, it never *would* occur to you!" but his tone wasn't malicious. He had spotted the Scotch on the sideboard. That Bill Benty might be pompous, but at least he was as good as his word, and Merv wasn't going to be stuck with that dumb champagne, which tasted like Seven-Up with aspirin. An oblong of pinewood lay piled with ham so thin it wrinkled in waves. The caterers had set parsley here and there, and sprayed mist over everything; they set one tiny chip of ice on each butter pat. "Those caterers just left that chutney preserve that Mrs. Wells brought right in its mason jar," Doreen whispered to Merv. He smiled and whispered, "Shut up, Doreen." She whispered back, "If you get drunk at this party, I will never forgive you."

When all the relations and friends had gathered into the living room, Bill Benty tinkled a glass and asked them to drink to his grandchild. After that, people glanced about, weighing places to sit.

Then the one thing that neither the host nor the hostess had foreseen happened: no one sat in the little groupings Lois had arranged. Nor did people pull up chairs to what free space there was at the dining room table. They gravitated to the messy screened porch off the kitchen. The caterers obligingly swept away all their trays and used foil. People dragged out dining room chairs; other people camped on the old wooden chairs already out there.

The morning's breeze had held. Some of it worked through the gritty screens. People relaxed and felt cheerful. They kept passing the baby about, not letting any one relation get to hold her for too long. Father Geoffrey kept boring people by re-marking that it was the most pleasant baptism he could remem-ber. Suddenly Lois Benty pointed across at Chad's and Jodi's plates. "Don't *tell* me you two aren't eating the lobster!" she screamed. "Lobster is not meat, you know!"

Both Chad and Jodi gave the smile that experienced vege-tarians keep ready for arrogant carnivores. "Well, you see," Jodi said with mock shyness, "we asked the caterers—you see, we did ask. The lobsters weren't stunned first!"

Father Geoffrey said pleasantly, "And delicious they are, too. I've never tasted better."

Jodi said, "They were dropped in alive, you see. . . . So it's a question of their agony." Then Jodi said in a hurried, louder voice, "Mrs. Benty, please don't worry about us! We always bring our own food, so we're all set." She reached into her back jeans pocket and brought out two plastic bags of couscous and sunflower seeds. "We are more than O.K.," she said.

Lois asked people if she could bring them another touch of this or that—the ham, at least? she said, smiling at Mrs. Oppedahl.

"Oh, no!" cried Mrs. Oppedahl. "I've eaten so much! I'd get fat!"

By now Merv had had three quick, life-restoring glasses of Scotch. For once he felt as urbane and witty as Bill Benty, even if he wasn't the boss of a chemical industry.

"Fat!" he shouted. "Afraid you'll get fat! Don't worry! I like a woman fat enough so I can find her in bed!"

He looked around with bright eyes—but there was a pause. Then Bill Benty said in a hearty tone, "Oh, *good* man, Oppedahl! *Good* man!"

Quickly, the baby's great-aunt said to Jodi Plathe, "Those little bags look so interesting! Could you explain what's in them? Is that something we should all be eating?"

Bill said, "Go ahead, Jodi. Convert her. That's what I call a challenge. If you can get her to set down that plate of lobster and eat bulgur wheat instead, you've got something there, Jodi!"

Jodi gave him a look and then said, "No, you tell *me* something, Ms. Wells. I was wondering, why were you crying at the baptism this morning? Somebody said you never went to church at all, and yet . . . I was just wondering."

"Oh," Lois Benty said, getting set to dilute any argument, "I bet you mean during the chrism."

Molly Wells happened to be holding the baby at that moment. Above its dreaming face, hers looked especially tired and conscious. "My dear," she said, "that is a long story. I just know you don't want to hear it."

"Let's have the story, lady," Mr. Oppedahl said. "My wife is always so afraid that I'll tell a story—but the way I look at it is, people like a story. You can always ask 'em, do they mind a little story? And if they don't say no, the way I look at it is, it's O.K. to tell it. So go right ahead. Or I could tell one, if you're too shy."

"Never mind!" cried Bill. "Out with it, Molly!"

Father Geoffrey said gently, "I know I for one would surely like to hear it!"

Molly Wells said, "I have to confess I was mostly daydreaming along through the service, thinking of one thing and another. I never liked church. Unlike Bill here—Bill's my first cousin, you might not know—I was raised in the country, and my dream—my one and my *only* dream—was to get out of the country and marry a prince and live happily ever after.

"The only way I could think to escape at seventeen was to go to Bible camp. So I went—and there, by my great good luck, I met another would-be escaper, Jamie Wells. We cut all the outdoors classes and then used those same places where the classes met to sit and walk together when no one was there. We met in the canoe shed. We sat on the dock near the bin of blue and white hats, depending on how well you swam. We met in the chapel, even, during off times. Wherever we were, we were in love all the time. I recall Jamie said to me, 'There is nothing inside me that wants to go back to the old life, Molly. Is there anything inside you that wants to go back to the old life?' There wasn't, so we ran away. Away meant to stay with his parents and sister, who were at a resort in the Blue Ridge Mountains that summer. We told them we wanted to be married, and they were kind to us. We married, and we lived in love for thirty years.

"It was so pleasant—in the little ways as well as the big ones. Jamie found a hilltop that looked over the valley and across to two mountains—Pisgah and The Rat. He told the workmen how to cut down the laurels and dogwoods and just enough of the armored pine so that you couldn't see the mill down in the valley but you had a clear view to the mountains. We spent hours, hours every day, sitting on our stone terrace. We even had Amos and George bring breakfast out there. I remember best sitting out there in March, when the woods were unleafed except for the horizontal boughs of dogwood everywhere! They looked so unlikely, so vulnerable, out there among all that mountain scrub! The ravines were full of red clay, and the sound of the hounds baying and baying, worrying some rabbit all the time. I remember how we always made a point of taking walks in late afternoon, and I would never stop feeling dazzled by the shards of mica everywhere. And Jamie did have the most wonderful way of putting things. He said mica was bits left over from the first world, back when it was made of pure crystal, when it was made of unbroken love, before God made it over again with clay and trees, ravines, and dogs. I recall when he said that kind of thing my heart used to grow and grow.

"Nothing interrupted us. Now, Jamie's sister, Harriet Jean, always wanted me to do social work for her, but she forgave me when she saw I wasn't going to do it. I expect she understood right off from the very first that I loved her brother, and all a maiden lady really wants from a sister-in-law is that she should really love her brother. We three got along very well. One day, on Amos and George's day off, we had a copperhead on the terrace and Harriet Jean was over there in a flash, and she shot its head right off with her twenty-gauge. She was so good about it, too: I remember she told us very clearly, 'I want you and Jamie to just turn your back now,' and she swept up its head and slung its body over the dustpan handle and carried it off somewhere. She had a good many projects with the black people, and she would have liked me to help her with those . . . but after a while she said to me, 'Molly, I see that you have your hands full with that man, and I mean to stop pestering at you,' and she was good as her word. Different occasions came and went—the Vietnam War, I certainly remember that clear as clear. It was in the paper, and when Amos and George came out with the breakfast trays and brought that paper, Jamie said, 'There is a time when a country is in a kind of death agony, the way a person could be,' and I felt a burst of love for him then, too. No one in my family could ever observe and think that clearly."

At this point, Mr. Oppedahl said in a loud but respectful voice, "I didn't just get what you said he did for a living."

Molly Wells said, "Oh, that. He had a private income—that whole family did. Of course, he had an office he had to keep to tend his interests with—but it was private income." She shifted the baby, and seemed to rearrange herself a little as she said that. It didn't invite further comment.

She took up her story. "Everything went along all those years, except of course we just wept uncontrollably when George died, and Amos never was so springy serving us after that.

"Then one day we found out that Jamie had inoperable cancer of the lung."

There was a little pause after she said that. They could all hear the footsteps of people on the sidewalk, outside. The wind had cooled a little.

"They wanted to do radiation on Jamie, because there were some lung cancer cells in his brain. Well, so we had the radiation treatment. I drove Jamie all the way to Asheville for that, twice a week. It was a very hard time for us: he was often sick. When he wasn't actually sick, he felt sick.

"They managed to kill those lung cells in his brain, and gradually, after many months, he died, but not of brain cancer.

"Well, now," the middle-aged woman said. "Three occasions all came to mind during that baptism service for this beautiful little girl this morning. First, after I had been married not two months, I noticed, the way you gradually get around to noticing everything there is about a man, that the flesh in his upper arm was a little soft, just below the shoulder bulge. I could have expected that, since Jamie just wasn't interested in sports at all and he didn't do any physical work. But still I remember thinking: That bit of softness there will get a little softer all the time, and after twenty years or so it might be very soft and loose from the muscle, the way the upper part of old men's arms are—which kills a woman's feeling just at the moment she notices it. Right away, of course, if it is someone dear to you, you forgive them for that soft upper arm there, for not being young and handsome forever, but still the image of it goes in, and you feel your heart shrink a little. You realize the man will not live forever. Then you love him even better in the next moment, because now—for the first time—you pity him. At least, I felt pity.

"The second occasion is when he was sick having all that radiation. He vomited on our living room floor. It was Sunday evening. We always let Amos go home to his own folks on Sundays, so there wasn't anyone to clean that up—but Harriet Jean was there, and she offered to. Suddenly I remember almost snarling at her—I just bayed at her like a dog. I told her to keep out of it. I would clean up my own husband's mess. Of course she was surprised. She couldn't have been more surprised than I was, though. That night in bed, I went over it carefully, and I realized that the only physical life I had left with Jamie was taking care of him, so his throw-up was a part of my physical life with him. Not lovely—but there it was.

"The last occasion was about a half hour after his death. The hospital people told me I had to leave the room, and I remember I refused. Finally they said I could stay another ten minutes and that was all. Now, you all may know or you may not know that they have their reasons for taking people away from dead bodies. I laid my forehead down on the edge of the bed near

Jamie's hip—and then I heard a slight rustling. My mind filled with horror. I lifted my head and looked up to see a slight change in his hand. It had been lying there; now the fist—just the tiniest bit, but I wasn't mistaken—was closing a little. When a person looks back coolly from a distance on a thing like that, you know it is the muscles shrinking or contracting or whatever they do when life has left. To me, though, it was Jamie making the very first move I had ever seen him make in all my life with him in which I had nothing to do with it. He was taking hold of something there—thin air, maybe—but taking hold of it by himself. Now I knew what death was. I stood up and left.

"This morning, in church, I was daydreaming about him again. It's a thing I do. I was not going to mention it to any of you.

"I told you about this because I was so surprised to find how my life was not simple at all: it was all tied up in the flesh, this or that about the flesh. And how is flesh ever safe? So when you took that palm oil," she finished, glancing across at Father Geoffrey, "and pronounced our little Molly here safe—*safe!*—in our Lord Jesus Christ forever . . . well, I simply began to cry!"

She sat still a moment and then with her conventional smile looked across at the younger godmother. "Well, you asked the question, and now I have answered you."

In the normal course of things, such a speech would simply bring a family celebration to an absolute stop. People would sit frozen still as crystal for a moment, and then one or another would say, in a forced, light-toned way, "My word, but it's getting late. . . . Dear, we really must . . ." and so forth. But the Benty family were lucky. A simple thing happened: it began to rain finally, the rain people had been wanting all summer. It fell quite swiftly right from the first. It rattled the ivy, and then they could even hear it slamming down on the sidewalks. Footsteps across the avenue picked up and began to run.

They all noticed that odd property of rain: if it has been very dry, the first shower drives the dust upward, so that for a second your nostrils fill with dust.

Then the rain continued so strongly it cleaned the air and made the whole family and their friends feel quiet and tolerant. They felt the classic old refreshment we always hope for in water.

A Committee
of the Whole

SINCE her middle-aged daughter had died before she did,
Alice Malley expected only sorrow, increasing solitude,
and eventual decrepitude. Instead, she found herself in the
midst of twenty-three friendly people enthusiastically bent on
any number of projects, one right after another. While Linda
was alive, Alice had paid no attention to the other residents at
Saint Aidan's: they were simply vague background—people you
saw greeting one another at the elevators, people accusing each
other of cheating at checkers or hearts, people forever coming
up with smiles, handing her computer graphics called "Housekeeping Update" or "Our Week's Events" or "This Week in
the Duluth Area."

There was a happy, rather drunken couple among them,
Charles and Martha. There was a loner, who kept himself to
the one third-floor room Saint Aidan's had. There was the community paranoid, LeRoy Beske, who had a strange conviction
that all the world was divided into the lucky Shattuck School
graduates and the unlucky, who were principally LeRoy and his

grandson. When Charles or anyone else tried to explain to LeRoy
what a small part of the world's population was made up of
Shattuck graduates, he snarled, "You can call 'em what you
want—Andover, Saint Paul's, whoever—they're all Shattuck in
my book, with their feet on the neck of the poor!"

As long as Linda was alive, Alice Malley's world shook and
woke itself at the moment when Linda swung into her room,
grinning with her great fair fifty-year-old health, her bluff man-
ner, her armfuls of organic-gardening manuals. In the spring
she generally had a cardboard box or two of cuttings or bare
roots. The last time Alice saw her, she had brought dwarf-pear
stock to espalier on the parking-lot wall. Meals, nights, walks,
were simply the distance between Linda's visits. Sometimes
Linda telephoned from K.C. or Atlanta to explain she was stuck.
She told Alice exactly when she could get home and visited
Alice exactly at the time mentioned.

One day Petra, a woman who lived next door to Linda,
came. It happened to be a Wednesday morning, when Saint
Aidan's residents were gathered in the Fellowship Lounge, so
Petra sorted her way through people folding up chairs, finding
canes, taking turns using the elevators. At last she found Alice
trying to drive a beanpole firmly into the gravelly soil of the
residents' garden. Petra told her that Linda's plane had struck
another plane.

After that, Alice stopped keeping herself apart from her surroundings and the others at Saint Aidan's. She had grown up
in Duluth, so Lake Superior, with its spit of land making the
harbor, was familiar to her. But now the landscape touched her
as it hadn't before: she took in everything—the queer aerial
bridge, the cold water strung across with whitecaps, the harsh,
curiously medieval rooftops of the West End. She saw everything inwardly. Alice made herself join everything going on at
Saint Aidan's. She saw that people pretended to be much more
interested in one another than could possibly be true. They
smiled at each other a good deal. They were patient with LeRoy

Beske. Linda had been killed in late spring: by midsummer Alice
was secretary of the group that a social work student convened
each Wednesday. She donated her daughter's library to the Seamen's Mission. By autumn she joined the protests against the
Saint Aidan's manager's various schemes to remove the residents' privileges.

Nearly all meetings and programs were well attended.
Everyone except Jack Laresstad went to everything. A few people, especially Martha, who drank in the mornings, nodded off
during slide shows of third world countries, but they politely
woke themselves during the Question Period and tried to have
eye contact with the speaker. Mr. Binner, the manager, brought
in a good many fourth-rate speakers for them. Each one was
introduced as a "very, very special person," whom they were
lucky to have right there, as a rich resource person. Someone
told them how cruelly used the third world sailors were on
oceangoing boats. A marine biologist told them what could live
and what could not live at the deepest levels of Lake Superior.

Each Tuesday Mr. Binner held house meetings, which he
liked to call "Housekeeping Updates." Everybody tried to pay
close attention at the Updates, in order to spot and forestall any
planned loss of privilege. LeRoy Beske was sure that Mr. Binner
invested their monthly payments, as well as the grant money
Saint Aidan's got, in gigantic firms whose fingers went deep
into all the money pots of the world and delivered the booty
into Mr. Binner's personal account. Each Wednesday they had
"Group." Nearly every day they had a cocktail hour of sorts,
in Charles and Martha's room, where Malcolm the minibus
driver left off cases of vodka and beer, wrapped in Eddie Bauer
camping bags. They had parties, everyone holding a toothbrush
glass or a glass taken from the Fellowship Lounge. Charles called
their parties "celebrations." They celebrated defeating the manager in his attempt to plow over their gardens. They celebrated
defeating the manager in his plan to authorize Malcolm to drive
them into downtown Duluth only twice instead of three times

a week. They celebrated after the Housekeeping Update in which they voted that Mr. Binner take the sunflower seed for Saint Aidan's ten bird-feeding stations out of his operating expenses instead of insisting the residents pay for it themselves. Charles was forever shouting, "Celebration, folks! Martha and I want you all to come to our room! Five sharp!" as if life were a succession of marches under the Arc de Triomphe.

Their recluse, Jack Laresstad, mainly stayed in his third-floor room, monitoring the harbor with binoculars. They had one bellicose member, LeRoy Beske. Like most paranoids, Beske made strong use of *Robert's Rules,* bringing them in even when the meeting was not formal. "Call the question!" LeRoy would shout. "Call the goddamned question!" in just the mix of fury and expertise to waken even Martha, who generally had her head on Charles's shoulder throughout any meeting. She would raise herself gently, like a mermaid trying the air. She would cry out charmingly, "Yes—oh, yes! Call the question!"

"We need to adjourn the goddamned meeting," LeRoy said. "We need to reconvene as a Committee of the Whole!"

"So the chair can't stop you from talking? Not a chance, my boy!" Charles said with a laugh.

"I am sick of being pushed around by a bunch of snobbish old Shattuck grads!" LeRoy flung back at Charles. "My grandson's trying to get started in business, and who cheats him clean? Gentlemen! Shattuck graduates who think they're so good they don't have to pay their bills!"

Everyone knew about LeRoy's grandson. Everyone knew about everyone else except for Jack Laresstad.

Alice, amazed at the folly of her life, took part in everything. She did not cultivate a friendship with Jack, because he was solitary. He was the only chance of a serious friendship, so she saved him for last, whatever last should be. The grief of Saint Aidan's was that you ran through any one person's repertoire of wit and wisdom in two weeks. You knew the names and circumstances of their relations, you knew whether or not a harsh wind off Lake Superior would make them complain or talk about neuralgia. You knew of all the blizzards they and their friends or family had nearly died in. Alice was saving Jack, therefore, so there should be something other than LeRoy Beske's tantrums to differentiate each day.

She knew he had taken it in that she was now among them all, in a way she had not been before. He greeted her, and she responded, in the affected raillery that Saint Aidan's residents used with each other: it was a slightly unnatural formality, which seemed to say, At some point in my life I lived a little more elegantly than I do now, and the elegance remains inside me.

At the elevators Jack said, smiling, "Madam!"

"Sir!" Alice said.

"May I ask what your energetic group have on for this frigid, blustery day?" he said. The elevators of Saint Aidan's did not go to the third floor, where his room was, so he had come down a flight of stairs and now waited with Alice to descend to the Fellowship Lounge for breakfast. He was very neat in his white shirt, open at the neck, not a lumberjack shirt. He had just a bit of white hair. He had the habit of bending toward anyone he spoke to, actually seeming to listen.

She told him, "We constantly fight against crime. Last week it was Mr. Binner's crooked deal with some landscape company that wanted to do away with our gardens. Today we have to save Helen's job."

Jack said, "Who's Helen?"

"Our social worker. She helped us fight Mr. Binner about the landscaping, so he left in a temper. Now he has asked her supervisor to come be at our meeting. We know that he intends to disgrace her. She is doing something called a 'practicum.' "

"You garden, don't you?" Jack said. The elevator slowly lowered them.

Alice turned the conversation away from gardening. Her instinct was not to talk about the subject of greatest interest.

"What's out on the lake so far today?" she asked him.

"Something big moored sternwise to us, sailing under a Libyan flag. And fourteen hundred gulls at last count."

No sooner did they emerge on the main floor than Charles came rapidly forward. "Oh, Alice!" he cried. "Hello, Jack. Oh, Alice! LeRoy is saying he won't go through with it!"

She had to follow him over to the window, where a few of the residents had set their trays. Beyond their heads the November day looked rather bright, whity and fragile: there was a slight frosty lick on the rock outcropping just below Saint Aidan's, a slight shine to the steep-pitched roofs on the hillside. The lake still lay motionless under its morning fog.

LeRoy looked up. "I'm not going to do it," he said. "It's goddamned humiliating. Besides, it's blackmail. What do I care if Helen loses her job or her practicum or whatever it is? Lots of people lose lots of things! Look how many people have cheated my grandson!"

Charles tapped LeRoy's hand with his fork. "We know about your grandson, you know. Cheated by Shattuck graduates!"

"Sneer all you like!" LeRoy shouted.

One of the maids came over. "Can I help with anything, Mr. Beske?" she said.

"Oh, hell!" LeRoy said. "Why should all you city slicks care about one poor kid trying to make a living at a wrecking business?"

Alice said, "Doing our best, LeRoy. *You* work this morning, *we* all work to help your grandson this afternoon. We do care!"

People always went to their rooms after breakfast. Then the elevators clicked and clicked over their safety catches as the residents returned in twos and threes and fours to the Fellowship Lounge for Group. Helen Pool, their young social work student, got the chairs set around in a circle. This morning a sensible, kindly-faced woman of fifty or so stood talking to the manager near the Fellowship Lounge doorway.

When everyone sat down, Helen said in her terribly young,

not particularly resonant voice, "Before we *check in,* I would like to introduce a very, very special person to you."

The Group waited, unaffected.

"This is my supervisor, Ms. Dietrich," Helen said.

Charles leaned over and said to Alice, "This is it!"

Alice couldn't decide whether she felt pleasantly excited at the adventures they had planned for the day or if she felt depressed at the stupidity of all their agendas. Since Helen had introduced Ms. Dietrich to Group, they were to go with Plan B. LeRoy was very red in the face, but he swung into his first speech.

"Hi, Ms. Dietrich!" he shouted.

"Good to have you with us," Charles said.

"Before we *check in,* can I say something, Helen?" cried LeRoy. Now he was on his feet.

"You know you don't have to stand up to speak out at Group, LeRoy," Helen said.

LeRoy sat down. "Helen," he said very loudly, "I want to say what a difference it makes that you come have these sessions with us. Before you started Group with us, we never shared any of our personal concerns. We had negative feelings and nowhere to go with them. We acted out. The bottom line is, we didn't bring anything out into the open."

LeRoy paused. Alice heard Charles say very low, "I know that I myself had trouble with . . ."

LeRoy manfully took it up: "I know that I myself had trouble with how I conducted myself in this room. I would feel angry that my grandson Terry didn't visit me more. Or I'd feel angry the way this place is run. It always seemed crazy to me that people accused me of cheating at checkers when I always felt that Mr. Binner, over there, was cheating the residents here in any way he thought he could get away with. Of course, that was just a feeling of mine. I had angry feelings."

"It is O.K. to have angry feelings, LeRoy. We've talked about that," she said.

LeRoy was grinding forward. "I'd be still feeling angry that someone had cheated my grandson—see, Helen, there is this optometrist downtown that cheated my grandson—"

Helen cut in: "We've talked about the optometrist, LeRoy."

LeRoy cut back in: "And I'd think about that and have angry feelings, and if the person I was playing chess with got up and went out, sometimes I would move one or two of their pawns off. If the person was a dumbbell or if they were some rich Shattuck School type, I'd try to slide their knight, maybe, off, too, and then stand it up with the other pieces which had been taken."

Charles did not forget his cue. "You cheat, LeRoy! You cheat! That was my knight you took, and when I said so you denied it, and in front of the whole Group, too!"

Helen said, "Did you want to respond to Charles, LeRoy?"

LeRoy said, "So I cheated sometimes. In hearts, too. If there were three, I would look at the kitty. I think I was under a lot of pressure but didn't realize it."

Charles: "Why are you telling us all this *now*, LeRoy?"

Martha, who had no assigned part, suddenly said very clearly, in a silvery voice, "How come LeRoy Beske is wearing a tie when he never wears a tie? I think it looks very sweet." Her head slid back down onto Charles's shoulder.

LeRoy said, "Helen makes it possible for us to work out this kind of stuff," he said. "Somehow I feel so much more in . . . in control of my life now."

Charles said, with his hand steadying Martha so she didn't sink into his lap, "I must say, I feel the same thing, Helen. I feel as if we can all get together and make the changes we want to make in our lives. I used to get depressed. Now when I feel depressed by something, I let it have its space, but I don't let it climb all over me."

"Like all my cursing and dirty language," LeRoy said. "I am cutting down on it, making a track record like you said,

Helen. But I am going to need help with this. So the rest of you can help some."

The ten who were in the Project kept a straight face, but a few of the others looked stunned. One woman, who had firmly slept through every Saint Aidan's program ever offered, was not only wide awake but on her feet, half her weight square over the four points of her cane. She studied the face of each speaker.

Alice Malley thought: Well, it stands to reason. When you are nine years old a skillful liar can fool you. But when you've lived another eighty or ninety years you have heard a good many people lie in a good many different kinds of circumstances, so most likely you can tell when you wake up in a room where four people are lying steadily.

LeRoy had one more speech, if Alice recalled the rehearsals right, then Charles, then she herself was to say, "I don't know if I can take in anything more right now, Helen—I think I'm winding down!" and then Martha was supposed to follow the two social workers out to the parking lot to overhear their reactions to everything. But Martha obviously had not obeyed Charles's request that she not drink anything just this one day when they had so much to do. Alice decided she would go to the parking lot herself.

She got past LeRoy, who was shouting at Charles, "How'd I do, big boy? How'd I do? Now it's *your* turn, big boy!"

It was bright and cold outside. Alice found Helen and Ms. Dietrich leaning against one of their cars. They had lighted cigarettes and were laughing and talking, not, Alice noticed, bothering to make eye contact. Eye contact was a bloodletting issue at Saint Aidan's Group: people hated being told by the twenty-three-year-old social worker they must make eye contact.

They smiled as she came up. Alice was delighted when Ms. Dietrich shook hands with her. She caught herself just in time before saying, "You remind me so much of my daughter—I noticed it all through the Group meeting! You remind me so very much of her! How much you remind me of her! It is the same rather hearty, frank face! I should not mention this, perhaps—but you remind me so much of Linda! Did you know that my Linda was killed?"

She did not say any of that.

Helen, who had a trick of not just looking at people but rather pouring over them, said, "Don't cry, Alice: it came out all right this morning! Really it did!"

Ms. Dietrich, still holding Alice's hand, smiled. "I have been telling Helen here," she said, "that she must be doing something right in her practicum. I have overseen a lot of practicums, but I have never yet seen a whole roomful of people lie themselves blue in the face in order to make a Master of Social Work degree candidate look good in front of her supervisor!"

They all laughed, and Alice wiped her nose.

"I gather Mr. Binner is a jerk," Ms. Dietrich offered.

They talked about the sleazy manager for a while, they shook hands again, and Alice spent a couple of minutes studying the parking-lot wall. She would need to furr out from the stone, with bamboo or other sticks, so she could progressively train the pear-tree branches as they came along. Now the little roots of them were curled, spineless still, safe under the gravelly dirt and mulch.

After a while she went in: for a half hour she had been lost in thought about the baby pear trees. She felt happy about it.

Charles caught her arm in the hallway. "Bad news," he said.

He led her over to the checkers table, away from people who were beginning to line up for the luncheon trays.

"LeRoy is very sick. Right after Group he apparently sat down on the carpet by the elevators and wouldn't get up. People thought he was having one of his paranoid tantrums. It turned out he was in a coma, and they've taken him to Saint Mary's."

Charles paused. "I guess that's the end of the afternoon plan."

Alice said, "Nonsense. Let's go ahead with it!"

"But what good will it do? What difference will it make to LeRoy? He's probably had a stroke! We'll go downtown and make fools of ourselves—and all for nothing!"

Alice said, "It's true we will make fools of ourselves. Let's go through with it, anyway. If LeRoy recovers, think how he'll feel!"

When the Special Committee of Ten gathered by the minibus, Malcolm checked their names on his clipboard. "LeRoy's not here yet," he said. They explained he was sick.

Alice went around to each person and made sure he or she had the right typed sheet: half the sheets had little else but figures on them; the other half had a couple of paragraphs of neat typing. Mr. Binner's secretary had let Alice use the copier, but she had had to pay fifteen cents for each copy because Mr. Binner had told her if they ever let the residents start making copies free, next thing everybody would do a whole book.

Malcolm drove them sedately down the Skyline Drive, then down one of the steep avenues to Superior Street, and then east.

"I'll be right here in an hour!" Malcolm told each person climbing out. To Alice, who got out last, he said, "Don't spend everything you got in one place!"

Alice had not lived in a jovial community for two years for nothing. "Spend all *what* in one place!" she jeered back in the right tone.

"Come on," Charles said. "We're on."

The man who owed LeRoy Beske's grandson $215 was Dr. Royce Salaco, an optometrist with an office facing Lake Superior on one side, the ground floor of a business building on another, and Superior Street on the north. Charles and Martha and Alice had been past it so many times they felt as if they knew it inch by inch.

No one wanted to get started: all ten clustered together on

the windy sidewalk, longing to be like the passersby—just private citizens not committed to some dreadful project.

Charles whispered, "Keep your spirits up! Here we go! Big celebration afterward in Martha's and my room, O.K.? O.K.! Let's go! O.K., Alice.

With Charles hanging a few feet behind, Alice went into the foyer of the building and turned left into Dr. Salaco's office. Out of the corner of her eye she saw the residents divide themselves into those who were to stay on Superior Street and those who were to stand about in the building. Charles waited at the office door, without coming in.

Throughout both rehearsals she had found Dr. Salaco to be simply another Scandinavian-looking Minnesota optometrist: he had rather coarse, neat, pale hair, expressionless eyes behind the rimless glasses. Now, as Alice crept over toward his counter, with its swivel seat for customers being fitted, Dr. Salaco looked like a film-version *Abwehr* officer—pale, blond, gigantic, with the snappy look of someone with lifelong skills in doing evil.

He said, "Can I help you this afternoon?"

"I've come about your account with Terence Beske," Alice said.

"How's that?"

"I've come to regularize your account with Terence Beske," Alice said.

"Lady, I haven't got the least idea what you're talking about!"

"Terence Beske," Alice explained, "is the young man who pulled your car out of the ditch you put it in on August 16, 1987. It was three-fifteen in the morning. Then he drove you and your lady friend to where you needed to go. He did it as a personal favor, charging you only for the gas, although you promised, at the time, to make it worth his while. Then, as contracted for by you, he replaced your Michelins with some old tires, since you told him that was all right with State Farm.

He presided over the assessment by the claims officer. He has
sent you a total of four billings since then, which—"

"Lady," Dr. Salaco said, "I don't know who or what you
are talking about, but I'm afraid I am going to have to ask you
to leave. As you see, I have a busy day, and there is a customer
waiting."

Alice did not look back. "The man in the doorway?" she
said. "He's with me."

As Alice and Charles had planned it, there would be nice
sass in the scene if she did not even look over her shoulder to
check if it *was* Charles who had come in. They had reckoned
that if someone else happened into the doorway just then, that
person wouldn't hear Alice's "he's with me" and, if he or she
did, wouldn't believe it had any application. If worse came to
worst, Charles could elbow in front of someone.

"Yes," Alice said, actually drawling now, warming to the
part. "He's with me. And those ones out in the street now—if
you'd look. Those people out there passing out sheets to passersby? They are handouts explaining how you didn't pay your
bill to a twenty-year-old entrepreneur. And the people in the
building lobby now . . ."

Alice waited while Dr. Salaco spun around and glared
through the lobby window of his shop. A few people were
waiting for the elevators. Four senior citizens were handing
sheets of paper to the others. A man stooped over the water
fountain: when he straightened up, an old person smiled at him
and handed him a sheet.

"Those people," Alice now said, "are handing out just the
figures—billing dates, a breakdown of Terry's services to you.
We thought people who do business right in the same building
with you should know the level of ethical unconcern you operate
on."

Alice moved over to a wall full of tiny shelves: each little
bracket held a model piece of eyewear. She ran her hand over

a few of the nose sections, then picked up one of the frames and put it on. There was no prescription, of course, which gave her an odd feeling: when she put the frames on, even though she *knew* they had no glass in them, she unconsciously expected to see better.

She wandered over to the window that overlooked the harbor.

"You're good at your trade," she said, loudly, so Dr. Salaco would hear although she was looking at the lake. "With these glasses of yours I can see so well I can see right into the portholes of that ship way out there. Libyan, I see she is. Right—and lying on the bunk is a guy from some African country who has been two hundred and twenty days aboard and can't even go ashore here because one of the ship's officers cheated him. You know," Alice said conversationally, "it is amazing how if someone doesn't have someone to look out for them, they get cheated by the rich. That poor sap in his bunk there, reading some book he probably got at the Seamen's Mission—yes—wait a second!" Alice took the glasses off and tipped them in front of her eyes, as if to sharpen the lens angle. "Yes," she said. "A book on land stewardship, how do you like *that!* Anyway, third world, no union, no ombudsman—no advocate!"

She came back over to the middle of the shop. "What surprises me is that someone of your luck and prestige and wealth should decide to cheat a helpless young person! Now, why would that be?"

She could feel Charles fidgeting in the doorway.

Dr. Salaco went around behind the counter. "How much do you want?" he said.

Alice thought fast. "Your account with Terry is two hundred and fifteen. If I were you I'd make it two fifty. You've given the man trouble."

The optometrist handed her the check and said very levelly, "I want both of you out of here in one second flat. Get out."

Alice turned to go. There stood Charles, with his raincoat

collar up, looking pleased as punch, exactly like the kind of man who explains to traffic cops that he is with the CIA. She felt happy as a girl that the whole job was over. She spun around and said, "Do you want us to explain to the people out there on Superior Street that you decided to pay up and be fair, after all?"

"That's all right, Doc," Charles said. "We're leaving."

Alice escaped from the celebration in Charles and Martha's room. When she knocked at Jack's door he called "Come in!" but turned to look at her with his binoculars still up to his eyes. It made her feel as if she had entered a tree shrew's apartment— and this ancient, owly creature was welcoming her.

"I understand all your day's projects went very well," he said. "Would you like some insty-pot tea?"

Yes, she would.

They drank the hot, mindless-tasting stuff.

Jack looked at her carefully. "There's lots to be depressed about," he said. "I understand that LeRoy Beske is seriously sick?"

She told Jack what she knew about LeRoy. She thought of him in the brilliant lighting of an intensive care unit.

Jack said, "I only know two tricks against feeling sad. And neither one of them works perfectly. Here's the first. What you do is, you shut off the lights in your room at this time of day." He got up and turned off his lights. "Most people try to brighten up the dusk—great mistake! Turn the lights *off*, and then the lights and everything else from the outside will come *in*."

They looked at the shadowy, chilled city. The last of the afternoon sun still lighted the lake some: it gave its surface a rounded, smooth look, as if the very surface of it were strong enough to support life. Alice and Jack couldn't see the slight chop that reminds one of what lies on the bottom of even inland seas.

"When the light outside is stronger than the light inside, you aren't so aware of yourself," Jack said. "All you have is nature, so to speak. . . . O.K. so far?"

"Better than O.K.!" said Alice.

"Then here is the second idea," he said. "Let's say a person feels the life leaking out of them. Day by day, here at Saint Aidan's. Now, here is what you do: You had better go on imagining the leak, all right, like imagining yourself a leaky cup. But instead of imagining your life leaking out of the cup, what you do is, you imagine the universe out there slowly, slowly leaking into you."

Alice nodded. "Those are two very, very terrific ideas," she told him.

"I think so, too," Jack said. "I think they're terrific. But they don't work completely. I have been going around and around about it," he said. "There are a couple of things that just keep coming and coming and coming, and you can put all the philosophy you like up against them, they still get through like dust. One of them is death, of course, and then the other one is just pure idiocy. That's what it is, just pure human idiocy."

An Apprentice

CROSS most of Saint Paul to take my violin lessons. Then I drive slowly around Georgia's half-block, along Hemlock Avenue, and through the north-south alley. I locate the regulars. They are of two kinds—the four men who generally are on their feet, laughing, shouting, dealing, waiting for the Hemlock Bar to open at six; and the three men who sprawl, elbows propped, right on the four low steps leading from the sidewalk up the low slant of Georgia's lawn. These are more languid than the crack pushers: they lie at ease and blow their smoke straight up, pursing their lips at the sky.

For my first two lessons, I gave those men the stairs: I climbed up the grass slant, keeping a good ten yards between them and me. But by the time I was learning the third position and could do "Go Down, Moses," with harmonics on the G string, I thought: If Georgia Persons doesn't give way to these guys, neither will I.

So I make myself pick a way between them up the concrete stairs. They never move an inch, but they always stop talking, and their eyes creep over my black plastic Hefty bag. Inside it, my mother's old violin case does not bulge the way garbage would. I have my music-stand top, since someone, when breaking into all the apartments of Georgia's building, went off with one of hers. I have my chin support, the Friml and Kuechler and Handel sheet music, and *A Tune A Day,* my violin lessons text. I am nervous that the smokers think: Why *not* knock over that sturdy, timid-faced woman of forty-one? Why *not?* She might have a ten or a twenty in the chipped shoulder bag, even though she wears her grubbies. And they must think: Whatever's in the Hefty isn't garbage. Who'd bring garbage to 4303 Hemlock, where there are generally several sacks of it on the front-porch floorboards, not to mention the sacks left in the downstairs hallway for weeks at a time. I step through these men prissily, lifting my bag over their pot-fragrant skulls, and I imagine their brains as indeterminate magma. Whatever thinking they do, the thoughts haven't cooled enough to be distinct, the way the central metals of our planet aren't quiet, reliable rock yet.

Georgia has opened the screen-and-torn-plastic door a couple of inches as soon as she has seen my car, so I will know she is there to let me in. She and the other tenants of 4303—the born-again on the ground floor and two men a flight above Georgia—have decided that the usual mechanical voice-check and relay lock aren't safe enough: they arrange for their guests' arrivals by phone. Then they crouch on the unlighted staircase inside until their guests' heads show through the scrim of door curtain.

Now Georgia opens the door wide for me. I bound in, taking the Hefty sack safely past her. She gives the street and yard a last wide scanning, like a bridge officer just leaving the conn. "I see the Boy Scouts have their troop meeting on my steps today," she says in her friendly, sardonic tone. "Good fellows that they are," she adds, "they invited a goodly number of policemen to their meeting in the alley yesterday—yes, they did—and finally the policemen invited a goodly number of them to a picnic somewhere; at least, they all climbed into two vans together! Very nice! Very nice indeed!"

Her ironic style restores my humor. It seems right that a disciplined artist should use archaic phrases and should nurture indignation against slobs. I follow Georgia's huge behind up the stairs. She always wears print dresses with dark backgrounds and large flower patterns: in the unlighted stairway, the white peonies and hydrangeas on her skirt lead the way.

Georgia is only ten or fifteen years older than I am, but her face if full and soft from her having taken prednisone for a year and a half. She has temporal arteritis, and the drug saved her eyesight in the first weeks. Now the doctors keep lessening her dose: they consider her much improved. Georgia wears hearty makeup—eye shadow bright as poster paint, paste rouge on each huge, viscous cheek. I try to draw her out, since I am interested in serious illness, but she explained the symptoms, the diagnosis, and the regimen to me once and refuses to go into it further. On what I have to guess are her bad days, all her makeup—shadow, rouge, and lipstick—looks lightly positioned, temporary, like an airplane parked. It might easily lift away.

She won't complain, even when I deliberately, hopefully, role-model complaining for her. I think of myself as someone coming to her only to learn the violin. I ought to be glad of having this discrete task as an escape from the rest of my life, but I have the slack-focused habit of dropping personal anecdote into our talk. I tell her about the first, even the second, laser vaporization I have had, a procedure for treating precancer and cancer of the cervix. Georgia waits through my talk. I try to intrigue her with bits of lifestyle at the In and Out Surgi-Center at Saint Alban's. When I stop talking, she says, "If you will hand me that Strad of yours, I'll tune it for you."

She turns sidewise to me and whines my violin strings with her thumb while striking her piano's A, E, D, and G keys with her free hand. At one of our sessions I told her I had not practiced very much because my ex-husband had asked the eldest of our children to tell me to have the younger children clean and well-dressed for his wedding that week. Old friends of mine were going to the wedding without a qualm. When I was through talking, Georgia said, "It is impossible to have a good lesson if you do not practice." She added, "Impossible." Then, after a little pause, she said, "Men are repulsive. As always."

She is a martinet of a violin teacher—the only kind, I decide. At first I thought she wore her makeup and her rayon, floriate dresses for her one other adult student—a dentist. But it turns out that she despises him because he wants to learn the Handel immediately and will not do any of the exercises in *A Tune A Day,* which Georgia assures me is the definitive violin study book, better even than the precise exercises of Wohlfahrt. During my first few weeks of lessons, she told me how little the dentist practiced. By the time I was in the third position, and starting the third position and learning the languid, swooping vibrato of beginners, I heard no more of the dentist. I expect she has dropped him. Now she has only me and her several dozen Hmong and Laotian children, many of whom do not speak English. I imagine her extending her arms like fat bridges to them, pressing their half- and three-quarter-sized fiddles to their necks, and pouring all her theory of bowing and fingering, in English, into those full, black eyes. Once—*only* once—I exclaimed, "How good you are to them! What wonderful patience you have!" Georgia promptly jammed her violin into her throat. "*They* do not have trouble with atonal music. *They* are not hobbled by preconceived ideas about where *do* should be," she said.

I vow to be her best student. Sometimes, when I have mastered something difficult, like sliding thirds cleanly across two strings, Georgia says, "That's *very* good. *Very* good. Also, it is pleasant that you do not ever tell me that your mother forgot to put your *Tune A Day* into your bag. And that your mother forgot the rosin so you could not practice." At long intervals I get hints about the rest of her teaching life. "Ah! you've practiced very well!" she says, looking at me from the center of her serious, drug-changed face. "Why have you practiced so much? Have you only just now arrived from the boat and therefore haven't learned yet that there's welfare and you needn't do a lick of work, ever?"

It sounds like such a friendly opening, I pick it up quickly. "Then are the earnest Asian people learning to rot in America?"

But Georgia is back to my bowing. "Wrists! Wrists! Wrists leading lightly," she says. "You needn't get revenge on the violin. Play it gently. *Especially,* be easy on that tiny, slender E string."

At other times she notices I am doing something right when I least expect it. Several times, when I have thought she wasn't listening but was putting her feathery handwriting under my country-day-school manuscript printing in the assignment book, I find she has been listening. "Ah! Lovely! Very nice sound, that! Very!" she murmurs, still writing. "You must always do good work. If it sounds bad, go back and get it right. You must play at concert level all the time." Then she gives her small laugh, drops the assignment notebook onto the piano bench, turns to accompany me with her own violin. "It is just a question of time now! Before Memorial Day, I would say!"

She drops her soft chin onto the chin support; the spidery fingers, so thinly hung to the flesh of hand and wrist, make their hummingbird-speed vibrato. One good violinist can make another violinist sound better: in fact, you can have three or four indifferent players playing, provided at least one of them can do the uncompromised bowing and vibrato that thin a string's sound to its lyric bone.

But I am too curious to continue. I stop and ask, "Before Memorial Day, what?"

"Oh," she says. "The Saint Paul Chamber Orchestra, of course. They will call, probably at midnight, wanting you for concertmaster, and of course, like Cinderella, you will have to go. Naturally you will mention to them that I am your teacher."

Georgia wanted to charge me four dollars a lesson. I told her that was absurd. "But I don't need more," she said. "I have my salary from the school"—where she teaches the Hmong and Laotian children—"and I have another private student. I have Minnesota state employees' health coverage."

I tell her that other violin teachers assure me that any musician of musical integrity must charge starting students twelve dollars. Each month I hand her a check for forty-eight dollars.

"This will pay for your lessons through the 1990s," she says each time, dropping my check into the little velvet lining of her violin case. I envy that velvet lining, with its blood-colored fur and its neat little zipper. I would buy one with part of a child-support check, but I am loyal to the ugly case I inherited from my mother.

"Now the Handel," Georgia says briskly.

It is in E major, but the first movement is adagio, so I have a little chance. From somewhere under the cry and grind of my efforts, I begin to hear Handel's lilt. It isn't pathos that makes Handel so tuneful: it is character. Under my fingers and crimped bowing, his beauty is only beginning to show. Even so, I can hardly believe I don't live in a state of gratitude all the time.

Georgia refuses to play it all through once so I can hear the full beauty. Fat arms go up—but drop. "No, no," she says. "You make it beautiful yourself. The first time you hear it all through and it sounds beautiful will be when you yourself do it. And now," she says, "that is enough for today."

She looks ill. I put everything away as fast as I can.

"I will let myself out," I tell her.

"No, no!" she says, in her singsong ironic tone. "I will see you safe into your car," and she follows me down the stairs.

Of course it is a relief to get away from one's teacher. No matter how good a teacher she is, it is a relief to escape. Once I am in the car, I daydream of going back to smoking. I daydream of stopping for some greasy fast food. I sing a descant, which, like Girl Scout camp descants, rides its resolute third above the melody without break, ruining any music it attaches to. I want to feel the *easy* emotions: I drive along in my car, leaving behind slatternly Selby Avenue and Hemlock Avenue and Dale Street, and I sing "You Want to Pass It On," a tune from twenty years ago, when I was a born-again Christian. My thoughts get silvery and loose like fish. I think of my mother, who died when I was a kid. I was not allowed to have violin lessons. She said it was ridiculous: I had no gift. Why give lessons to someone with no gift? Right, I think, without rancor, and I start humming "Abide with Me," imagining the fingering for the key of D, key of G, key of E. I do an upside-down vibrato on the left side of the steering wheel.

I have been home two hours when a man calls and asks who I am. Then he asks, "Are you a relation of Georgia Persons?"

"She is my violin teacher. Why?"

"I am a policeman, at 4303 Hemlock Avenue," he says. "Is Georgia Persons a close friend? Just your teacher, or what?"

Right now my children are my close friends, but I am trying to ease them more and more away, into their father's care, just in case. I make it a point to think of them only a few quarter hours a day. Old college friends are close friends, but right now they avoid me because divorce might be catching. And whatever makes people have surgery once and then surgery again and even again might be catching too. Sometimes on the Hardanger plateau, in the endless landscape of scraped stones and freezing creeks high above the treeline, you see a walker in the distance walking another path, which won't cross yours. The other walker may stay within view for as much as two hours. You feel an affinity for him or her, because you are engaged in the same energetic project. The people who feel like friends to me at the moment are Georgia and the nurse-anesthetist at Saint Alban's.

"She is a close friend," I tell the policeman. "You had better tell me what is going on." I am now recalling Georgia's pallor.

"We will send someone around to pick you up," the man says. It is clear that Georgia Persons is dead.

I always wore the shabbiest jeans and tees to take my lessons from her. I meant to give the impression of someone without a nickel, so the alley and sidewalk folk would leave me alone. Now I put on a silk orange shirt, a silk jacket, and a flowered silk skirt: it is full and has the huge roseate flowers of spring 1990 styles. I put on stockings and a new pair of yellow high-heeled pumps. "Well, Georgia," I say as I dress, "it's for you, since you won't get to hear me play for the Chamber Orchestra, after all. Do not feel bad," I say, trying for her exact ironical note. "Everyone in the Saint Paul Chamber Orchestra may not have musical integrity, even though we have to admit they sound as if they do."

The policewoman's car is astir with air-conditioning. We ride in great comfort to Hemlock and Dale. "It was assault, and she died," the policewoman tells me. At Georgia's house, not only are all the regulars there, on their feet for once, collected into a little group, with two policemen watching them, but all the alley types are standing around on the grass. Three police cars are parked askew in the street, with blinkers going. All around and in neighboring bits of yard, people hover in groups, not a single person smoking anything.

"We're using his apartment for now," my cop says, jerking her head toward a man standing beside a policeman on the porch. I realize this is the born-again Christian.

In his apartment, three people approach me and stand close around. Was I there two hours ago? Yes. My lessons started the better part of a year ago. Was anyone else ever in Georgia Persons's apartment when I was there? Whoever stole her music-stand top, I think. I decide I had better mention that. They listen, as they do to everything I say, taking no notes. I mention the dentist. Yes, they have his name already, but he refused to come. He said he was not a friend and had quit taking lessons from Georgia because she did not "address his needs." All the while we are talking in the middle of the room, I must have seen that there is a slightly raised stretcher on the floor, but I avoid the idea, thinking of ways I will insult the dentist someday if I live so long. I will find time to insult the born-again Christian, too. It turns out that a first-rate violinist was assaulted and killed and her body left drooping over his pileup of garbage bags in the staircase landing. I tell myself how much the author of Ecclesiastes would disdain the born-again Christian. Of course none of that does any good: the policewoman takes me gently over, and I am shown a three-cornered opening to Georgia's face. The fine craft of her brain, whatever of her that can fly, clearly has got away.

The following week, I am to have two laser vaporizations and one small ordinary surgery done at the same time. All three procedures can be taken care of in the In and Out Surgi-Center, as before, but I feel like a girl at the Scout meeting who is a little too old and really should join the serious organizations of adulthood. I know that any future surgery they have to do will be in the main, serious part of the hospital, where patients survive or they don't.

As before, they hand me my papers, a folder called "Welcome to the In and Out Surgi-Center," and a zipper bag long enough for my clothes. I undress in a cubicle and emerge to claim a comfortable lounge chair in the waiting area. There are several of us, our chairs spaced informally about. We all have our angel robes and light-blue dressing gowns over them. We are mostly graying or white-haired or bald. We look so much alike it is a reminder that our insides—cervixes, kidneys, veins—are more alike than not.

I note how kindly each of us is treated: white-dressed people lean over to drop a word; someone brings a magazine. It crosses my mind that if the Saint Alban's In and Out Surgi-Center were part of a gigantic lab experiment in human outcomes, we would probably be the control group—the ones you handle kindly but don't give any of the hopeful treatment to. None of us has eaten in twelve hours, so we give one another shy, starving smiles. We doze in the marvelous chairs. From time to time, a nurse wakes one or another of us to go to a curtained area, where we get anesthesia on a gurney.

In my curtained area, I find the same nurse-anesthetist I had last time.

"Oh!" she says with a laugh, entering the IV. "I'd know you, all right! You're the one who is learning the violin! It isn't everyone you meet that studies a tough instrument like that, I can tell you!"

"I remember you, too!" I crow back.

Now she tells me in a triumphant tone, as she disappears around behind the drip stand, "I remember that you're fussy about what we do for you! You told me to give you something that would leave your brains in good condition, that would kill pain but leave you conscious, because you wanted to experience the procedure—and you didn't want Sodium Pentothal, which we don't have anyway, because you were afraid you would use foul language. You thought I'd *forget* all that?"

I tell her, "I also remember that you told me the ordinary dose of fentanyl is one cc, and I told you I wanted half, and you said, 'Oh, just relax'; you had already entered the full dose into the intravenous. Tricky, I thought."

"I know," she says in her gentle, nurse's tone. "And I have done it again."

She has come back to my side. "How are the violin lessons going?"

"Very well," I tell her. "I have one of the best teachers in the city, it turns out. It is important to study with the best, especially if you yourself are not particularly gifted."

"Gifted schmifted," the nurse says. "What's gift?"

Now the tremendous boost of the fentanyl, not to mention the sugar hit of the glucose drip, comes into my elbow. After its overnight fast, the body is pathetically grateful. "I feel my IQ not only not *dropping* but actually going up," I tell the nurse.

"Could it go up?" she says with a laugh. "I didn't know they got any higher than what you came sashaying in here with."

It is precisely the tone in which Georgia Persons had told me that the Chamber Orchestra would need me by Memorial Day of 1992 if not 1991, no question.

The drug makes me every second more airy. I like to keep everything in a kind of bullety focus, so I monitor the drug working in me as sensibly as I can. Yes, you are getting smart-ass with the drug, I think, but *intraveno veritas,* I think, too, and I notice I am dissolving into smart-ass peacefulness. The world looks unrealistically softened, but the scrim over everything looks like wise scrim, and I raise myself up to lead my bow hand gently with my wrist, not sawing, not vindictive, gently taking the right wrist forward and back down right, upward and left again. I keep the left elbow bent in the required, absolutely unnatural position under a violin, with the wrist bent the other way so the fingers can work.

"What's going on?" cries a cordial-enough male voice.

I hear the nurse explaining that I am demonstrating how much more difficult it is to hold a violin than any other instrument—than a cello, for instance. Anyone can hold a cello without tiring. You are working at it against your knees. One can nearly droop above a cello.

But now I am a little lost and notice only that other people in white or green go drifting by outside the furry edge of my cubicle. One of them is my surgeon. It crosses my mind (though now I am wafting a good deal) that if he loses me in the end, it might hurt his career. No, I reply to myself, coming to sense by main force of will now, nothing hurts anyone's career. People continue to do whatever they now do. The Hemlock Avenue Boy Scouts, as Georgia called them, will continue to smoke mild dope and sell serious drugs. The born-again Christian will go on explaining to new tenants at 4303 that the last thing in the world he would do is take credit for God having chosen him, rather than someone else, to work through with His gifts.

The born-again Christian will continue leaving his garbage in the tiny hallway and on the front porch. And at Saint Alban's, the nurse-anesthetist will go on letting patients ask for .5 cc while she administers 1 cc.

And I will go on being afraid of death all the months that lie ahead of me, even though I have had Georgia Persons as a teacher of courage. Now I imagine her as hard as I can, because the nurse is wheeling my gurney into the actual icy surgery itself, where a crew of people dressed up in green insect costumes are engaged in bee tasks here and there. And now I remember what it is that lifts us above the flower patch of our fears: it is our good teachers, of course, but behind them it is the artists themselves—Handel or Friml or Kuechler, doing their work. Georgia was right: men are repulsive. And women are repulsive, as well. But there are always a few artists ghosting around who invite us to do the work of beauty, and who give us back our humor when we are terrified.

The Tender Organizations

Nature is so rife with life that tender organizations can be
serenely squashed out of existence like pulp. . . .

—HENRY DAVID THOREAU

THERE is a natural, satisfying enmity between ecstatic
people and practical people. The Marthas of the world
know the Marys are goldbricks. The Marys, smiling at
their gurus' knees, would never trade their numinous excitement
for housewives' depression.

Where we go wrong is in supposing that it is the ecstatic
people who find the practical people boring. They do, of
course—but not nearly so boring as the practical people find the
ecstatics. Of course anyone skilled in breadmaking and other
kitchen work gets irritated by the ecstatic people's pouring oil
over the mentors' feet or at the way the ecstatics wait silent until
their mentors stop speaking, and then give off an odd singsong
trill of admiration. All that is merely irritating: what drives the
practical people to exasperation, and finally drowsiness, is the
way ecstatic people can't get hold of a project and do it simply.
In parish churches all over the world, not just in Clayton, Minnesota, practical people go straight to sleep while the ecstatic
people cry, "Oh! Oh! How *shall* we get people to *feel* the loving-

139

kindness in our beautiful universe!" The practical people simply drop off to sleep, right there in the Lady Chapel or the Guild Hall or the Fellowship Room.

Sally Thackers, the Episcopal rector's wife, was a methodical sort. She was twenty-eight, a healthy-faced woman who went about in a Hollofil vest in the wintertime. In the summer she was a raiser of perennials; in the winter she planned to develop beds of the sparer flowers: she planned where she would put Carpathian harebells, and how to present their slight flowering as delicate, instead of simply scant. She was pleased to spend a lot of time in the kitchen—rather more pleased to be there than participating in her husband's discussions before the rectory hearth. She had nothing striking about her looks: her hair was already turning pale, and her healthiness seemed just that: healthy, rather than decorative. Her plainness was not all bad. She found it easy to slip from the rectory living room to the kitchen, with a deprecating wave—"There is the bread to be looked after"—hiding in her persona of Jack Thackers's practical wife.

In the last week before Saint Andrew's Feast, she hovered at the kitchen window, listening to the hushed sleet tick on its panes. She half overheard the men's conversation in the living room; she half sang a nursery rhyme to her unborn child. She sang sotto voce its violent plot. She sometimes pretended that life was as it had been before these seven and a half weeks of her pregnancy. She pretended she was a freestanding person, at liberty to be lost in the universe. She wished that her husband's few, slight failings—his fear of dogs, his belief that God answered personal prayers—struck her simply as touching, the way they had before her pregnancy. Now that she was to be a mother, she saw him as the loved, honored father of her child but also as a man not one hundred percent reliable. She would have to stay on tippy toe.

She and Jack had a slightly older friend, an oncology nurse named Mercein. Mercein's brother Dick had come to the rectory this morning to share with Jack that he had laid out the fleece for God, and God had answered. Dick must be forty-two, Sally thought, old enough to know better. Dick had told God that if God wanted him to move from Clayton down to the Twin Cities, as Dick's wife wanted to do, God was to give a sign. If no sign was given on the designated day, the man would know it was all right to stay in Clayton, where life was so pleasant, with the mixed forest to hunt in and all the calm, low-paying jobs. Dick went hunting up around Route 6 all day. He checked out the little lakes near Emily, and Outing, finally standing in a blind on Lawrence Lake, but he never got a shot. When he got home he told his wife, and she agreed what it meant, even though she had wanted to be in the Twin Cities so much. Now Dick wanted Jack to know that he had spoken to God, and God had spoken back. It was O.K. to stay. Dick gave Jack and Sally a Williams-Sonoma bowl.

Sally listened a little from the kitchen, her lip curled. When she went into the room with a tea tray, she saw Jack nearly weightless on his seat, his body bent toward Dick. His face was guileless and vacuous; he prompted Dick's story nearly in a whisper. Sally had trouble even thanking Dick for the bowl. Born-again Christians would never just give you something. They never said, "Sally, here is a bowl." You had to listen to their rhetoric, as well. "Sally and Jack, I really feel as if you two are really Servants of God, you know? I feel as if I can really tell my feelings about God to you—here is a bowl."

It was hard for the Thackerses to find a whole morning, or afternoon, or even a whole evening, to be alone with each other. Two days after Dick's visit, Jack brought in an armful of the dry ash firewood from 1988 and announced that they were going to spend the morning hanging out. Since Sally felt nauseated, he would make the tea.

The wood came from an eighty just north of Carolyn's animal hospital, straight across from the regular people's hospital. Two summers ago, George, Carolyn's husband, who had the

Super Valu store in town, and Carolyn, and Mercein (the hospice nurse), and Norma, the new UCC minister, had taken down eleven trees. The following January they stood in the snow, brushing against the spiny redwood bushes, and Swede-sawed up all the trunks. Now the wood was perfect.

Just as Sally and Jack settled down to waste the morning, Mercein called up to say that the Otto Schlaeger situation had become intolerable and would Jack please get on the stick and use whatever clout he had with the Schlaeger family's pastor to intervene. And also get the daughter home. The man was dying fast.

Aloud, Sally said to Jack, "You can have him over." To herself she said, Goodbye, hearth, for *this* morning.

A disadvantage of clerical life was that Jack couldn't use the statement so handy to people in the women's movement: *Sorry, I need to do something for myself*—so would you please take your problems with the Schlaeger family somewhere else? Jack's $24,000-plus package deal made him a professional, the way the president of Merrill Lynch was a professional.

"Too bad," Jack said, lingering in the kitchen doorframe. "I really thought this time we could just drink a lot of tea and get nervous and enjoy the fire. Now we have Kurt instead."

He dutifully dialed the Missouri Synod church number. Sally heard him say in a full, open-throated voice, "Sally's baking something with raisins in it that smells wonderful! How about making it over here in a half hour or so?"

Kurt would come. He was a huge, comfortable man, whose body dropped fast into any inviting space. He always took Jack's recliner when he visited the rectory. If the chairs were unevenly drawn up to the fire, he inched his forward until it was fair. He was interested in the arms buildups of all countries—not just of the big ones. He knew, for example, that Afghanistan rebels had repulsed Soviet helicopters with their mix of rifles, even old Enfields, as effectively as they would have with SAM Sevens.

Sally said, "I had better go ahead and bake something with raisins that smells delicious, then."

Jack looked apologetic, and then smiled. "How is the baby?" he asked.

They had not told anyone they were expecting a child, so it was still a mysterious happiness and pathos of their own. Sally imagined the baby somewhere on the wall of her vaulty, blood-colored womb. She imagined the egg and the seed still so newly joined they were curious to have found each other: they were binding themselves together as fast as night. She imagined the baby hanging on for dear life, now in November using only the tiniest part of the space reserved for it. The womb must feel very rangy to the baby.

She and Jack found their rectory a little rangy, too. There it stood in their town of 2,242, a fake-half-timbered-English house rough in its sleety grapevines, in the police catchment area of Saint Cloud, in the hospice catchment area of Jack and Sally's friend Mercein, in the mental health catchment area of Mora, in the Anglophilia catchment area of the Episcopal church. Its walls were hung with British servants' hall hangings, in the way that Missouri Synod Lutheran parsonages have Dresden flower stollen plates, or barn-owl steins made in West Germany.

In Jack and Sally's house the kitchen hanging said that any servant caught feeding dogs under the table would be fined threepence halfpenny. Any servant coming to dinner without his jacket would be fined twopence. "It's not evil—it's just silly," Jack said to Sally. "Any object from a revered place feels *holy* to people. People revere England, period." He no doubt recognized the expression on her face: he said firmly, "We are *not* either just a museum piece of Anglicanism."

Now they clung together a moment. "I am singing to the baby every day now," Sally told him. "And using less bad language. Today the music is the Magnificat, half *tonus peregrinus* and half faux-bourdon, and the nursery rhyme is 'Three mice

went into a cellar to spin—Puss passed by and Puss looked in.' "
She added, "On with the raisins and white dough."

A half hour later, she shamelessly eavesdropped as she spread
an ironed piece of old Fair Linen on a tray. Jack was explaining
the Schlaeger situation to Kurt.

"There's old Otto Schlaeger in horrible pain now, from the
cancer, and apparently Vi is secretly not giving him his pain-
killers. She *tells* Mercein she has given it each time, but when
Mercein shows up, Otto is often in outright agony. Apparently
Vi is skipping the every three or four hours' morphine dosing.
Mercein says the idea is to give the meds at exactly the same
time intervals. Vi isn't doing it."

No sounds for a moment.

Then Jack's voice again: "If you skip one of the scheduled
times, the pain gets so out of control it takes a shot to bring it
down. Shots are not the idea," Jack went on, obviously relating
information exactly as the hospice nurse had recited it for him.
"Oral meds is best. Then suppositories. Third, injection."

"Yeah? Suppositories?" Kurt's full, friendly voice.

Good, Sally thought, taking out the white-dough-and-raisins
muffins. Kurt is taking an interest.

Kurt's voice again: "Suppositories, huh? I would hate to have
to have a suppository."

Jack's voice: "So Mercein said to Vi, three days ago, that
she absolutely must *not* fail to give Otto his meds. Vi told Mercein to get out of the house. Mercein couldn't even get back in
this morning. So that's where we are with this now," Jack
wound up.

Kurt said, "A difficult time of life for those two—very, very
hard going, I know. I remember when my dad got his cancer. . . . Well, now—Otto and Vi Schlaeger. Much to be said
on both sides, Jack . . . much to be said on both sides. That
isn't a marriage that's always been easy. I don't think I am talking
out of school when I say that."

Jack's voice: "Easy marriage! Easy marriage, Kurt! Holy shit,

Kurt! Otto's been beating Vi for twenty-six years! The grown daughter won't even come home!"

Kurt: "These things are so darn difficult to judge from the outside. Naturally I've heard some about this, and I'm not at leave to pass all of it on. But I will say that Vi came to me twice, saying how hard he was on her."

Jack's voice: "Just twice?"

Kurt gave a small laugh. "She wanted me to look at a mouse she said he'd given her. Both times. Same thing. My feeling was then and is now that I'd want to hear both sides of these family things before I moved on it."

Jack: "So did you hear both sides?"

Kurt: "Otto never came complaining to me, so I figured they'd worked out something. I know that I sure gave them focus in my prayers, for quite a while there. Well, Jack: it does take two to tango, it really does. I know Vi is supposed to be a wonderful homemaker—all that canning and gardening and all—but there isn't any rule says a woman can't put on a spot of lipstick once in a while, or get herself done up a little."

Sally carried in a tray of the muffins and coffee. Kurt smiled happily and took two. She went over to Jack. They mentioned the sleet and how it would freeze soon and Interstate 94 would be a mess. Sally knew they would keep making small talk until she left the room.

"Schlaegers have a wonderful dog," Kurt remarked. "Airedale bitch. It'd be fun to have a really smart dog like that along for hunting. I'm not one of your hunters who has to have a dog to *work* all the time! I'd just like to have it for the companionship. A lot of people forget that hunting is supposed to be recreation and that goes for the dog, too. They treat it as if it were just work, work, work."

Sally slid back into the kitchen and regarded the sleet out the window. It lay in shining fur along all the basswood branches.

Then she heard two clear thuds in the living room. She put

her head around the door. Kurt had dropped to both knees on the Belgian rug. Now Jack, not very willingly, was sinking to his knees, too.

"Almighty Father," Kurt said. "We would ask that you intervene in the hearts of Vi and Otto Schlaeger in this time of their need." His voice was solid and good-willed. "Guide Vi to set aside her angers. Guide her to know and rejoice in your love of her. . . ."

In the kitchen closet, Sally found her Hollofil vest and a sou'wester hat and let herself out the back door. She drove very carefully down Main Street and then over to Seventh Avenue, to George's Super Valu.

The frozen-foods manager told Sally that George was out back somewhere. A shelf stocker told her to try the office, all the way back, past all the crates in the warehouse part of the building. Sally barged along the huge, shadowy warehouse aisles, where the air was snappy and smelled of old ground. She knocked at George's little ply-and-bare-studs office door. Inside, it was all bright light, sudden heat from the electric strip, and George's work spread out on a desk—claimed coupons, bad credit notes, truck vouchers. He poured Sally a cup of boiling water with a beef-flavor cube in it and listened to her story. He made a telephone call. Mercein, he told her, would be there in five, and thank God someone was doing something.

George and Sally made negative, catty small talk as they waited. They and their group—Carolyn, Jack, Mercein, and Norma, the UCC minister, and even George's frozen-foods manager, who was also VFW post commander—had too high profiles to gossip in the usual places: at coffee parties on Eighth or Ninth avenue, or at the VFW, or during dishwashing at Men's Fellowship or at Guild. Therefore it was delicious for them to assess and criticize when they could. George told Sally that as far back as he knew, the Schlaegers were the worst family in town. They weren't the worst in the conventional sense—that

is, they didn't live in an AFDC addition and they didn't miss
church because of hangovers. They were quite respectable. In
fact, Otto was the one who first proposed that everyone on
Eighth Avenue mow their lawn on the same day of the week
so that the grass height from lot to lot would match. Once he
had gone around to Mercein's brother, Dick, and told him to
set his mower height lower because it wrecked the look of the
whole street. The Schlaegers were middle-class, but everyone
in town was sixty percent sure he beat his wife whenever he
had three beers, and for all anyone knew, the kid as well. That
would be his daughter, George said, looking up, thinking: who
must be something like thirty-five now. Gone away to the Cities.

Sally offered, Beaters are beaters. In the Episcopal church,
the wife-beater was the guy who made sure they ran up the flag
of Saint Andrew every November 30. Sally said, How is Carolyn? George told her he didn't see much of his wife this time
of year, when the rich went to McAllen or Waco to get away
from the Minnesota winter. They left their domestic animals in
Carolyn's kennel.

Sally and George gave each other the superior look of people
who stay through the winter. Then Mercein burst in, bright
from the cold.

"What're you two hatching up?" she said. "I could tell from
your voice on the phone." She gave Sally a fast appraisal. "How
are you, Sally Thackers?" she said.

Sally instantly saw that Mercein knew she was pregnant. So
much for that secret, she thought.

George said, "We have a solution for the Schlaeger problem.
You move in, Mercein. Nights. Tell Vi that Otto needs round-
the-clock nursing care."

"Tried that," Mercein remarked. "As soon as I saw Vi was
trying on purpose to make him suffer. For revenge! I told her
I would move in, but she threw me out."

Sally explained the fine points. "We force her," Sally said. "We threaten to call a psychiatric social worker from Mora if we have to. That ought to work."

Mercein heard them out. "O.K.," she said. "But I don't go over there alone. This last time she offered to set that airedale on me."

George said, "Sally and I go with you."

Sally said, "No—I go with you. George stays here. George, we save you for *heavy metal* if we need it later. And our backup plan is to haul in the whole ministerium if we have to."

Mercein said, "That's no good. The Schlaegers' pastor won't do anything. And he's a fourth of the ministerium."

George said, "That's right, and we can't use Norma, either. She's had that UCC job less than a year, and she can't get in trouble with breaking and entering, in case Vi goes to court. Speaking of clergy, Sally, are we telling Jack about this?"

Sally said, "Jack needs to not know. If Vi calls him, he can draw a complete blank. It'll have to be just us, Mercein."

Sally thought, as she and Mercein moved out through the drafty warehouse, past all the piled vegetables far from wherever they were grown: This is an untoward business for the baby. On second thought, though, she decided the baby was still so very small—only a scant eight weeks old—it couldn't be paying even the most unconscious, most inchoate attention to her projects. Still, she felt that the activist flavor was not right for in utero people. She would counteract the tone of all this with some bland song, the moment she got free.

Mercein and Sally stalled outside the Super Valu window. "We had better take both our cars," Mercein said. "I may need to stay a while, if we ever get in there today. By the way, this might get tough. If it gets tough, Sally, you do exactly what I tell you to do, and you do it right away."

"What nonsense," Sally said. "I am stronger than you, and I've seen grievouser and worse things in the world than you ever thought up in a bad dream." The moment she had said it, however, she couldn't make a mental image of one grievous thing she had seen. She felt like a faint, ridiculous child, brought up in a childish way, helping other people live childish lives, and now carrying a still fainter and more childish child inside her. It all seemed rather wonderful, if stupid.

Mercein said, "People who are expecting should stay out of fights."

Sally felt as if she were watching a flare slowly sink down above her.

Mercein said snappily. "For goodness' sake, I am a nurse. I know you are pregnant. I can tell a birth or a death months ahead."

"How nice to be a prophet," Sally said.

Mercein said, "You know we're stalling, don't you? We're both scared to death. Let's go over there and get it over with."

Each got into her own car and drove through the new slush to the Schlaegers'.

Mercein stood to one side of the storm door; Sally rang the bell. The moment Vi Schlaeger opened the inner door to see who had come, Mercein whipped around and put her foot in the storm door opening. She was an old hand: she put her boot in so that when the home owner slammed the door on it, it hit the soft part, not the anklebone.

Vi was a German-American immigrant's grandchild. She had the remarkable horizontal eyebrows and forehead width of thousands of northern faces. The eyes were gray-blue, with handsome dark eyelashes; the mouth was wide. The straight, abundant hair, now gray, was drawn back. Every single feature was handsome and powerful, yet the overall effect made your blood run chill.

"Told you before, I'm telling you again: you get out, and you're not coming here anymore. He don't need you, and I don't need you," Vi said to Mercein. She ignored Sally.

Mercein said, "I am moving in. Otto needs round-the-clock nursing, and that's what he's going to get."

The infuriated wife cried, "He don't need no round-the-clock nursing, period!"

Sally geared up for her lines and said them. "Mrs. Schlaeger, I am here as a witness. If you refuse entrance to the oncology nurse, I will act as witness. It is your legal right to know that."

Vi Schlaeger did not know much about American justice, but she watched the American average of six and one fourth hours' television each day. She knew that words like "witness" and "your legal right" had grave muscle. She opened the door.

Vi's bit of living room was dark and heavy, like the inside of a cave. Sally was aware of dreary lampshades, their bulbs unlit, of at least a dozen plants with wide, drooping leaves hanging above the clay rims.

Otto Schlaeger lay curled on the sofa, legs pulled up, his whole body rocking frantically. Mercein went over to him immediately. When she said his name, he jerked his head around and he cried, "For Christ's sake!"

The nurse was on the floor by the sofa, bag open, fixing her syringe. "Better in two minutes, Otto," she said.

Sally hovered a few feet behind her. She heard Vi mutter, "Hurts, does it, huh?" When Sally swung around, Vi looked back at her, steady as a column.

Sally then paid attention to everything Mercein did, interested in the earmarks of a new trade. "Just like a hobbyist," she then told herself, "learning how people do what they do—give medicines, bake bread, run stores, decorate churches. Why don't you just live your own life?" Only a part of her mind said that, however. Another part went on watching how Mercein kept her hand on the man's forehead and kept talking to him, waiting for the morphine to take. Mercein also talked to the patient's wife, in a friendly, Scout leader tone. "Vi? Let me show you this. Say you're going to put an afghan on a patient. That afghan on the chair. Would you bring it over?"

Mercein said a little louder, "Vi, bring over the afghan."

"He don't need an afghan. He's all sweaty anyhow."

"Sally—you bring me that afghan, would you? Now. You pull it up not just *to* the shoulders but all the way over, because that's where the chilling gets in. And Sally, would you bring my bag in? And Vi, would you tell Sally where to set my things so they will be out of your way? Bad enough to have houseguests without they don't leave their stuff around!"

Mercein kept up everything in a singsong. "We'll keep Otto on these meds, every four hours, day and night, so the pain never gets ahead of us. The three of us can manage perfectly well. And if Otto needs it, he can have a bump now and then."

"A bump!" cried Vi.

"Extra morphine," Mercein said. "Everyone knows you take pride in your work, Vi. All that canning. All your house-cleaning. Well, I take pride in my work, too." She kept talking.

Presently the dying man's knees relaxed. Sally thought: He doesn't look so much like a cause now. He simply looks like an ugly person asleep, who is neither interesting nor kind when awake. There must be millions, millions, of men like Otto. Sally told the baby, It's bad luck, someone like Otto. But your luck is already better.

Suddenly Vi said, "Now you get out, you the one that's not nursing or anything."

Sally said, "I *am* going home now. But Mercein is going to stay. And if you give her any trouble I am going to call the psychiatric social worker from Mora, and you know what I'm going to do, Mrs. Schlaeger? I will tell her that you live at 314 Eighth Avenue instead of 312 Eighth Avenue, so the social worker will knock there first, and explain who she is, and ask where you live."

Vi's cheeks shook. "You get out, or I'll set Hoffer on you."

Sally now realized that a large dog lay behind the vertical leaves of the dining room table. Its head arched forward about two inches above its paws. It kept one eye squeezed shut, or perhaps the eye was missing. Sally thought: Not just a bad thing for the baby, bad for me. Although she was only half as fright-

ened of dogs as Jack was, she was still frightened her full half-
share. The airedale, however, didn't move when Mrs. Schlaeger
spoke its name.

Sally said, "If you try to kick us out, we are going to call
the police, Mrs. Schlaeger. Not the police which is that fellow
that goes to your church, either. The real police. In Saint
Cloud."

"You can't call the police," the woman said, but her voice
wobbled, and Sally, with one eye on the dog, now felt that
everything would be all right.

"I'll walk you to your car," Mercein said.

The translucent sleet was turning to real snow. In the quarter
hour—which seemed like hours—that Mercein and Sally had
been inside, the snow had been disposing itself in its own tendrils
and handsome ganglia along all the ash and maple trees.

At Sally's car door, Mercein said, "Now listen to me. Here
is how you look at this. You keep your mind on how really
peaceful and painless old Otto looked on the couch. That's *all*
you think about. You remember this, Sally: in all the rest of his
life—one week, ten days—he isn't going to feel any pain ever
again. You understand that?"

Mercein paused a moment. Sally thought she was about to
comment on the weather, because she looked about her, at the
little street full of cold lawns and trees and some cars parked.
But Mercein said, "Forget Vi. All her life she has had a mean
husband, and her daughter ran away and never writes home, so
she's mad. But the mean husband is dying, so her problems are
over. I will go back in now, and talk to her some, and also try
to find out where the daughter is. I'll be in touch."

In the next ten days the weather deepened. George's Super Valu
staff grease-marked the front store windows: REMEMBER LAST
SUMMER? WELCOME THE MOISTURE! HAPPY HOLIDAYS! Sally re-
covered from morning sickness and went on a whole-grain baking binge. Outside her kitchen window the snow did the one

thing we want snow to do: it turned the twentieth century back into the softer nineteenth century. In this softer, quieter landscape, the snow said, technology is nothing, industrialization is nothing; surely the hole in the far south sky will heal . . . everything can be managed.

This is your first snow, Sally told the baby, since how would it know, otherwise, hiding in there, as it did, self-centeredly growing its brain, its nervous system, its stomach, still keeping its beginnings of hands curled inward.

Jack said, "Kurt just called. Of all things, he called to say that God has answered our prayers about Vi Schlaeger."

Sally heard the "of all things" as Jack's willingness to join her in a small jeer at the Missouri Synod Lutheran pastor. She also saw that Jack leaned a little springily in the kitchen doorway, his elbows sticking out, one hand touching along the back of the other in front of his stomach. "Did you know—" he went on, "perhaps you didn't know—that Kurt and I prayed Vi would find it in her heart to let Mercein take over the care of old Otto?"

Sally felt Jack's mind alternately flaring and shrinking in front of her, wanting her to agree to this mysterious outcome, that something had come of the two men's prayers. He wanted her to agree to it, of course: worse, he wanted her to feel wafted away, as he seemed to feel. Once, in their five years of marriage, she had pretended to get more pleasure in bed than she had felt at the time. It was a February night, as clear as stars in her memory. She had gone to sleep early, exhausted from housecleaning the whole rectory. She had made herself get through all the cleaning, knowing that once bathed and in bed, she could look over the new garden catalog. She had her pen and paper and a clipboard lying alongside her, on Jack's side. She carefully drew all the flower plots and drew some brick layouts. She planned how to keep something white and something blue in bloom throughout the summer. She liked flowers that had a good deal of green, with space between the blooms, rather than crowding flowers, like daisies. She wanted Carpathian harebells.

Jack's lovemaking had not distracted her from her thoughts. Therefore she had lied a little. Now, looking toward him from the kitchen worktable, she lied again: that is, she gave him a smile, but she squinted her right eye, hoping it would make the smile into a kind of twinkling, good-natured grin.

Jack then said, "Funny fellow, Kurt. He calls me up to tell me about the Immanent God, but he gets onto deer hunting, deer hunting, deer hunting."

Nearly five hundred of Clayton's two thousand and more people sat in Saint Paul's for Otto Schlaeger's funeral. The great, bluff pastor told them that Otto Schlaeger's father had come to America so he would not have to serve in the Kaiser's army. Kurt's sermon went on, quietly, undeniably giving its own kind of consolation. It connected the little town with the great world outside. It connected the past of Germany and America with this death. If that German had not emigrated, Kurt told them, he might well have dressed in field gray, and he might have shot at our Clayton, Minnesota, men who met Germans at Château-Thierry. That man's son, whose life among us we celebrated today, might never have served as a rating on the USS *Mississippi*.

As Kurt began to maunder, Sally let her thoughts shift here and there. She told the baby she would teach it history, because learning history—it was a simple fact she had not thought of before—makes people happy. She daydreamed about that idea for all the rest of the service. It spared her getting irritated when Kurt got lost on one of his hobbies: he was listing Navy ordnance options to this funeral audience. It spared her feeling sardonic at the grave, when George's frozen-foods manager and a young guardsman stretched and yanked corners of the flag, put it roughly into its triangles, and then took it, a pad of cloth now, and marched, squaring imagined corners across the undertaker's green cloth and the snow, to Vi Schlaeger. The post commander presented the flag to Otto Schlaeger's widow on behalf of the

President of the United States. Clearly the widow didn't know what expression to arrange on her face. She seemed to try two or three. In the end, she settled on the expression of people returning to their pews after they have taken Eucharist.

As they came away from the graveside, Jack put Sally's gloved hand into the crook of his elbow. "Tomorrow I am going to make a fire and we are going to sit around our house, *alone,* all day. There's no one in the hospital. No one is getting married."

"I will bake whole-wheat rolls with oat bran in them," Sally said. "On the other hand, there is something really depressing about oat bran."

"That's true," Jack said in a happy voice. "Oat bran sucks."

The next morning, however, someone banged their door knocker before ten o'clock.

It was an energetic-looking woman in her early thirties, with springing hair, glittering eyes, an expressive mouth; she was made up fully—there was something of everything: shadow, liner, mascara, blush, and lipstick—yet the woman's focus was so strong, even aggressive, that the makeup couldn't gentle it.

"Mrs. John Thackers?" she said loudly. "They said over at the church that your husband was home today."

She jammed her way in past Sally. That was close, Sally said to the baby. She felt cheery. Whoever this visitor was, Sally meant to throw her out after fifteen minutes. Sally had been a good rector's wife: she had gone to the funeral, even out to the cemetery, instead of waiting in the Saint Paul's basement with the old, the pregnant, and the greedy. Now this was her and Jack's day off. Besides, the woman had thick, strong hair. She probably had a coarse nature, Sally decided.

"I don't guess you'd know who I am," the visitor said. "I'm Francine, Vi Schlaeger's girl."

Jack came in with an L. L. Bean canvas full of fireplace wood.

"This is Jack Thackers—Ms. Schlaeger," Sally said.

"We didn't know you'd got here for your dad's funeral," Jack said.

"I wouldn't come for his funeral!" Francine said with a laugh. "I drove up from the Cities this morning. Just to pick up my mother and take her to stay with me a week or so. Just to put the dog down and get the stuff out of the refrigerator. But then, on the way up, I had an experience. A direct relationship to God."

Jack motioned toward the chair Sally usually sat in, by the fire. Sally started to ease out to the kitchen, as she always did as soon as people started talking about having a direct or personal experience of Jesus Christ. She did so not so much to spare herself the thrilled, self-congratulatory voices but because people having a religious experience always want to tell it to someone in authority—a clergyperson—not to a spouse who happens to be there.

But Francine called after her. "Don't go away! I won't be long! In fact, my mother's waiting out in the car!"

"Waiting in the car!" both Jack and Sally cried, going toward the door.

Francine raised and dropped one shoulder. "She wouldn't come in," she said. "She doesn't want to hear about the way God spoke to me! I don't know why I am surprised. She wouldn't even listen to ordinary-life things I tried to tell her as a child. And things I tried to tell her about . . . Anyway," she said. "Anyway. And I couldn't go to Pastor Kurt, because of course he's gone hunting or trapping. And anyway . . . there was some nurse that took care of Dad hanging around the house this morning, and she said to come to you."

She stopped, giving Jack a look.

"Now," she said, I hope you don't *mind* hearing about a personal religious experience?"

You're in luck, Sally thought, looking at the woman. It's too late for *me* to get out of the room, but Jack not only does not mind personal religious feeling; he likes it very much. Sally felt like a Martha who has been told she absolutely may *not* go out to bake the loaves: she *must* stay, like Mary, and pour oil and be admiring.

Francine had driven out of Minneapolis very early in the morning, before full light, if you could call any daylight in December full light. She was half asleep on Interstate 94 when a voice said very clearly, Keep a sharp eye out for animals on the right side of the road. Now, Francine was very surprised, since she thought the only person who heard voices was Joan of Arc, a Roman Catholic. Francine didn't particularly *want* to hear voices. This voice persevered. It insisted she watch for "beautiful animals on the right." Well, all right, she told the voice, but I don't expect anything out of this. Now Francine said to Jack and Sally, "I expect very little of God and very little of people of God, too. The one time I ever went to the pastor in need, he told me I should be a good girl and not go around carrying tales about my dad."

She'd kept driving and presently whizzed past a crow, which stood right beside a fair-sized carcass, a dog or something that size. As roadkill goes, it must have been very fresh. It was a cold day, but the entrails, some of which hung from the crow's beak, were still bright red and flexible. The crow was so pleased with its find it scarcely budged as the powerful car shot by.

Francine then said to the voice, "If that is your idea of 'beautiful animals,' forget it."

The voice said monotonously, "Keep watching for beautiful animals on the right."

Another ten or fifteen minutes later, Francine's car fled across the Rum River bridge. There, far on the right, with their skinny black legs silhouetted against the white ice, stood a buck and several does. The bridge noise startled them: they pawed once, and the buck bobbed his head so Francine saw his full rack.

Now her face, under its no-nonsense permanent, was bright. "So you see? . . . You see?" she nearly shouted at Jack.

Jack said steadily, "That is a wonderful, wonderful story."

He spoke in a companionable, respectful, calming tone, but Sally felt his excitement as well. And his right foot went lightly pigeon-toed and back several times.

Eventually Jack let Francine out of the doorway. Sally heard him say, ". . . something to hang on to for a lifetime."

Sally told the baby, Well, your father is an extraordinary man. He would be delighted to have such an experience himself. He always nearly comes out of his chair when someone tells such stories. But he never, at least not ever that Sally knew of, let on how much he wished *he* saw visions or heard voices or got any proofs of anything numinous.

By the time Jack had closed the door, Sally had her Hollofil vest on. "I'm off for just a half hour," she told him. "Then I'll be back, and we will still have the whole day."

He held her shoulders. "Where are you going?"

"Out." she said ironically. "You don't want to know where."

Then he said, "Don't slip. It melted last night and then froze up again this morning."

Carolyn's animal hospital and kennel were at the north end of Clayton, past the flower shop, past the nursing home and hospital. As she drove by it, Sally gave a respectful glance at the hospital's maternity wing. A part of her fate had already moved in over there: it was much the way a part of her fate had moved into the rectory when Jack first showed it to her, before they were married.

She found Carolyn examining a cat. The vet kept one hand on its breast and reached for things behind her with the other.

Sally said, "We just got a telephone call from Francine Schlaeger, of all people. She said she'd been trying to reach you, but the line was busy."

"It wasn't," Carolyn said briefly. "I've been right here, working on this fellow."

Sally relaxed. "I suppose she had the wrong number. She

asked me to tell you she has changed her mind about that airedale of her dad's and she wants you to give it to me. Along with a leash and a couple of days' food. Then she will call me and make other arrangements later."

Carolyn said, "She wanted me to put that dog down, I thought. She said it was vicious."

Sally said brightly, "Well, she's changed her mind."

"She has, huh?" Carolyn said. She molded her hands around the cat and laid it in a small cage. She went out back and re-emerged with a one-eyed animal, which Sally recognized as Hoffer, the dog under the Schlaegers' dining room table. It looked huge. Could it have grown in two weeks?

Carolyn took a leash from the wall. "Now, you want to be careful with this one, Sally. She's been knocked around some. Ill-fed, too. My guess is, if you feed her and water her a lot, right from the first, she'll make her home with you. Don't move fast around her at first. Did Francine Schlaeger tell you what to do with the nine-dollar check for the Nembutal?"

"Oh," Sally said, "she certainly did. She absolutely wanted you to keep it, in return for your trouble."

Carolyn grinned and said, "Yeah, she did, huh? Well, here's enough dog food for until Ms. Schlaeger decides to relieve you of the dog. Now . . . in case she changes her mind *again* and doesn't relieve you of the dog, bring her back in so I can give her some shots and check her over for you. Airedales are aire-dales. I thought you were scared of dogs, hey."

Sally thought: If I put the dog in the backseat, it might bite me in the neck as I'm driving. Also, I would see it in the rearview mirror and get scared. But if I put it beside me, as a passenger, it might leap at me. Life, she told the baby, is made up of the greater evil and the lesser evil. She put the dog beside her.

At the rectory, Jack took Sally's vest and hung it on the visitors' coat tree. He also took the leash and said, slightly in his falsetto, "Hello, Big Fellow. Welcome."

"Big Girl," Sally said. "Her name is Hoffer."

Jack dragged the fifty-pound feed bag to the kitchen. He came back with the Williams-Sonoma bowl, filled to the top with dried dog food. He made another trip and returned with a bowl of water. He set the food and the water between their two chairs before the fire. The fire reflected a little in the water. Then Jack and Sally sat down, leaving the dog at the back of the room.

"You see what a first-rate husband I am?" Jack said. "Do you hear me asking any questions? No. And after a while, when I recover from the cold sweat that animal put me in, I will go to the kitchen and make cocoa. Then we will not have any more adventures all day."

Sally and Jack heard a series of thuds. They turned to see.

Hoffer had lain down bonily, with the idea of thinking everything over. She knew that eventually she would creep forward; eventually she would do that, and eat some of that food and drink about half of the water, if that's what that was in the other bowl. She also knew she would kiss the hands of these human beings, the male one and the female one, who had left their fingers hanging off their chair arms, in full sight. She would do that, although they were nearly strangers. She had seen and scented the female only once before, and the male not at all.

Life doesn't offer perfect choices. When Hoffer lay in a pile of puppies, her mother had told them all: Look, you either *adore people* or you live your whole life in the Great Emptiness. You take what people give you, kisses or blows or both, because if you don't, you know what you'll end up with? The Great Emptiness—that's what! The puppies didn't know what that was, but it sounded execrable.

Hoffer obeyed her mother. She spent about two thirds of her life being beaten by the male of her people, sometimes by the female. Once, even, the male of her people set upon the child of her people, and Hoffer had had to make the only decision of her life: her nose had raged with the scent of the same blood on both sides as they struggled. Hoffer, in terror, elected to save the child of her people. She leapt upon the male. In return for her trouble she lost one eye. Then the child went away and Hoffer went on being beaten by both of the others, but less and less frequently. A sorry business.

Now then, these new people: Hoffer's jaws were already wet with her plan. She meant to creep forward and thoroughly kiss their hands, between all the fingers and up to the sweater cuffs. She decided on the female of them first, then the male. She had a notion, which she knew she couldn't get across, but she had the idea, anyway. It was that she would explain with her tongue how close to death she had been; she meant to explain with her tongue how life always looks much more ordinary than it really is—how its dangerousness, and its ecstasy, scarcely show.

Amends

SOMETIMES I feel as if I spent my whole childhood and high-school years around people who wanted some old golden era to come back. My parents were always talking about "back when farmers had good values," and our priest would remember when people really respected the Church and wanted to obey the priest. Our debate coach wanted people to have an old-fashioned education in the classics. Even now, when I am thirty and a mother of five, and busy helping with Joel's business at the store, I can't help noticing that some of the mangy dairy farms along County 10 where my mother still lives used to be less poor. When I told Joel, he said, "Ja, well, that was then and this is now." Some of those farms are more just absence of forest in the middle of the forest than presence of farm.

My parents brought me up in this same township, Agans. We sat around the vinyl tablecloth, looking out at the spiky swamp spruce and the wild cherry bushes. My parents recalled the *good* loam of southwestern Minnesota, where, as my father repeatedly remarked, you could *grow* something—as opposed to this northern wilderness. He seemed to have forgotten that he lost his farm before anyone else lost theirs. In 1955 anyone could make money farming in Lac Qui Parle County, where he and Mama started out, but we don't have good judgment in our family. One year, a neighbor called up to say he found a pile of his shelled corn was heating in the farmyard and maybe Dad should check his. "I'm not going out there," my dad said, "and that's the end of it." Because he didn't go out there and push the corn apart with the tractor and blade, he lost three thousand dollars' worth of shelled crop in two days. It blackened up, from the inside out. Dad went credit-broke before anyone else. And then, instead of going to Minneapolis like other broke farmers, he and Mama decided they would try it up here in northeastern Minnesota. Up here the soil is so stony and acid, and the growing season so short, even the smartest small-farm operators just barely made it. But Mama and Dad had another quality: they loved natural beauty, so half their conversation was longing for good old days and half was enjoyment of birdsong and the look of the forest going yellow in late August. I grew up thinking: I will end up on some good land. I would marry someone who would take me to a prosperous farm.

I never did. I ran around with my high-school friends, who just joked through everything all day. On the side I made time to talk to some serious people—Coach, for example, and our priest, of course, Father Matt, and old Mrs. Moen, a Lutheran who planted flowers. My high-school friends were the same friends Joel and I have now—Bernice and Leland and Leland's phony sister, Melanie, and Wayne Schackli, who was much older than the rest of us because he had run away to the Marine Corps when he was only fourteen. We all liked Wayne for his moxie: he had convinced recruiters he was seventeen. He was six foot seven even at fourteen. "They didn't really care if I was of age or not," he would tell us, leaning on the appliance crates in his freight warehouse. "They wanted anyone my size because

I could hurt more people faster than someone only five foot seven."

I always liked it about Wayne that he told surprising truths like that. Only Wayne and Father Matt and the Lutheran Sunday-school teacher, Mrs. Moen, said philosophical things that you had not heard before. Years later, I leaned against a stack of crates at Wayne's loading dock. He was leaning on the other side. We were only planning a mud-wrestling event for Agans Crazy Days, but I felt Wayne's body pounding against his side of the crates like waves against a seawall. Of course, it was my side doing the pounding. But there was that in Wayne which started it. I had kept clear of him in high school because he slept not just with the dirty girl from a small farm north of us, Oralie Stett, but with everybody—even back then with some adults' wives in town. Later, when we were in our twenties, we would see Wayne's truck parked in front of houses where the man was away for the day. It was a joke among the fellows at the VFW: "Seen Wayne's truck in front of your house today, Leland," someone would say, curling up the corners of his mouth. "Hell you did," Leland would answer. "You had better blacktop your driveway so he don't get stuck at *your* house." Then someone else would say, "You could take that two ways if you wanted to," and everyone would laugh, because as soon as anyone, at least in Agans, said you could take something two ways, we laughed.

Jokes, as much as anything, drove me to liking the people around the edges, the ones who were serious. Old Mrs. Moen. Or Coach. He was our debate coach, college counselor, volleyball coach, art teacher, and driving instructor. We would take Affirmative or Negative positions on issues we didn't care anything about and work hard for Coach because he was so nice. When I was fourteen, all fall I read up on farming so I could take the Negative of whether corporate farming was better than family farming. I had to stop asking my parents for help: my father's face would fill with blood. He was sure he had been ruined, personally, by the Farm Home Administration.

Coach got strange ideas. When we were all in junior high school (which in Agans is the same school building as the elementary and high schools), Coach got pamphlets from a place that he said was of the highest quality and then he got a scholarship to that place for Oralie Stett. We were all surprised. The Stetts were not anything. I knew about them more than other people because their little dairy operation was next place north of my parents' place. In the winter, I sometimes saw old lady Stett, Oralie's and little Sue's mother, wandering around on County 10 in her Sears jacket. Sometimes she had a black eye. She was a thin, graying woman with a very good figure even in her forties. My parents despised Mr. Stett because he poisoned bait for wolves and was a fundamentalist Christian.

The Stetts were so poor they were barely visible. In school, Oralie was a stringy, mousy kid. Those of us in the "good" kids' group—Wayne, Leland Newhouse, Leland's sister Melanie, and Bernice and me—thought she was stupid. It is perfectly possible that old man Stett was no poorer than my father, but my parents kept me dressed like other girls. Oralie Stett wore long hand-me-down skirts from somewhere and looked as if she had been slapped around some.

You can't talk psychology or philosophy with people like Joel Haft and Wayne Schackli and Leland Newhouse and his twin sister Melanie and even my best high-school friend, Bernice: they haven't any ideas about anything. Unlike my parents, theirs didn't mourn at the kitchen window for a golden age. I said (we were all fourteen at the time) that I thought it was wonderful that Coach was going to get Oralie Stett into this unusual, very good school and she would escape and become something really big.

Joel said, "Yay, Coach. And Janis Joplin's going to move to Agans, too."

"Escape from what?" Leland said.

And Bernice really stuck her neck out for her, and said, "It sounds really different." Leland's sister Melanie was a horrible person, already at age fourteen a snake: when only girls were in the room, she worked you for what she could get. She would borrow money from anyone who would lend it; she always told you exactly when she would return it—and then never did. She would look at you with her beautiful blue eyes, the same blue eyes her twin brother Leland had, and say, "Maggie, I am going to have this back for you by tomorrow, because I am baby-sitting tonight." I would *know* it was a lie. No one let her baby-sit, anyway: she was the first kid in town to smoke pot, and she'd been seen spaced out in her dad's car at stop signs. But she spoke in such a frank tone I would want to believe her. I would lend her more than I lent people I trusted and liked. I once lent her five dollars—a whole five dollars, which I never saw again.

When the boys were in the room, Melanie curled and re-curled herself in any armchair she was in, or snaked her legs around each other differently at five-minute intervals, and arched her back. By the time we were fourteen she had tried to get Joel away from me (we had been going steady since we were eleven), and the very next year she tried to make Wayne Schackli marry her.

When we were fourteen, two bad things happened. Coach took all the correspondence with the fancy school and drove his car out to the Stetts' place. Old man Stett told him they were a Christ-centered family, and no daughter of his was going to no atheist high school. Coach told me about it the next day. We sat together on the iron rung that kept cars from driving over onto the pine seedlings near the football field. The wind blew in the white pines there—it made the silvery hiss of wind sliding along the millions of needles.

"It's not an atheist school," Coach had told Mr. Stett. "It is the chance of a lifetime."

"What do you think, Bill? What do you think, Bill?" Mrs. Stett had keep saying.

"This is a major decision," Mr. Stett snarled. "You want to know what I think?" He took some of the material that Coach had taken along and tore it in half. "She ain't going there to turn out a bad girl. Girls don't need an education or whatever they've got there, anyhow," Stett said.

"You sure, Bill? You sure, huh?" Mrs. Stett said.

"You want me to show you how sure I am?" he said. He half rose.

"I'd like to go, Daddy," Oralie then said. Her younger sister hovered over by the old cook stove they had. Poor people who had them called them trash burners so it would sound as if they had a regular gas or electric, too, and kept the wood-burning thing out of sentiment. It was all the Stetts had.

Mr. Stett started to scarf his big arm around all that pamphlet material to take it to burn it. Coach told me, "I couldn't let that happen, Maggie. I stood up and said, 'Nope, Mr. Stett, you don't get that,' and I brought it all back with me, along with their letter saying they were very interested in Oralie Stett because of her excellent essay and good math record and they were interested in her background. See," Coach said in his sad voice.

I rebalanced myself on the iron rod and carefully took the papers he handed me.

"I wouldn't mind going off to a place like that, Coach," I said in a very casual tone. He didn't pick up on that, probably because I had an ordinary mind and that Oralie Stett was a genius. I studied a photo of about twenty-five boys in red-and-white football uniforms. In the center, first row, two of them held footballs. Their faces were sweet. They all wore the same expressions our boys put on for team photos, but they looked kind of gentle, anyway. I felt a pang on top of the disappointment that Coach wouldn't wrangle *me* a scholarship to that school; the pang was that Joel never really had a sweet expression

on his face. Once, when he got stunned during a scrimmage
and they had him on a low stretcher beside the field, I hurried
over and his face looked gentle—eyes closed, so you saw the
long, wonderful lashes and his face dark rose; one hand hung
off the stretcher rod like the hands in pictures Coach showed
us in Art. But when he came to, the first thing he said was he
was going to get the fuckhead that busted him. Joel didn't talk
like anyone's knight in shining armor, so when I looked at these
boys in the picture, who Coach assured me lived a totally different life from ours—an old-fashioned life full of what Coach
was always calling "classical values"—I felt a pang.

The other pictures were of brick school buildings with white
woodwork and ivy growing up. In Agans we didn't have one
building like that, and they didn't in Nevis, either. I never had
seen Duluth yet, so I couldn't speak for there. Coach passed me
over the letter. "We would be very happy to hold a place for
Oralie Stett in Exeter's Class of 1978."

I handed it all back to Coach. "Is that really an atheist place,
Coach?"

He snorted. "That place would allow Oralie to develop her
wonderful imagination! That place," he repeated more loudly,
the way he had shown us to do in Debate, "would teach her
how to think freely. She wouldn't have to cower, because her
parents wouldn't be around! She wouldn't have to act dumb so
other kids would like her!"

"Aw," I told him, "it's her clothes, Coach. You know?
Clothes. Those people in those pictures there. They going to
like Oralie's clothes any better than we do here?"

He paused. He said, "I would have taken care of that. I'd
have just got the money from somewhere and we would have
sent her off looking O.K. and her whole life would be changed."

Then he seemed to put all that away. "You want a driving
lesson? Come on, Mag."

In addition to everything else, Coach was the Driver's Training person in our school. He was the teacher who stamped purple markings on your hands when you had paid your way into the basketball games.

He put the passenger's seat way low and laid himself back in it gingerly, as if he had a fever. "Drive me around, Mag," he said, shading his eyes. "Drive safely. Don't scare me."

"Belling O.K.?" I asked him.

"Yeah, Belling," he said.

Our town was two thousand people at the edge of the north woods; Belling, another eleven miles north, had only five hundred population, if that. U.S. 53 took you past County 43, where I lived, and then swung peacefully northward through pine forest and Holstein pastures. Belling was just a town where boys took you to the movies, to get out of our town. You were with a nice boy if he took you all the way to the movie—some violent thing of his choosing. You'd sit through motorcyle murders and Regensburg monster movies and afterwards carry your pop to the Belling Public park. It was a soft, grassy place, the grass growing the luxurious way it does in failed small towns and on retired people's farmsteads. There was an old gazebo in that park, where years earlier, when there had been culture in small towns, people listened to the band play adagio movements on Friday nights. My parents were big on explaining how all culture had leeched out of Minnesota like gasoline through a stock grate.

I liked the gazebo. Other people stopped to park on the way to Belling and never got to see the nervous-mafiosi or the hay-wire-scientist movies at all.

When we were in high school the pine forests were only beginning to pale and dry out from acid rain. The white pine stood green where it hadn't gotten blister rust. The swamp spruces looked good, and the birch didn't have their present blight. The oak wilt was just something in the Twin Cities we heard mentioned. Every time Joel Haft took me to the movies in Belling, I thought: The country certainly is pretty, and if Joel would just agree to live in the country I would marry him. He had started asking me to marry him when we were in the fifth grade.

Coach was not the only person it was fun to talk to. Our church had a mild-mannered priest, Father Matt. He had been there as long as my family had lived in the Agans area. It was interesting how young a man can go on looking as if he never changes his insides at all. Father was of course regarded as a closet gay by all the men in town, but we women had more to do with him and knew better. He was simply a passive and chaste person. He had a distaste for anyone who spoke up strongly. His pale-brown hair fell like a little boy's over his forehead, and you could see he didn't fill the shoulders of his cassock. His eyes were warm, but Father Matt would look at you and then out the window. No matter where we were, in the church basement getting a banquet ready, or even during the Power Through Prayer meetings that caught on later, Father Matt was always gazing away. My friends and I grew up in the 1960s and 1970s; in the 1950s, my parents told me, priests were actually respected. In those days they didn't have to dodge what came at them from the bishop or from the Protestants in town or from the born-agains in their own parishes. When the homicide detectives came to our town, rumor was they didn't waste ten minutes altogether with Father Matt.

I liked Father Matt because he and I had a secret longing: we both wanted to be idle. I can't tell you what a pain it is for a naturally idle person to be industrious. I don't *have* those feelings of pride that Bernice and the others get when they have done a good job of serving roast ham, raisin sauce, buttery peas, and mashed real potatoes to the Agans football team. I just would rather be home. And I wish my home were in the country. But I could never get Joel to listen to me. He doesn't understand how much plain natural beauty means to people who are lazy.

But Father Matt did. Like Coach, who liked to pretend you needed more highway practice so you could run up through the forest and pastures toward Belling, Father was always organizing us CCD (Confraternity of Christian Doctrine) students into field trips. He would take us to some godforsaken unused pasture, and the boys would play baseball. The girls were supposed to stand along the side and cheer. Sometimes, when I was first going with Joel and Bernice was going with Leland Newhouse, I would pretend to cheer when someone stole a base, especially if it was Joel. But what I really liked was ambling tactfully over to where Father Matt lay propped up against a down log.

"What a wonderful day it is," he would say.

He told me about saints who were being tortured and how they would ask for just one more dawn—to see one more day. He said he knew exactly how they felt. Daytime is beautiful.

Odd incidental conversation means a lot in a little town. I never heard any saints' lives before I talked to Father, and I never heard any from anyone else. What if I had not been a Catholic? Then I never would have heard any at all. It is interesting, if you are naturally lazy, to hear stories of sacrifice, because you feel that if you had been brought up in some finer place, you, too, would have had noble causes that helped others and then they would kill you for it.

Even Wayne Schackli, who prided himself on being a tough guy from the age of fourteen up, liked to tell unusual stories about people who made huge sacrifices. In a little town, you live on those stories. It's them or it's farm accidents—about how some guy got tired and it was nearly quitting time so he didn't turn off the picker. When it got a cob stuck in the intake, he put the gear to neutral and reached in with his arm. The picker picked his arm just the way it does a standing corn plant: the rollers grab the plant and squeeze along it until they hit something hard. Then they tear it off and throw it into the hopper behind. That's what happens to farmers' arms.

Bernice used to egg on Leland to tell stories like that. "Oh, that just makes me . . . I don't know!" she would cry, shivering.

Leland said, "Women! They want to hear about something; then they can't take it. Lucky you got me, Berns—lucky you!" and he'd grab her. She mewed into his shoulder. One time, when we were all on a picnic date and she was afraid of ticks, she got Leland to tell how if a lion is wounded by a falling tree and stuck there, red ants will slowly kill it. She gave a lot of shrieks as he told it, but I could see half her face over Leland's shoulder, and the expression in it was absolutely composed.

It is strange when you find that your best friend doesn't care two cents for the man she is going with. You are torn. We should feel like women in this together; on the other hand, it is hard to trust a liar, and Bernice was an amazing liar. I shouldn't say amazing, because she told only the same lies people tell all over the world—such as "I am crazy about my guy." It's just that she told *all* of them. If there was any pose going around, Bernice took it up. She was afraid of insects in 1974 and 1975, when small-town girls were supposed to be afraid of insects. Boys would grin and look pleased. But once in our CCD religion class room, in the girls' section, a basement beetle climbed up on her when just she and I were there putting down paper for one of the athletic banquets: I saw Bernice take up that beetle and carefully pull it apart. Then she said in an ordinary tone, "That should take care of that little shithead."

The unspoken secret of small-town life, or course, is that there isn't much choice of people, so you have to be friends with whoever is there, and eventually you marry one of the people around who is single. How little we had to go on! I couldn't just look around for some nice boy who would go into farming. So I went with Joel.

"Hey, how's Joel," other kids would ask. As if his health were in danger.

"Great," I'd say, putting on a very animated expression.

When Wayne and Leland and Bernice and Joel and I were seniors at Agans, we had some wispy sex; the boys, lost in themselves, scarcely touched the girls' lugubrious consciousness that whatever happened would be very different from the sex that Oralie Stett did with the boys. We referred to the "Oralie Stett kind of thing," which we "wouldn't buy." It sounded like a clearly identified behavior, the way we spoke of it; yet we had no clear picture in mind. We didn't think of Oralie as lurid or passionate or easy. Yet we took on such cynical airs when we talked about her, we seemed to be referring to some evil that was perfectly understood by us all.

Coach was working up Negative with Oralie and me (I was the backup) on whether the U.S.D.A. served land stewardship as well as it served agribusiness. Right in the middle of going over my index cards, Coach said, "Don't do high-school sex, Mag, don't do it."

"I figure it isn't any of your business," I told him.

"I know," he said in his sad voice. "I know, I know. Hardly anything *is* my business. I've got all these visions about farming, and no one wants to hear them. I even offered to have a program of you debaters doing a kind of off-season debate for the vo-tech school farmers, and were they interested? They told me, 'Forget it, Coach; our people are *practical*.' "

Coach kept after me to take the college prep stream. I let him talk on, until the very last minute. If I told him we had no money at all and I couldn't go to college, he might stop letting me hang around his office, with the colored pictures of young people servicing helicopters and getting educated at the same time through the Army College Fund. It was great to sit in Coach's office and listen to him mention distant places. Whenever he looked like slowing down or wanting me to respond specifically to anything, I would set him going again without committing myself. "Now, that Duke," I'd say. "What kind of place is *that,* anyhow?" "Where the heck is Gambier, Coach? It sounds like some castle in a Harlequin. 'The last he ever saw of her, she was combing her hair behind the mullions at Gambier. He knew he would never fold his arms around Amherst again, but he smiled as the dark carriage thundered past.' "

Our town was getting a little poorer all the time. In the past, some kids had gotten to Saint Olaf College or Saint John's University, in Collegeville. By the time I was growing up, even the less-poor kids went to the University of Minnesota at Duluth or to Morehead State College. Every year a few more didn't go to college at all.

In the end I would have to tell him we didn't have two cents and my father had cancer and my mother had asked me to stay home for now. I could go maybe later. I'd explain all that in a dead practical voice so he would shut up. Coach looked at me while I was showing him my research for the debate in Duluth. (We got to District and then to Region, which was pretty good. We would have got to State, except for what happened to Oralie.)

Only Coach thought of Oralie as someone to be saved. He secretly bought her clothes for the out-of-town debates. She changed into them at his place. If that had gotten around Agans, Coach would have been strung up to the Royal Café awning. Or old man Stett would have gone after him.

After we got through Region in Duluth, Mr. Stett stormed into town. He went straight into the principal's office. He told them he was not having his girl driving around nights with an unmarried teacher, no matter it was debate or what it was.

The principal's secretary and the Title I lady at the copy machine heard the whole thing. It went all over town.

Coach begged. It didn't do any good.

We were within two days of State. I realized I was next in line, so I needed Oralie's cards and I needed a conversation with her or Coach or someone if I was going to do her argument. "You can do it all right, Mag," Coach said. But he seemed distracted. "Mag, I can't go out to that farm to ask Oralie to hand over her debate cards."

I visualized her ratty farmplace, with the mother skulking around, shoulders forward like a cave overhang, and the little sister Sue, who was just as lean and miserable-looking as Oralie, and the father, who kept two Bibles on their table. They did not have running water, and old Stett kept sheep right up to the house. It was a class thing about Agans: people who kept animals right up to the house instead of fencing them away. Word around town was he did it to be mean to Mrs. Stett so she couldn't have a flower garden.

"I'll go get the cards, maybe," I said.

"No," Coach said. "I don't want you anywhere around that place and that man."

In the next year or two, Oralie became Agans's fast girl. All over America the sexual revolution may have been going on, but we didn't have it in Agans: there was still a division between the fast people and the regular people. Later, when we were in our twenties and Wayne Schackli had affairs with married women all over town, the affairs counted as Wayne cuckolding other men—not as a sexual revolution. Oralie started wearing her debate clothes—blazer and skirt and the linen dress—to our physics, English and art classes.

Coach got some money from the Minnesota Arts in Education. He showed us charcoal drawings by famous painters. One of them struck me: it showed a thin young man, not what we girls called "built, really built," because he didn't look so heavy and motionless, dropped into his shoes, the way our football guys did. His arms were flung upward—and he was curved a little to one side, as if for ballet. His skin was dead white, his hair done in black blotches, so his body was in contrasts—the pale and the black; his arm bones nearly showed, twining inside their light flesh. This sounds strange, but it is true: I had not made a mental image of a man looking any way other than the photos in magazines or the way the boys looked when we sneaked into their locker room—that is, I had never seen an artist's *impression* of a man.

It changed my life this way: when Joel and I finally shoved off in our pathetic little dinghy of love, I was moved by the look of him naked because he looked like the charcoal drawing Coach had shown us. I had thought Joel would be more or less tawny all over; when I saw Joel's darkness and whiteness, the contrast so much like the charcoal drawing, I saw that Joel belonged to the *idea* of male beauty. I was really happy with him for a while. Since he never asked, "Are you bored with my mind and my jokes and my plans to take over Dad's store and do you love my body only because it resembles a charcoal drawing?" I didn't have to lie to him.

But soon I was bored with our physical lovemaking as well. I looked around for things to be interested in. Mrs. Moen was supposedly planting the original wildflowers of Minnesota at one end of our park. I walked all the way there from school to see her and missed the school bus home. People kept slowing and shouting out their car windows. "Hey, Maggie, you want a ride?" but I waved them off. I wanted to walk my ordinary life out of me so that when I got to where Mrs. Moen knelt in the prairie dogwood, there would be nothing left of it. It was not very interesting to watch an old woman using a trowel and an iron fork with the handle sawn off, but I knew she had a sharp tongue and a good mind. I decided to wait out the flower planting so I could have coffee in the Royal with her.

I noticed that Oralie Stett was often in the girls' lockers, although she wasn't on our volleyball team. I made friends with her. She confided that she kept the good suit and dress Coach had got for her in a locker and changed into her old clothes to take the school bus home at night.

"Well," I said, searching for the acceptable thing. "Coach is nice."

"*You* should say so!" she said.

"What's that mean, then?" I asked.

"He talks about you all the time."

"That's nothing," I told her. "He talks about *you*. He says you are *far and away* the most imaginative person who has ever gone to this school. He wants you to go to a very good college somewhere."

I went over to hug Oralie but only because she was crying. I knew it would be painful to hug anyone so thin and sad. The hugging I had done before, aside from those phony embraces we debaters gave debaters from other towns like ours, was hugging my parents, who were at that time so hefty you felt the affection didn't make it from you through all their lumberjack shirts and muscles and their ongoing dreariness about things.

We found out in the fall of senior year that Oralie had been making love to just about every boy in high school. I don't know how she did it, since we saw those boys on Friday nights and sometimes on Saturday nights. Apparently they hunted her up.

It came out because she was found dead one Monday morning, in the old unused gazebo behind the Odeon in Belling. By noon everyone knew she had lain there all night dead, with her arms raised, each bent at the elbow, the hands frozen into fists— the agonized position of strychnine victims. The examination showed she was pregnant. Everybody quoted what Doc Heimlich said.

Father Matt called in the senior and junior boys who were Catholics. He told them special police were coming from the Twin Cities. He made them pray for the soul of Oralie Stett. No one respected the sheriff very much; like other towns, we had our stories against the sheriff, as natural as foam on beer. One was that a homicidal maniac escaped from the Twin Cities; the police down there called up our sheriff and said they thought this guy was heading our way, up Minnesota 73 or 65, and would the sheriff watch for him. Our sheriff collected his wife and mother-in-law and went to Duluth for the weekend instead. Years later, when people tried to stop a farm foreclosure, our sheriff got urban-riot vehicles and twenty deputies to take after those farmers. So he was not a respected man.

Murder put stir in our town life: we all woke up as if from a drugged sleep. Our minds whirred in a light misery. Coach, especially, went around looking haggard. Nobody could draw in art class. "O.K.," Coach said. "Philosophy instead, you guys." He read to us about Socrates and the poison.

"I'd be scared if I was Coach," Joel said in his blustering, matter-of-fact, already man-of-the-world way. We were driving over to the VFW because it was closed for Monday night and some kid had sneaked a key. We crept in quietly and down to the basement. Our policy was we weren't going to touch the grownups' booze down there: we brought our own. "Coach is prime suspect number one."

I felt disloyal to Coach that I was so thrilled. If you have been watching TV murder movies all your life and nothing came of it, it is exciting to have something real going on. We all felt alive now that we had genuine violence in our hometown. We pulled the VFW shades down and closed the nubbly plain curtains. We turned on the lights. It was a bare-floored room with a couple of rows of auditorium chairs, an American flag in a stand, and against one wall the Minnesota flag, with its dumb picture of someone plowing with a moldboard behind an ox, and a French slogan underneath, which Wayne told us meant "Toil of Nerds." We stood around, grinning at everything, poking at trophies in the corners. "This place gives me the creeps!" Bernice said, going into one of her clinging-to-Leland acts.

Wayne took the flag out of its stand.

"Here, give me that, Wayne!" Joel said. "I'll do my VFW sergeant-at-arms gig, hey!"

The boys gulped whiskey and handed the bottle around to us girls. Joel reached for the flag.

Wayne knocked Joel straight to the floor with a flick of one wrist. I knew I should be sorry. I couldn't keep from watching Wayne, though. Wayne stood braced. He held the flag in front of him, then raised it, then tipped it forward and butted its staff end against his belt. He picked up his right foot, toe-touched smartly behind his left boot heel, and about-turned to face us. " 'Up! 'Errrup!" he snapped. The boys wavered about him, not knowing how to take it. Joel was still sitting on the floor. Wayne kept his eyes a little crossed on the flag right before his face. Then he started off. He marched the flag around the room, squaring all the corners, ordering himself, "By the right flank! Hrupp!" for each turn. He made mincing steps to allow an imaginary column to swing around him. He made a little hiss, timed with his right foot striking the ground.

"O.K., O.K., Wayne, we got the point!" Leland called after a couple of minutes.

But Wayne kept on. Leland is a lightweight.

"O.K., big boy," some other kid said. Another lightweight.

The others went back to their bottle, but Wayne kept marching.

Wayne always had some new girl with him—usually someone from some other town. That night she was an unfriendly blond from Nevis. Now she started humming the second part of the Marine Hymn. Wayne rolled his eyes at her as he passed her with the flag. The rest of us women started humming it with her.

Joel muttered to me, "Just because he ran away and did some big-shot soldiering when he was a juvenile delinquent."

"Never mind!" I said. "Give me that," and I took a swig. Joel looked at me.

"That's my girl!" he said. I kept watching Wayne.

After a while Wayne set the flag back into its holder. Then he clicked his heels, took two steps backward, and said to the flag, "Begging for dismiss, sir. Thank you, sir. Yes, I thought you *would,* sir," and came ambling, smiling, over to the circle of wooden chairs we had made.

We gave him the bottle. We talked about Oralie and how everybody in town would have to answer questions.

Joel turned to Wayne's girl. "I don't guess anything like this ever happens in Nevis, does it?"

Wayne said, "Something wrong with Nevis, Joel?"

Leland said fast, "We have to all stick together. None of us killed Oralie, but they are going to try to pin it on one of us, so we have to stick together."

A month later Leland borrowed money from his father to buy Bernice a ring.

"Leland's chicken," Joel told me. "He got engaged so they wouldn't think he was the man who killed Oralie."

"Maybe she killed herself. Maybe her mean old father did it," I said.

Joel said, "Or maybe she knew all sorts of guys from all the towns around. Once her dad wouldn't let her go to college, maybe she went crazy."

"Lots of people can't go to college," I said.

"But Oralie was an intellect. Everyone said so."

By March, Oralie was a wraith floating among us. People started saying that she had carried off those long, dreadful skirts with innate grace. People even tried to be especially nice to her eight-year-old sister, but if you spoke decently to Sue, she just stared and asked you for a loan.

The police detectives were both good-looking men, about thirty-five. They hung around town for days. Their pattern was, they would leave and then be right back, hanging around again. We saw them go in to talk to Father Matt. Everyone wondered if someone had confessed killing her to Father Matt and now the police wanted it out of him.

The investigators' clothes were sharper than Agans men's outfits. Their manners were better. They would courteously ask a few questions and listen to any amount of response. They were from another world. We stopped wondering who had killed Oralie and slipped into thinking of ourselves as a unified community of decent people being unfairly pinioned by these big-shot types from the city.

Soon they stopped asking everyone. They now returned to talk only to Wayne Schackli, Leland Newhouse, Joel Haft, and Coach. So they suspected *those* four! people said in the VFW. But no one was ever indicted.

In April, Coach's contract wasn't renewed at school. He drove out to my house one wet night: we had had snow and then rain, then bright cold sky, then more rain. The rain had slammed his hair against his face: he looked older than twenty-nine or thirty.

My mother and father went into the family room—but what good did that do? They were listening. "You said you were going to show me the stereo with the Brahms on it," I said.

"That's what I'm here for!" he said loudly.

We went out and sat in his car. The Brahms came mournfully from the right-hand speaker. "I've been fired," Coach said. "I was going to ask you to marry me this spring."

"You were?" I said. "You *were*?"

"I couldn't go around with you," he said. "Any teacher caught dating a student would be washed up. Now I'm washed up as it is. They found out I bought Oralie the clothes for debate. Well, of course they found out. Everyone knew. But the principal decided I bought her the clothes because I was sleeping with her and then when she started the baby I killed her. That's what he said! He actually said that!"

I was unnerved to see an older man so vulnerable. I think was more upset by that than by the idea he wanted to marry me. I had never thought of him.

He gave a rough laugh. "All I wanted to do was help her."

I joined in. "You even had that fancy school in mind."

He said, "Well, anyway, I can't ask you to marry me now, unless you'd like to run away with a man who hasn't got a job. I don't think I'll get out from under the cloud of this until they find the man that did it. And how will they ever find him?"

"And what if it's a woman?" I said.

"Or a woman," he said. "Would some girl be that jealous if Oralie was starting a baby fathered by her boyfriend?"

I thought of Joel. "I don't know if they would."

We listened to the Brahms for a few minutes. Intellectuals like Brahms certainly live differently than we regular people do: when they are mournful, they are still in focus, gathered and plunging in some one direction. When we regular people are sad, we smile all the more and slide jokes across at one another like nachos.

As I sat there with Coach I thought about seriousness, what a nice thing it is to be serious, but I didn't feel anything for Coach. It was odd he asked me to marry him. What I *felt* was self-pity, because my friends, whom I intended to spend my whole life with—Joel, Bernice, Leland, and Wayne, and even Father Matt—joked all the time. I felt self-pity because my father now had a terminal illness.

Coach's voice came along to me gradually, as if it were separate light particles. "So are you going to marry me or not?" I had been thinking: Perhaps I could teach that wonderful seriousness of Coach's to Joel. Perhaps I could. Who said just because a boy's conversation was shallow and he started moving the car forward while you were still getting your right foot off the ground to climb in—who said he couldn't turn out philosophical? If I could make Joel philosophical I could still have my regular life—my gang of old friends, my Agans life the way it had always been.

At the same time, I realized that I liked the rather rusty coloring of Coach. His hair was nearly the same color as his skin. I had tried to like Joel's body by thinking of it as a longish white smear at dusk, with its black smears—like Impressionist artwork. But the fact was Joel's body revolted me. I felt a second kind of revulsion for him. His contacts, or sometimes just his Friday-night sousing, gave his eyes a round red outer rim. I hated the rabbit look of it next to the dark eyelashes. His mouth hung nearly always slightly ajar, as if ready to drop a joke easily, as a pitcher can drop a splash of anything waiting in it. Joel liked to jut his head and shoulders forward on his body, as if he were about to blaze away at some enemy. Coach, on the other hand, stood up straight. Still, I couldn't imagine saying, "Actually, Bernice, I am engaged to Coach." I couldn't hear it.

I turned to him. "I don't guess I could do that, Coach," I told him.

"Coach!" he exclaimed in a whisper. He gave a low laugh, which sounded good-natured to me. "Coach!" he repeated. He added, "I suppose that's understandable enough."

He rolled down the car window on his side. He turned off the Brahms cassette, and we listened to the rain hitting the leaves near our driveway. It slammed into the water already trapped in the ruts. It was the last real talk Coach and I ever had.

In May our church did the athletic banquet for the boys. Like all Agans occasions, it was in a basement, this time in Saint Thomas's. While I stirred the vat of raisin sauce for the ham, Father Matt hung around, as he always did, praising now one, now another, of us junior and senior girls who were signed up to cook and serve.

"Ah, if it isn't Maggie stirring the pisspot," Father said with his grin. We all called those ladies' aid raisin sauces pisspots, because the recipe was amber.

Agans boys pretended to hate athletic banquets in church basements, but they showed up early every time, and two or three would wander into the kitchen, where we girls were lining pans with foil or slicing oranges for garnish. They would lean over the table of potato peelings and the pot of raisin sauce. Wayne Schackli, years before, had made an exaggerated gesture of sniffing from the sauce, and said, "Have you read *The Golden Stream,* by Mr. I. P. Daly? No, I thought you hadn't!" Father Matt, with that loneliness for vulgarity which all the clergy in Agans had, shouted in a joyful tone, "Now, whatever made you think of that!" We had all giggled for him. I noticed that Father Matt brought in dirty language whenever he could.

Our two huge ovens were full of roasting hams, got at forty percent off from the Catholics' grocery store. In the 1970s, our stores were still divided up into the Catholics' stores and the Lutherans' stores; by 1980 it all came to an end, because Catholics were practicing birth control and Lutherans were doing guitar music in church. No one was obeying any orders handed down by anyone over forty. Agans had a Catholic grocery and a Catholic furniture store (Joel's dad's). For a little while, seven years later, we had two Catholic furniture stores.

Father Matt put his hands on my shoulders. People didn't sue priests for putting their hands on your shoulders back then. "How can we get this girl to college?" he said to me in a low tone.

"I don't guess you can," I said.

"It's where you belong, Mag."

"Tell me about it, Father," I told him. I stirred the raisin sauce with a hot splash and moved over to check on the potatoes.

He followed me, slouching in his cassock. "I can talk to counselors at the university. Duluth or Minneapolis. These things can be worked out."

"Coach tried. My parents said no. Talk to *them*, Father."

"I did. What have *they* got to do with it? You're eighteen."

I foresaw a year of sticking around home. Besides, I meant to feel cheerful about a future with Joel. I saw myself trying to get Dad to listen to music. I was going to hang out with him while he gardened and pretend to be interested in his organic theories and memories of better farm soils. He had a Lady Eve Balfour compost pile. Can you imagine, some lady in England with a recipe for compost—six inches of green crap, two inches of manure, one inch of dirt, one scattering of wood ash, and the whole thing over again? I was going to spade compost for him while he choked and coughed and looked grateful and gradually got sicker.

Boys began to fill the Fellowship Hall. I leaned out the doorway of the kitchen to watch them. In their plaid sport jackets and white shirts and bright ties, they kept turning energetically to one another as if listening carefully to what each person said. They were acting. Two of their coaches were there; the best athletes danced attendance on them. The lesser athletes minded an age-old protocol: they wouldn't dream of claiming coach time at a social occasion.

Joel came in with Wayne. Any room changed when Wayne entered.

He would hulk over to someone important and then grab their hand in his huge paw and bellow some cordial thing. Joel stood beside him in a navy-blue wool blazer. His black hair was combed coarsely; it was in perfect order but in thick, moussed strands. He caught sight of me and dropped his jaw in a big just-off-the-fan-bus cartoon smile. I grinned back. It would be all right, I thought. This kind of life.

The police kept returning from the Twin Cities. One day, when Joel was driving me up to Belling to see a stakeout movie, he told me it got on his nerves. I liked it that he said something personal, instead of his usual bravado about how he was going to improve the store as soon as he got out of high school. "You got to try new things. Christ, you can't just do the same old stuff year after year." That was his usual talk.

"Like what?" I would ask dutifully.

"Like for one thing, we got tourists going through here like mad. Are we doing anything about it? *No!*"

At eighteen, he had wrathful convictions about business.

It was almost delicious when Joel spoke softly and let himself be simply a person. It made him fun to talk to, the way Coach had been, or the way Father was—instead of just a guy to go with.

"Why do they keep questioning *me?*" he said. "Why *me?*"

"My guess is they are keeping on asking questions, asking everyone who had anything to do with Oralie. Even once."

We had had it out already: he only took Oralie once, he said, far too long ago for her baby to be his baby.

"Hey, Mag," Joel said now. "How about getting married?"

"I don't know," I told him. I didn't want to lie and say I loved him.

Bernice had always been a liar, but since so many of my friends were liars I didn't pay much attention to it. It causes a sadness around a person when you know she will say whatever sounds good. Bernice wasn't much interested in Leland. Why should she be? He never had any idea of what to do. Even his summer jobs, when he had them, were dumber than other people's summer jobs. One year he farmed a little with my dad, and even my dad had to let him go. Leland ran the WC when it was out of oil. And he jawed all the time they were baling. Dad sat on the tractor; Leland lurched around on the baler-trailer, grabbing the bales with the hook as they slid toward him, then lifting them into neat stacks at the rear end. Leland kept shouting to Dad about new equipment you could get now where no one had to lift bales by hand. When Dad got him to help hook and lift bales to the loft, Leland told him how some guys had an elevator that did the same job ten times better.

The evening he fired Leland, Dad told me, "You know, there's people around, you never notice how beautiful the earth is. Then when they go away, suddenly you hear the birds singing and everything smells good. Lilacs. The sky."

On the morning of the prom, every girl who had been invited had her formal lying pressed on her bed. Bernice told me what happened. She had gone over to school to get something out of her locker, and there was Wayne Schackli.

He backed her up against her own locker, gently, like someone setting canvas to easel. "Bernice, you little screwball, you aren't going to piddle away the dance of your life with Leland Newhouse! Let's face it. You're going with me. I am sure not going to face that dance with anyone but you, and you aren't going to suffer through it without me."

While Wayne's body moved against her leisurely and tend-

erly, all she thought of was her formal. She thought of how her
formal lay waiting upstairs at home, the bodice of it flat on the
chenille bedspread, and the lower skirt part hanging vertically
over the edge like a woman dancing with a man who likes to
suspend a woman backward over his left arm in a deep swoop.
"I just knew!" she crowed at me.

She went to the dance with Wayne and was lovers with him
all spring and half the summer. No one expected Wayne to
marry any of the people he made love to; in July he dropped
Bernice, and she and Leland got engaged. Bernice insisted to
everyone that she had uncontrollably fallen in love with Leland.

That summer I decided that I was good at artwork. I particularly liked designing stationery. Someday I will go to Duluth, I thought, and make something of myself. I thought that
when I saw the tourists drive by. Iowa people looking for woods
and lakes and cool air. *They* got to move about the country; I
wouldn't stay forever up here.

Yet, I thought, if I go to Duluth, I might not meet any men
at all. Leland's revolting twin sister Melanie went off right after
graduation to study real estate in Minneapolis; here it was August, and she hadn't found anybody.

Joel took me to the movies, the one in town, the one in
Belling. Idealistic young scientists were eaten by large blobs,
which turned red just after they had emulsified some human
being inside them. We watched the special-effects scorpion ex-
plode out of a patient's stomach as he lay on a surgical table.
The surgical nurses' and doctors' eyes grew round over their
masks.

Joel liked cynical jokes. "You can use any bad actor for those
parts," he said. "With the mask, you can't see what they look
like, so they use cheap help."

I wasn't crazy about the movies, but since we were there, I
liked imagining the plots were real. From time to time I took
Joel's hand out from between my legs.

*   *   *

In late August my whole life took a change because of a farmer, someone I had never met and never would meet.

Coming home from the Belling Odeon, Joel and I parked. A farmer had sickled and half baled up the ditch grass along 73. The incomparable sweetness of cut grass floated into the car. It reminded me of things that softened my heart. My father was dying; I took in the seriousness of it. I was no longer a schoolgirl: *that* felt serious. In the darkness I couldn't see Joel very clearly. He wasn't making any jokes.

"You know," he said, "eventually one of those guys is going to land on someone, and that someone will go to jail for a long, long time."

"Which guys—who?" I said.

I was a very young woman. A few years later, when I wanted silence, I didn't encourage a man to speak. But at just eighteen, I still had all the promptings of habit and upbringing. Some boy starts up something, you help him with it—even if you'd rather smell the fragrant night.

"The police, Mag, the police!" Joel said. "They will decide somebody here in town fixed old Oralie, and they will hound that person into jail."

I imagined Oralie coming into Coach's house. O.K., take these boxes upstairs, maybe he said, and try on this stuff; and the thin rail of a girl, with a tiny, pretty figure, went up, like Cinderella—Cinderella! that's what she was!—and came down looking radiant.

Joel was saying, "I'd wanted to be happy this summer. Going with you and all. Everything's wrecked."

I said a little lanquidly, "You're doing all the things you wanted to do with the store. You got the tourist trade."

He had made a deal with a guy running beef cattle and with some deer hunters. They were giving him the feet of cows now and would bring him deer feet—heels and all—in the fall. Joel

was getting them stuffed with mortar and preserved. Then he
would spike them to the legs of maple chairs and footstools. I
helped. I designed very nice tags about the furniture, explaining
it was made by local craftsmen right here in Agans, Minnesota.
I got the idea we should put in a little quip about the town. I
described how this town was full of people with *ideas*—we had
organic farmers who were experimenting with compost, we had
a homegrown Sunday-school teacher who had replanted the
virgin forest part of the town park with the flowers of a hundred
years ago. We drew a two-inch-by-two-inch map, showing access from U.S. 53. We put these few paragraphs of sell into a
one-fold card, on brownish stock. I went down to Duluth just
to arrange that for Joel and his dad. They said, We sure got to
pay you mileage, Maggie. I told them O.K.

"Anyway, I hate the pressure from these cops," Joel said
now. "It is miserable, if you want to know the truth."

The beautiful grass smell kept wavering and ghosting
through the car. I saw Joel's face in outline: he had lost the casual
fat of last fall's football player who keeps eating heavily throughout the winter and spring. His chin was a clean line. He wasn't
wearing his bullying expression. He wasn't making a joke.

I could marry him, I supposed. I knew it would be a little
lonely, because Joel was like the other boys in town; his real
friendships were with men, not women. Sooner or later, after
the honeymoon, he would start begging me for weekends off
to go over toward Grand Rapids, hunting with the guys, putting
out trap routes.

He said, "I want you to be my wife."

If he had said, "Hey, how 'bout getting married?" the way
he had earlier, I'd have decided to go to Duluth and *really* learn
graphics. Commercial art, since I gathered from Coach that I
was intelligent but didn't have any big talent.

Joel used dignified, dead-simple language, so I agreed. The
rest of August and September, I decided I would not lie the way
Bernice did about her engagement to Leland. She went around

saying, "My guy just doesn't like hot dishes!" or "I guess I fell for a guy who doesn't like plaid jackets!" She was building aloud, with a phony tilt, a legend of her having fallen for Leland. In her myth, Leland was a man of strong tastes in a good many areas, and she was the woman whose passion left her clinging to him despite all—the way birds curl their claws around a wind-swung telephone wire.

All of us knew that Leland hadn't any opinions about any-thing: he was just looking for something to do. Bernice's ex-clamations gave the impression that she was hopelessly in love with a man who couldn't *stand* the old roast-plus-gravy diet; he loved garlic and basil, she said. He spent hours, she told us, preparing the comment for Masses (by then we had lay members called commentators, who were supposed to prepare some ideas for the parish). If there was one thing Leland couldn't stand, she told everybody, it was crookedness in a car dealer. In Sep-tember, Leland started at commission only with the man who had the Ford garage and imports, both. "I just don't know," Bernice would tell me in a light, slightly fretful tone, "how it will go with him at the lot. You know, when a man is com-pletely, completely honest—well, the others might take it out on him some. I tell you, it isn't easy. I have to say this for my guy, though: he knows how to take it."

"Niagara Falls—I don't know," Bernice told me. "Where are you two going? Leland really doesn't like the usual crap. He likes something more original, you know the kind of thing."

Joel and I were just doing two nights up to International Falls, because Joel and his dad were up to their ears in Octo-berfest at the store.

In the first year of my marriage, I had a baby. My father grew worse, but more slowly than we expected. I visited him in the hospital night after night. Dad went in and out of a coma. Mother would sit in the room with him. She rubbed his legs or his stomach. I hovered around his tubing stand, and said his name a lot, but he was nearly always dozing. I walked down the hall a way, as we do in those small hospitals, and found that Mrs. Moen, the old Lutheran Sunday-school teacher, was dying in 108. A woman came out as I stood at the door. "I couldn't get a thing out of her," she said from under her permanent. "We brought candy and everything. We should have known. She's past eating candy, I can tell you."

I went in feeling partly half-assed. What business of mine was her death? Yet, because I had a baby and was already expecting another, I felt a kinship with first things and last things.

"Mrs. Moen," I said, "do you feel well enough to have a visitor?"

She looked at me, but didn't speak.

"Well," I said, trying to be ingenious, "if you want me to stay and talk with you, blink twice, and if you are exhausted and I should just come back tomorrow instead, will you blink once, then?"

She blinked twice and I looked gratefully into her dark eyes that were full of pain. It was as if I were in a movie, one of the serious ones. I was terribly happy. I leaned over and smoothed her hair but with only two or three fingers, because I didn't want to touch her hard. She looked as if she had in addition to her own skin a fragile outer web made up just of pain.

I sat beside the bed, remembering how she planted woods flowers all around the Agans park edges. What a strange thing to do! I had two opinions at once: that is a strange and stupid thing to do—why didn't she just keep house and be a happy married woman with her husband?—and when I get old I am going to restore some part of nature, too. I will not always be a regular Catholic wife around town. I will do strange stuff.

"Will you promise to blink once when you are tired and want me to go?"

She blinked twice.

"Mrs. Moen, I want to tell you that you are one of the people around Agans who keep us all from being bored. When I think of the things you do and the free way you do them—I realize you make a huge difference."

I told her about working with Joel at the store, not mentioning the cattle feet nailed to make footstool legs. I told her about our baby. I told her about how Leland got fired from the car lot, so he tried insurance selling, but his own family already had policies, so even they wouldn't switch over to him. Anyway, we had a State Farm guy in town whom people liked: why would they buy insurance from Leland when they wouldn't buy a '72 Chev from him in 1976 for four hundred dollars. Everybody knew that the dealer had said, "Is this right, Leland? You offered one of my good cars at four hundred dollars and it didn't go? Who the hell'd you try to sell it to—the head of First Bank in Duluth?"

After a while I said, "I don't know why this is true, but it is: it was great talking to you. I will come again tomorrow. My dad is here in the hospital, too."

Mrs. Moen blinked twice. Then I never saw her again, not even at her funeral because Joel wanted me to deliver some of the new things—ten footstools, ten plaques, and ten watercolor paintings—down to Duluth.

He and I looked over my clothes. "Good, you don't look pregnant, yet," he said.

"Is that right?"

"Yeah. You and I love the baby, but fact is, women with bulging bellies don't sell good." We agreed on a navy-blue cotton-and-rayon dress and dangling earrings. "That's right," Joel said, standing away from me a little. "Half business, half arty like."

"What about Mrs. Moen's funeral, though?" I asked him.

He looked at me with his slightly red-rimmed eyes. "I don't know," he said. "I guess that'll have to slip."

*   *   *

We had five more children. There was nothing much wrong
with my life except the boredom. We and our friends were all
twenty-eight or twenty-nine years old, Wayne Schackli about
thirty-five. The others had to put up with the boredom, so why
should I complain? Like when Joel and I decided it would be a
good thing to do some art thing. Father Matt was talking about
how you could get the Saint Paul Chamber Orchestra to come
all the way up here and do "some services." He wrote a letter,
and some of us in town, the Auxiliary Committee, Christian
Mothers, and the VFW Auxiliary, looked it over. For five thousand dollars we could get the orchestra to come play two pieces
and then accompany us (both Lutheran choirs and our Saint
Thomas's Catholic one put together) in Vivaldi's *Gloria*. Members of the orchestra would go to our school and the Nevis
school and show kids about violins and cellos and all. Nevis
didn't want in, or we forgot to ask them, but the county com-
missioners went along. Then we went out and hit up all the
businesses.

Joel said, smiling, "Gee, the guys run to the other side of
the street when they see me coming." He was the principal asker
for money. He figured it wouldn't hurt his store to be the big
arts backer and community backer. He was right. People never
forgot that Joel had done so much to bring the orchestra here.
It took a lot of patience, though. And when Joel and all the guys
did so much to get the orchestra in, they expected the gals to
do just as much for the stuff they wanted. Joel planned the
biggest mud-wrestling event in our part of the state; he planned
it for the hot part of August, when tourists and people who had
cabins around would be bored and could be seduced into coming
to town for things.

Bernice and I pretended to enjoy the mud-wrestling. It was
all right. I suppose they found those trashy girls in Duluth or
somewhere. Anyway, they climbed all over each other and
rubbed mud and muddy water into each other's ears—and one

girl seemed genuinely angry. Often, you know, they straighten up after being wrestled down, and you can see they are completely cool and are simply relaxing their backs, and that their thoughts are in some completely different place. But this one time, this girl opened her mouth (a thing not to do in mud-wrestling), and she went for the other girl and slugged her in the stomach. The Agans guys and Bernice all went, "Booooooooooh!" and the girl who got slugged lay on her back with her arms bent and her fists tight, slogged with mud as they were. Then she rose up like an avenging blob out of a horror film and went for the other girl. The Activities Committee (which was the men's group, like our women's Auxiliary Town Committee) gave the girls an extra fifty dollars each because of the show. They didn't want to, but Joel said, "Look, guys, you know? The laborer is worthy of his hire? You know?"

They all slapped him on the back, and downtown in Main Street guys would grin when they saw him and say, "How's the laborer doing, Joel?"

That whole orchestra business and the mud-wrestling didn't hurt our store or the town at all.

Another couple of years went by, and then Leland's twin sister, Melanie, came back to town. She didn't actually come back to be what you would call "in the town." She was a member of a huge company that was buying up outlots in Minnesota.

Outlots are the acreage behind but adjacent to lakeside properties. Usually they are disused meadows, being sold by dairy farmers going broke. Reagan had got in, and there was a new combination of milkhouse laws, which wrecked a whole new category of small-herd operators. Each time Land O'Lakes or whoever had your milk deal called and said there was going to be what they called an "informational meeting," you knew you were going to lose your shirt in some new way. When you decided you had to sell, Melanie Newhouse was there with her firm to make you an offer. She was a beautiful woman now;

she had always been fast, pretty, and rude-looking. Men liked to make sexy remarks about her. Joel had told me that way back in high school. "You don't respect her, see," he had said, "but she gets to you some way."

Now she was stunning—very Twin Cities–looking. She had not had any babies. She was picking up these outlots, and then her company platted them for subdividing and sold them high. They always finagled to get one lake lot, which they would use as "access" for the outlot people. Joel lay awake at night telling me the kinds of deals Melanie did. "See, what they do," he said in the dark, "is they buy, say, two hundred feet of lakefront. Then they have to sell lots not less than a hundred fifty feet, so they sell one fifty of it at lake frontage price, but they don't tell the guy that the other fifty feet are going to be graveled or concreted over so the outlot people can put their boats in right next to your cabin and their water-skiers can blast around in front of your nose all day."

"That's horrible," I said, tired, just barely able to decide whether Joel wanted to hear it was horrible or wanted to hear it was clever.

He rolled over and said right at my cheek, "You don't need to judge her, either. She's a born-again Christian, and she's starting a Power Through Prayer group right in town, too."

Melanie got the Saint Thomas basement for it, Wednesday nights. Everybody got sitters, and we all went. Well, in a town that size, we all went to everything. Besides, it wasn't deer hunting or Christmas or winter trapping anymore.

We all sat in a circle in the church basement, and Melanie, in a beautiful actual-wool red dress, with a flowered scarf dropped over one shoulder, told us that her land sales went up after she found Jesus. This joy could be ours. She explained that we might have the wrong motivations, like wanting Christ only because we wanted success, but that he would forgive us. *He* didn't have the wrong motivations. She meant to pray for this joy she had for all of us.

In our group, the only one who got the infilling of spirit was Leland—what we least expected. He stood up and raised his arms and started shouting in some foreign language.

"It's tongues!" cried Melanie. "Leland has been gifted!"

He started backing up, shouting and crying—but very happy. His chair went over, and Wayne reached around fast to get it out of his way so he wouldn't trip. He backed up into all the long tables that we Christian Mothers had been laying white shelf paper on for the Winter Athletes' Banquet. The table Leland hit slid screeching into the next one, which hit the next one, and all the neat white paper that we had pressed down with our thumbs rode up and got mangled.

All through February and March we had those Wednesday-night prayer meetings. Other people asked for infilling of the spirit. Bernice didn't ask; she told the group that Leland was head of her household and that was Christian blessing enough. One night even Wayne told some story about something that happened to him in the Marines. I couldn't see that it was anything but the story of two guys getting into a fight, but everyone seemed to see something in it that I missed. "Glad you shared, Wayne," they said in syrupy voices. Men thanked Wayne—men who normally respected Wayne because he bed-hopped so much and could knock anybody out with one hand tied behind his back.

In that prayer group, people put their hands on other people's hands.

Wayne put his hands on Melanie's hands a lot. I saw Joel noting it, too. "Did you see how Wayne and Melanie kind of held hands?" I said.

Joel said in a cross tone, "This isn't the VFW lounge you know, Maggie. This is a prayer group. Things mean different things."

"Yeah? Is that right?" I said. "Well, say fifteen years from now our little girl goes to a prayer group someday and Wayne's in it. Will that be something different, him pawing her over?"

Joel looked at me. "The devil is holding out in you," he
said. "The devil is trying to keep you from feeling His love."

In April the snow lay on the ground, but one Wednesday
night the moon was out full. At the prayer group, Melanie said,
"I have a new idea for us all: let's climb the old fire tower on
County 10."

"Yeah? Yeah?" the guys said. "You serious, Melanie?"

"The moon is wonderful tonight," Melanie said. "You
know, I don't want to sound sappy, but moonlight really is one
of God's blessings. O.K., O.K. Now you've snickered and all,
let's be serious. Moonlight is beautiful. Let's go up there—I
drove by there the other day during work and noticed you can
still get up. Let's go there and bless the whole countryside if we
can. How about it?"

Of course they loved the idea. It was a surprise. If there's
one thing our lives were missing, it was surprise. We all got
into cars, with four people in each car so we would save gas.
It meant I couldn't tell Joel I thought the idea stank.

At first, it felt good to be exercising, pulling myself up the
iron ladder of the tower, though I didn't trust the rotted wood
steps, some of which hung loosely off their bolts like windmill
sails. Joel and I went first, me ahead of him, both of us well
ahead of all the others. We heard their giggling from farther
and farther below. Then I got unnerved.

"Oh, hurry it up, will you?" Joel snapped, not calling me
by name. He kept nagging. "Hey, why don't you pray for
courage or just for some plain guts?" It was strange how his
steady irritation kept smoking up at me in the night. I pulled
myself upward, with new handholds, and Joel scolded away. I
could feel his irritation almost physically. I decided—absolutely
in one split second—that his fury was sexual.

In the next split second, something else happened. He completely stopped talking. I kept forcing myself to go up. I decided
that Joel had stopped talking because he was *thinking*. What was
he thinking then? I asked myself. I decided—in another split

second—he was thinking that the others were so far below us that they couldn't see what we were actually doing. Joel could push me off. It would be a frightfully sad accident. Then he could go after Melanie. I even briefly felt sorry for him: that his body had never seemed interesting to me in itself—except the one time when Coach had shown me a charcoal drawing of a man's body. And here we were almost thirty, making love though I didn't like his looks and he was bored with mine.

Now he began shouting up at me again. I decided he had stopped thinking about pushing me off. I was able to get my hands moving faster and reached the top—a safe high-railed little lookout platform. Two by two the others came up, and we lightly cuffed one another and joked about the frightening climb. Melanie took over. "Look around you," she said. "Listen, fellows and girls. Why don't we be utterly silent for two whole minutes—no jokes, no snickering, no nudging and shoving—and look all around us. There is our snowy countryside down there. And think of all God's blessings you wish for everyone down there."

The snow had melted off narrow surfaces like pine needles, so the forest showed black around us. Our town, Agans, was a smear of light to the south. You could make out Belling to the north. Everywhere else was dark forest or moon-whitened field and a few farmers' yard lights on, like cats' eyes. It was utterly beautiful.

Melanie then brought our silence to an end. "Amen," she said. "God bless us all."

"Amen," people said shyly—half hypocritically, half really wanting to express their liking for the world. The moon shone on, and we hung around up there, pointing out places we thought we knew.

"There's Doc Heimlich's place," Leland said. Leland, always gumming up whatever he took on, the sap.

"That's not Doc Heimlich's," Wayne told him. "That's old man Stett's place."

Of course, I thought, looking where Leland and Wayne were looking: it was just a single farm yard light. Of course, *Joel* had killed Oralie Stett. Of course! That is why I felt such terror as we climbed up here! When someone gets in Joel's way, he shoves them *out* of the way. In the dark I couldn't see his head jutted forward, but I imagined it. Of course, I thought, getting the feel of the idea. It was Joel.

I stared down at the forest and the spot Wayne told us was the Stett farm.

But I am a person of habit. It takes me a long while to make up my mind to anything. For the next few weeks I was very busy, anyhow. Two of my children caught chicken pox at school, and Joel was doing a new promotion at the store. I didn't get around to thinking my idea through, coolly and clearly, until June.

Then a plan came to me only by happenstance. The high-school commencement had come and gone. It didn't mean much to me, since Joel and I and our friends were so long out of school, and our children were still in grade school. We took note of the commencement, however, because there was always an all-night party after it, and we had to watch the store. Sometimes pickups tore down the streets until morning, and boys and girls flung eggs everywhere. The cops tried not to be too hard on them, which means we store owners had to look out for ourselves.

On the Monday following, a young girl came in to ask for work. We went through this every spring, of course. It was always the kids who had just graduated and who couldn't plan on college—at least not yet. They divided into those who lied about being interested in a permanent position and those who really did want one. This girl was dressed in a pink polyester jacket over a pink-and-gray plaid skirt. There was no blouse under the jacket, but she wore four strands of good-looking imitation pearls. Her hair was done beautifully—which helped.

It was her hangdog look that made me recognize her. I was in the store alone; the carpets guy was out to coffee, and Joel had gone off in a truck. We had this advantage of our customers: on a hot summer day, the store is shadowy, and it has so much furniture in it, people entering keep seeing edges and corners and lamp stems and unfamiliar shapes in the gloomy light. It gives us, sitting coolly toward the back, a chance to look them over. This girl was Sue Stett, the younger sister of Oralie.

As she gave me a now-on, now-off smile that showed her nervousness, and began to lie to me about how interested she was in furniture, I got my plan fast. Yeah, Melanie, I said to myself, you can tell that prayer group all you like about getting the gift of God when you least expect it—suddenly and all. This idea was not the gift of God, but I got it suddenly—and it was complete. It was my plan to make amends for the murder of this girl's older sister. I wasn't going to leave my husband: why should I do that? He was all right. And my kids needed their dad. But I could do *this* much at least.

So I interrupted the little dumbbell standing before me. "Listen," I said. "Maybe we can give you some work. Maybe not. But how would you like to really get out of town and start a new life? I mean, how would *that* feel?"

"I can't," she said promptly. "If you're saying am I going to run out on you come fall and go to college, forget it. My dad won't let me go anywhere."

"Hey, you're eighteen," I told her, hearing Father Matt's voice again from so long ago when he had tried to set *me* on my feet.

"He won't let me," the girl said.

"Sit down," I told her. "You don't have to stand there. I don't know where my manners have gone. You say your father won't let you go?"

"He won't, Mrs. Haft, and that's the end of it."

"Would he slap you around?"

"It's Mom," she said in a limp voice. "He told me if I ran away to try to go to college, he would take it out on Mom, and how would I like that?"

My plan got clearer and clearer to me.

"But I don't want to go to college anyhow," she said. "I want to go to cosmetology school."

"Why not college?" I tried to remember what Coach had told me about education. "They teach you to think for yourself and have your own ideas about everything."

The girl looked up at me from her thoroughly made-up eyes. She had rimmed them so darkly that she looked a little owlish. The light blue of her eyes was surprising with such dark lashes. She used turquoise shadow.

"I want cosmetology," she said.

I quickly imagined again all the dumb conversations I have listened to in the beauty shops of Agans and the towns around. Even in Duluth. And that devitalizing odor of perfumed sprays.

"You sure?" I said.

"Sure," she said, smiling with so much happiness that she actually looked like a beautiful, nice person.

"O.K.," I told her. "I can give you some work. Not full-time, though."

Later, Joel said, "That's the dumbest thing you ever did. What can that dumb kid do around a furniture store?"

"Nothing," I told him sprucely. "She can run our house until five each night and take care of the kids, and *I* will help you run the store better all the time."

"Yeah?" he said. "Is that right?"

"It's a new idea," I told him, very upbeat, so he wouldn't put up any opposition. "You'll get used to it, hey."

"I guess," he said. "Well, start thinking, smarty pants. Guess what's happened. Leland Newhouse is going to start a rival furniture and tourist-items shop."

We went over it carefully. I told Joel I thought he should let

Leland do all the start-up promotions stuff he wanted. "Don't advertise against it. Just let Leland go."

"Why not nip him in the bud?" Joel said.

"Let him do a big start-up. He will cut prices to beat you out and *acquaint* everyone—our old customers, namely—with his stock. He'll spend every nickel he's got on coffee and dough-nuts and every other gimmick. He'll do that for about two weeks, and then he will start needing to make money, and he and Bernice will be exhausted with all the promotion."

"Yeah?" said Joel.

"Then you slash all your prices in half and leave them that way all summer."

"I'd lose my shirt."

"You'd run him out of business by August fifteenth," I said. "And I think we should take all our stock and sell it in franchises along Lake Superior or Highway 61 this summer. Can we do that?"

"I'll find out," Joel said. "But say we could: how can I be away all that time?"

"You can't. I will. Sue can watch the kids, and you can make supper at night and all."

I spent four days a week on the road, getting people to stock our animal-feet footstools and all the other light stuff. I had the retailers make out half their checks to me and half to the store, explaining that we paid the artists who invented the wooden stuff from our own fund.

It worked. At first, as I lay in a motel in Grand Rapids or Saint Cloud or Duluth, I felt guilty about cheating Joel out of all the money. I made myself remember what he did. I made myself think of Oralie, lying dead in the graveyard at Agans. The image would fade, though, so I had to keep reminding myself. "She would have liked to live, too," I would say loudly in the motel room. "Maybe Oralie would have liked to grow up and get married and have kids whose father loved them,"

I'd say in a harsh voice aloud. I kept a part of myself wrathful. It was exhausting, but on the other hand, running a business— even such a helter-skelter one—is such a beanhill compared to raising children, my health actually improved.

In Agans, Leland began to worry. He bleated to Bernice. When I was home on the weekends, Bernice sometimes dropped it to me that Leland was worried. Bernice and I had scarcely anything but our mutual concerns left, and now Bernice couldn't tell me her real thoughts because our husbands were in competition. I certainly couldn't tell her mine. Therefore I had to buy her a lot of drinks one night to make her talk at all. She and Leland were scared stiff.

"Is your store insured?" I asked her.

She looked back at me, her eyes drooping with drunkenness. "I guess so," she said. "I suppose it would be, I mean."

"Well, that's good," I said. "Because you never know. If some lowlife snuck in there and burned it down some night, there you'd be."

I saw her eyes sober up for a flicker.

Leland Newhouse is not one of the fastest-moving people in the world. They didn't have a fire at his store until November.

Like most other people in town, we had taken to spending a little while each Friday evening at the VFW. It gave everyone a chance to talk to everyone else. Wayne would be there, with whatever new girlfriend he had taken up with, and Bernice and Leland and everyone. I got myself into a booth with the State Farm guy, a classmate of Joel's and mine, who carried Leland's building and business insurance.

I maneuvered and maneuvered and finally got the conversation onto that fire.

"Yeah," the insurance agent said. "Those fires. We investigate fires all the time. You don't know until you look into them, and *then* you sometimes don't know."

"But if you found clues around?" I said. "I thought people left clues that told you."

He grinned. "Yeah," he said. "They leave matchboxes with the names of a competing company, so we will think the fire was started by their competitors. Oh," he said luxuriously, "what they don't do! *If* they start the fire themselves. We'd have a time in a town like this, where every single person swipes matchboxes from every store they go into! Anyway, Newhouse has the classical old bad thing. Bad wiring—and since he was warned about that, he don't collect."

I sat there with them for a while and then returned to where Wayne and Bernice and Leland and Joel were all leaning their heads over the table so they could talk low. Leland was nearly crying, and the others were trying to console him. "I thought my religion, I thought Jesus, would help me," Leland said.

Everyone drew back a little. Wayne said in his big voice, "Even he can't do everything, I don't guess."

I had to think seriously the next day. I couldn't do everything, either. I had this idea that I would get Joel blamed for something he didn't do, so that would make it fair somehow that he had never got blamed for the thing he did do. It was a stupid idea, but, as I've been saying, we don't have very good judgment in our family. And I am not so smart as I sometimes feel. I get feeling high, and I think I can do anything. I remember once, when I wasn't more than fourteen, asking Coach why he didn't recommend *me* for some fancy school. Who'd I think I was?

But I had one more idea. The next day, as soon as Sue got to our house and took over the children too young to go to school, I drove north to my old house, where my mother still lived alone, by choice, doing the same thing she and my dad did together when he was alive. She even kept up all his compost bins. At this time of year, she watched a lot of television, but like my dad, she watched good television—Channel 8. She watched people make canoes by hand. She learned how some guy made handmade leather boots for people who wanted them. She learned how men and women sewed a gigantic quilt for

AIDS. She watched innumerable movies about how wrong it was to trap or poison wolves.

"Coffee," she said, obviously happy I had come. "You didn't bring any grandchildren for me?"

"Not today, Mama," I said. "I come to ask a huge, just horrible favor."

"That's frank!"

I took coffee from her and doused it with honey and evaporated milk, the way she and Dad had it. The house was warm and dark. I felt glad to be there, glad to be asking this huge stupid favor and trying to be tricky.

"I want to borrow five thousand four hundred dollars," I said.

"I thought the idea is that you and Joel are making money hand over fist and I am the poor widow who is eking out on her husband's nearly nonexistent social security." She said that but she wasn't cross. "What do you want it for?"

I said, "I need the money to do a good thing. If I pay you back in ten years, would you lend me the money, no questions asked?"

She said. "You are my baby, and you will be until you die." She wrote me a check.

"What is this—your retirement fund?" I asked.

"Shut up and take the money," she told me.

We sat for a while, and I told her how I planned to pay her back: in what size installments at what intervals of time. She half listened. I promised myself, If one of my grown-up kids asks for a loan, I will give it, no questions asked.

After a while I got up and went out to my car. While the engine warmed up in park, I thought: Shall I wait for better weather or shall I go to Duluth now? I decided to go then, while people expected me to be away.

The people at First Bank told me they would have to wait to clear the check and then I could get a cashier's check. I went to A & E Supply and got the graphics I needed—rub-off lettering, colored tapes, heavy plain stock, and blue-squared stock.

Then I went home and began the project, which took two weeks in all. Late each night I worked hard on the certificate: it announced that the recipient had won a scholarship to the Horst Institute in Minneapolis, where she could complete the full course in ten weeks. Midweek I drove back into Duluth, got the cashier's check, and mailed the letter advising her that she had won a sweepstakes. I mailed it to Susan Stett, c/o Haft's Furniture, Agans, Minnesota, 55706.

"Mail for me? Here?" Sue said. She opened it. An ugly expression came over her face. "They'll try anything won't they? What is this? Some real estate trick?"

I took the certificate and the cashier's check from her and pretended to glance back and forth between them. "Nope," I said. "It's the real thing. Looks like the real thing. I suppose they trust a person's place of business more than their home."

"Really?" she said. "Really?"

After closing, I told Joel, "Let's go down to the VFW tonight. I need a break!"

"Yeah? That's my girl," he said.

I decided to get happily drunk because for once I had done all I could. All my life I never guessed right about what to do or what not to do, but I got it right this time. It would make amends. It was true that the Horst Institute was not Phillips Exeter Academy, but it was what Oralie's little sister wanted. It was true that Joel would keep on half lusting after that no-good pig of a Melanie Newhouse, and apparently I didn't mind living with a murderer. Anyhow, that was then, as Joel would say, and this was now.

"You sure got your tail up over your back," Joel said. We had our elbows on the clean tabletop. "Who you looking so smiley at, hey?" Joel said. He turned around, but there wasn't anyone at the bar this early on a weeknight except Wayne, talking to some out-of-town guy.

"Oh, no," Joel said in his sneering way. "All this good cheer isn't because of *him*?"

I was planning to write a postcard or even a letter, maybe, to Coach, if I could find his address where he finally got some job in Nebraska. I wanted to tell him about Sue Stett's good luck.

"No, I'm not smiling at Wayne," I said.

"I should slug him one day," Joel said as if daydreaming.

Leland came over, "Slug who?"

"He is going to slug Wayne," I said recklessly, "And really knock him down for good and all."

"What's that supposed to mean—you think I can't?" Joel said. Leland sat down. Since he lost his store, he was trying to take over the hatchery and see if he could make it in leghorns. He wanted to talk about it. He wanted to tell us what he had laid out in equipment and how much he thought he'd have to do in business before he would start taking in. He wanted us to assure him it was a good idea.

We asked him questions, and Joel was kind. I was too drunk to be kind, but I hazily remember thinking: Joel is being very nice to Leland. Leland couldn't make two bits selling Kool-Aid, so how would he ever make money when the hatchery guy, who knew something about chickens, couldn't keep it in the black? But we pretended we were interested. Joel made some little, low-tech suggestions.

The next day, while Joel and I were still in the house, Sue came early. She sailed around the room, hardly on her feet, even though she was carrying our littlest child in her arms. "Horst! Horst!"

"Horse!" our two-year-old repeated, laughing.

We both congratulated her. Out in the car, Joel said, "That's a nice thing to have happen for her. God knows what her old man will do, though. I've heard he won't let that girl go any-where except to work in town here."

"My God," I said. "I didn't think of that."

Joel looked thoughtful. I wondered if Sue reminded him of the older sister, and I felt stony.

Then he said, "You know what, Mag? I don't think we should let that guy keep that girl home. I'm going to call Wayne."

"And then what?"

"I'll tell Wayne, and the two of us will just go out there and explain to that guy that he doesn't stop that kid from going to beauty school."

"You can't do that," I said icily. "You can't just push people out of your way when you want them out of your way. You can't hit that old man—two younger guys like you."

"Hit him! Hit him!" said Joel. "Who's talking about hitting him? We'll just stand around and look scary and tell him about how his daughter is going to Horst, and then we will tell him the police have new kinds of chemical evidence and they're coming back out from the Twin Cities and they're going to pin him for the murder of Oralie. We'll tell him that. We won't have to hit him."

"There isn't any new evidence, though," I said.

Joel said, "No, but I've been thinking about that whole thing. It's not fair that that girl is dead under the ground and he did it and now he's going to ruin this kid's life too. It isn't fair."

"Did . . . the father do it, then, after all?"

"Wayne's always thought there isn't anyone else mean enough. I think he's right."

A little later, I watched as Wayne and Joel and Sue got into Wayne's pickup. I thought, I suppose, this is what life is—I *suppose* this is what people do. As I've said, we never had very good judgment in my family, and I didn't guess well. But I felt cheered looking at the heads of those men as they drove away, with the girl's head safely between them.